DEBBIE MACOMBER

Time for Love

mira

mira

Recycling programs
for this product may
not exist in your area.

ISBN-13: 978-0-7783-0929-1

Time for Love

Copyright © 2019 by Harlequin Books S.A.

The publisher acknowledges the copyright holder of the individual works as follows:

A Friend or Two
Copyright © 1985 by Debbie Macomber

The Trouble with Caasi
Copyright © 1985 by Debbie Macomber

For questions and comments about the quality of this book, please contact us at CustomerService@Harlequin.com.

Harlequin.com

Printed in U.S.A.

Also available from Debbie Macomber and MIRA Books

Midnight Sons

Alaska Skies
  (*Brides for Brothers* and
  The Marriage Risk)
Alaska Nights
  (*Daddy's Little Helper* and
  Because of the Baby)
Alaska Home
  (*Falling for Him,*
  Ending in Marriage and
  Midnight Sons and Daughters)

This Matter of Marriage
Montana
Thursdays at Eight
Between Friends
Changing Habits
Married in Seattle
  (*First Comes Marriage* and
  Wanted: Perfect Partner)
Right Next Door
  (*Father's Day* and
  The Courtship of Carol Sommars)
Wyoming Brides
  (*Denim and Diamonds* and
  The Wyoming Kid)
Fairy Tale Weddings
  (*Cindy and the Prince* and
  Some Kind of Wonderful)
The Man You'll Marry
  (*The First Man You Meet* and
  The Man You'll Marry)
Orchard Valley Grooms
  (*Valerie* and *Stephanie*)
Orchard Valley Brides
  (*Norah* and *Lone Star Lovin'*)
The Sooner the Better
An Engagement in Seattle
  (*Groom Wanted* and
  Bride Wanted)
Out of the Rain
  (*Marriage Wanted* and
  Laughter in the Rain)
Learning to Love
  (*Sugar and Spice* and
  Love by Degree)

You…Again
  (*Baby Blessed* and
  Yesterday Once More)
The Unexpected Husband
  (*Jury of His Peers* and
  Any Sunday)
Three Brides, No Groom
Love in Plain Sight
  (*Love 'n' Marriage* and
  Almost an Angel)
I Left My Heart
  (*A Friend or Two* and
  No Competition)
Marriage Between Friends
  (*White Lace and Promises* and
  Friends—And Then Some)
A Man's Heart
  (*The Way to a Man's Heart* and
  Hasty Wedding)
North to Alaska
  (*That Wintry Feeling* and
  Borrowed Dreams)
On a Clear Day
  (*Starlight* and
  Promise Me Forever)
To Love and Protect
  (*Shadow Chasing* and
  For All My Tomorrows)
Home in Seattle
  (*The Playboy and the Widow*
  and *Fallen Angel*)
Together Again
  (*The Trouble with Caasi* and
  Reflections of Yesterday)
The Reluctant Groom
  (*All Things Considered* and
  Almost Paradise)
A Real Prince
  (*The Bachelor Prince* and
  Yesterday's Hero)
Private Paradise
  (in *That Summer Place*)

Debbie Macomber's
Cedar Cove Cookbook
Debbie Macomber's
Christmas Cookbook

CONTENTS

A FRIEND OR TWO

In memory of Darlene Layman,
encourager and dear friend.

Prologue

"Miss Elizabeth?" The elderly butler's eyes widened, but he composed himself quickly. "This is a surprise. Welcome home."

"Thank you, Bently. It's good to *be* home." Elizabeth Wainwright felt comforted by his formality and British accent. She looked around the huge entry hall, with its elegant crystal chandelier and imported oriental rugs and sighed inwardly. Home. Would it offer her what she hadn't been able to find in Europe? Immediately doubts filled her.

"Would you see to my luggage?" she asked in a low, distracted tone. "And ask Helene to draw my bath?"

"Right away."

She looked around with a renewed sense of appreciation for everything this house represented. Wealth. Tradition. Family pride. With all this at her fingertips, how could she possibly be dissatisfied?

"Bently, do you know where Father is?"

"In the library, miss," he responded crisply.

Her smile faded as she started across the huge hall. She loved Bently. Nothing could ruffle him. She could recall the time… Loud voices drifted past the partially opened door, and she paused. Her father rarely raised his voice.

"I'm afraid I've failed her, Mother. Elizabeth is restless and unhappy."

Stunned, Elizabeth stood just outside the library door, listening.

"Give the girl time, Charles. She's suffered a great loss." Her grandmother's raspy voice sounded troubled, despite her words.

"She has no drive, no ambition, no purpose. Dear heavens, have you seen these bills from Paris?"

The sound of his fist against the desk shocked her.

"Elizabeth goes through money as if there's no tomorrow. I've pampered and indulged her since Mary died, and now I'm left to deal with it."

"But she's such a dear child."

"Dear, but hopelessly unhappy, I fear. The thing is—" her father's voice lowered and took on a slightly husky quality "—I don't know how to help her."

A twinge of guilt caused Elizabeth to lower her head fractionally. She'd thought she had concealed her unhappiness. And she couldn't argue with her father's earlier statement. Her spending *had* been extravagant the last few months.

"What can we do?" Again, it was her grandmother.

"I don't know, Mother."

Elizabeth had never heard such resignation from her father. "I'll talk to her, but I don't know what good it will do. Perhaps if Mary had lived…" he continued soberly.

Elizabeth refused to listen to any more. Her father rarely spoke of her mother. Mary Elizabeth Wainwright's unexpected death two years before still had the power to inflict a deep sense of loss on them both. Elizabeth's brother had adjusted well, but he was older and constitutionally more able to cope with his grief.

Thoughtfully, she climbed the long, winding staircase to her rooms. A confrontation with her father was the last thing she wanted. How could she explain this lackadaisical attitude that had taken over her usually cheerful existence? And as for the benefits of wealth, she was well aware of the privileges and even the power that came with having money. But money wasn't everything; it didn't bring happiness or fulfillment. The best time she'd had in her life had been the summer she bummed her way across France, when she'd barely had two euros to rub together. Not only was she intelligent, she was gifted. She spoke fluent French, and enough Italian and German to make her last visits to Rome and Berlin worry-free. But what good was any of that to her now?

Sitting on her plush canopy bed, she forced her spine to straighten. She was a Wainwright. She was supposed to maintain her pride and independence at all times.

A gnawing ache churned her stomach. She didn't want to talk to her father. She didn't want to explain the fiasco in Paris and her extravagant expenses. All she wanted was peace and quiet. The germ of an idea began to form in her mind. Her bags were still packed.

She could swear Bently to silence and slip out just as quietly as she'd slipped in. San Francisco sounded appealing. Her mother had spent a carefree summer there when she was about Elizabeth's age. With a renewed sense of purpose, she headed out of her bedroom door and down the back stairs.

One

The ever-present odor of fresh fish and the tangy scent of saltwater followed Elizabeth as she sauntered down Fisherman's Wharf. The wharf wasn't far from where she was staying at the St. Francis, one of San Francisco's most prestigious hotels. A little breeze ruffled her golden-brown hair and added a shade of color to her otherwise pale features.

With the morning paper tucked under her arm, she strolled into a small French café. It had only taken three days for the restless boredom to make its way into her thoughts. How could she sit in one of the most beautiful cities in the world with the homey scent of freshly baked bread drifting from the restaurant kitchen and feel this listless?

A friendly waitress dressed in a crisp pink uniform with a starched white apron took her order for coffee and a croissant. She wasn't hungry, but she had noticed this morning that her clothes were beginning to hang on her and decided to make the effort to eat more.

Lackadaisically her eyes ran over the front page of the newspaper. Nothing had changed. The depressing stories of war and hate were the same on this day as they had been the week before and the month before that. Sighing, she folded the newspaper and waited for the waitress to bring her food.

"Are you looking for a job?" the young waitress asked eagerly as she delivered Elizabeth's order.

"I beg your pardon?"

"I saw you looking through the paper and thought you might be job-hunting. I wouldn't normally suggest something like this, but there's an opening here, if you'd like to apply. You could start right now."

Elizabeth's pale blue eyes widened incredulously. What was this girl talking about?

"I know it's not much, but a position here could tide you over until you find what you're really looking for. The other girl who normally works with me called in this morning and quit." She paused to forcefully release her breath. "Can you imagine? Without a minute's notice. Now I'm left to deal with the lunch crowd all by myself."

Elizabeth straightened in her chair. Why not? She didn't have anything better to do. "I don't know that I'd be much help. I've never been a waitress."

"It doesn't matter." The younger girl's relief was obvious. "I can guarantee that by the end of the day you'll discover everything you ever cared to know about waitressing and a few things you didn't." Her laugh was light and cheerful. "By the way, I'm Gilly. Short for Gillian."

"And I'm Elizabeth."

"Glad to meet you, Elizabeth. Boy, am I glad." The breezy laugh returned. "Come on back to the kitchen, and I'll introduce you to Evelyn. He's the owner and chef, and I'm *sure* he'll hire you." With determined, quick-paced steps, Gilly led the way across the room to the swinging double doors. She paused and turned around. "Don't be shocked if Evelyn kisses you or something. He's like that. I think it's because he's French."

"I won't be surprised," Elizabeth murmured and had trouble containing her smile. What would Gilly say if she knew that Elizabeth spoke the language fluently and had lived in Paris?

A variety of pleasant smells assaulted her as she entered the spotless kitchen. As a little girl, her favorite place in the huge, rambling house had been the kitchen. The old cook would often sneak her pieces of pie dough or a cookie. Her childhood had been happy and untroubled.

"Evelyn," Gilly said, attracting the attention of the chef who was garbed completely in white and working busily at the stove. "This is Elizabeth. She's going to take Deanne's place."

The ruddy-faced man with a thick mustache that was shaped like an open umbrella over a full mouth turned and stared blankly at Elizabeth.

Giving in to impulse, she took a step forward and extended her hand. In flawless French, she explained that she hadn't done any waitressing but would be pleased to help them out this afternoon.

Laughing, Evelyn broke into a wild speech in his native language while pumping her hand as if she were a long-lost relative.

Again in perfect French, she explained that no, she wasn't from France or Quebec, but she had spent several years studying in his country.

An expression of astonishment widened Gilly's eyes. "You should have said you were from France."

"I'm not. I studied French in school." Elizabeth didn't explain that the school had been in Paris.

"You know, that's one thing I'm sorry for," Gilly said, thoughtfully pinching her bottom lip. "I wish I'd studied French. A lot of good Spanish does me here. But then—" she paused and chuckled "—I could always end up working in a Mexican restaurant."

Elizabeth laughed. Gilly was delightful. Amiable and full of enthusiasm, the younger girl was just the antidote for the long day that lay ahead.

Luckily, the two were close enough in size that Elizabeth could wear one of Gilly's extra uniforms.

After a minimum of instruction, Elizabeth was given a pad and pencil, and asked to wait on her first customers, an elderly couple who asked for coffee and croissants. Without incident, Elizabeth delivered their order.

"This isn't so bad," she murmured under her breath to Gilly, who was busy writing out the luncheon specials on the chalkboard that would be displayed on the sidewalk.

"I took one look at you and knew you'd do great," Gilly stated cheerfully.

"You took one look at me and saw an easy mark." A

smile revealed deep grooved dimples in each of Elizabeth's cheeks.

"Does everyone call you Elizabeth?" Briefly, Gilly returned her attention to the chalkboard. "You look more like a Beth to me."

Beth, Elizabeth mused thoughtfully. No one had called her that since her school days, and then only her best friends. After all, she was a Wainwright. "Elizabeth" was the dignified name her family preferred.

"Call me anything you like," she said in a teasing tone. "No, on second thought, you better stick with Beth."

A half-hour later Elizabeth was answering to a variety of names, among them "Miss" and "Waitress." Never had she imagined that such a simple job could be so demanding, or that there were so many things to remember. The easy acceptance given her by the customers was a pleasant surprise. Most of the café's luncheon crowd were regulars from office buildings close to the wharf. Several of them took the time to chat before ordering. A couple of men blatantly flirted with her, which did wonders for her sagging ego. A few asked about Deanne and weren't surprised when they learned that she'd quit.

The highlight of the afternoon came when she waited on a retired couple visiting from France. She spoke to them in their native language for so long that Gilly had to point out that there were several other customers who needed attention. Later Gilly was shocked to see that the couple had left a tip as large as the price of their meal.

"Tutor me in French, would you?" she joked, as she passed by carrying a glass coffeepot.

Elizabeth couldn't believe the time when she glanced at her gold wristwatch. Four o'clock. The day had sped past, and she felt exhilarated, better than she had in months. Tonight she wouldn't need a pill to help her sleep.

"You were terrific. Everyone was saying how great you were," Gilly said, laying on the praise. "A couple of regulars said they hope you'll stay. And even if it was your first time waitressing, you were as good as Deanne ever was."

After all the orders she had mixed up, Elizabeth was surprised Gilly thought so. Of course, she had eaten in some of the world's best restaurants and knew what kind of service to expect. But giving it was something else entirely.

"Would you consider staying on for a while?" Gilly's tone held a mixture of hope and doubt. "I'm sure this isn't the kind of job you want. But the pay isn't bad, and the tips are good."

Elizabeth hesitated. "I… I don't know."

"It would only be until we could find someone to replace you," Gilly added quickly. "That shouldn't be long. A week or two. Three months at the most."

"Three months?" Elizabeth gasped.

"Well, to be honest, Evelyn saw you with the French couple and told me that he'd really like to hire you permanently. I suppose it's too much to ask, with your qualifications."

What qualifications? Elizabeth mused. Oh, sure, she knew all the finer points of etiquette, but aside from her fluency in several languages, she'd never had any formal job training.

"Just think about it, okay?" Gilly urged.

Elizabeth agreed with a soft smile.

"You'll be back tomorrow?" The doelike eyes implored, making it impossible to refuse.

Exhaling slowly, Elizabeth nodded. "Sure. Why not?"

Why not indeed? she mused later as she unlocked the door to her suite at the St. Francis. Her feet hurt, and there was an ache in the small of her back, but otherwise she felt terrific.

The hot water filling the tub was steaming up the bathroom when she straightened, struck by a thought. There was no one she wanted to visit this summer, no place she wanted to go. There wasn't anything to stop her from working with Gilly. It would be fun. Well, maybe not fun, but…different, and she was definitely in the mood for different.

With the sound of the hot water still running behind her, she knotted the sash of her blue silk robe and eased her feet into matching slippers. Sitting atop the mattress, she reached for the phone. For the first time in months, she felt like talking to her father. He had a right to know where she was staying and what she was up to. Over the last year she'd given him enough to worry about.

Bently answered the phone. "Good evening, Miss Elizabeth," he said after she identified herself.

"Hello, Bently. Is my father home?"

"I'll get him for you."

Had she detected a note of worry in Bently's tone?

He was always so formal that it was difficult to discern any emotion.

"Elizabeth, dear." Her father spoke crisply. "Just exactly where are you?" He didn't wait for her to answer. "Bently said that you were home, and then, before anyone knew what had happened, you were off again."

"I'm sorry, Dad," she said, though in fact she wasn't the least bit regretful. "I'm in San Francisco. I've got a job."

"A job," her father repeated in a low, shocked tone. "Doing what?"

She laughed, mentally picturing the perplexed look working its way across her father's face. With a liberal arts degree as vague and unimpressive as her grades, she knew he doubted that anyone would want to hire her. "I'm a waitress in a small French café called The Patisserie."

"A waitress!" Charles Wainwright exploded.

"Now don't go all indignant on me. I know this is a shock. But I'm enjoying it. Some of the customers speak French, and the chef is from Paris."

"Yes, but…" Elizabeth could feel her father's shock. "But if you wanted to work," he went on, "there are a hundred positions more suited to you."

"Honestly, Dad, I'd think you'd be happy that I'm out of your hair for the summer. Wish me well and kiss Grandmother for me."

"Elizabeth…"

"My bath's running. I've got to go."

A resigned note she recognized all too well entered his voice. "Take care of yourself, my dear."

* * *

"This is working out great," Gilly commented at the end of Elizabeth's first week. "I don't know what it is, but there's something about you that the customers like."

"It's because I can pronounce the name of Evelyn's pastries," Elizabeth returned in a teasing voice.

"That's not it," Gilly contradicted with a slight quirk of her head. Her short, bouncy curls bobbed with the action. "Though having you speak French does add a certain class to the place."

"My French may be good, but my feet are killing me." She faked a small, pain-filled sigh and rubbed the bottom of one expensive loafer over the top of the other.

"Your feet wouldn't hurt if you were wearing the right shoes."

Elizabeth glanced at her Guccis and groaned. Heavens, she'd spent more on these leather loafers than she made in a week at this restaurant. How could they possibly be the wrong kind of shoe?

"If you like, we can go shopping after work and I'll show you what you should be wearing."

Gilly's offer was a pleasant surprise. "Yes, I'd like that."

"It'll give me an excuse not to go home." Discontent coated Gilly's normally happy voice.

"What's the matter with home?"

One petite shoulder rose in a halfhearted shrug. "Nothing, I guess. It's just that I turned twenty last month, and I hate living with my parents."

"So get an apartment." Elizabeth suggested the obvious, wondering why Gilly hadn't thought of that herself.

Gilly's returning smile was stiff. "So speaks the voice of inexperience. I don't suppose you've gone looking for apartments lately. Have you seen how high rent is these days?"

Elizabeth had continued to live at the St. Francis. The hotel was convenient, and what meals she didn't eat at the Patisserie were promptly delivered to her room after a simple phone call.

"It isn't that I haven't tried," Gilly continued. "I found a boarding house and stayed there until my mother found out about my neighbors."

"Your neighbors?"

"I admit they were a bit unusual," Gilly mumbled. "I never saw the girl in the room next to me, but every morning there were two empty yogurt cartons outside her door."

Elizabeth couldn't restrain her soft laugh. "Suspicious yogurt, huh?"

"That was nothing," Gilly continued, her own laugh blending with Elizabeth's. "The woman on the other side looked like a Russian weight lifter who had failed a hormone test. One look at her—or him, whichever the case may be—and my mother had me out of there so fast my head was spinning."

Elizabeth could sympathize with her friend. "I know what you mean. I moved away from home as soon as I could, too."

"And if I left, my younger sister could have her own

room and..." Gilly paused, her hand gripping Elizabeth's forearm. "He's back."

"Who?" Elizabeth glanced up to see a tall, broad-shouldered man enter the café. The first thing that impressed her was his size. He was easily six foot four. Yet he carried himself with an unconscious grace that reminded her of a martial arts expert. He wasn't handsome. His jaw was too angular, too abrupt. His mouth was firm, and even from this distance she noticed that it was slightly compressed, as if something had displeased him.

"Him," Gilly whispered under her breath. "How long has it been since you've seen such an indisputable stud?"

"Obviously too long," Elizabeth responded, picking up a menu and water glass. "But then, isn't one stud just like another?" she asked blandly. Although not strikingly handsome, this man was compelling enough to attract women's attention.

"One stud is just like another?" Gilly repeated on a low, disbelieving breath. "Beth, this guy is Secretariat."

Elizabeth had difficulty hiding her smile as she moved across to the room to deliver the ice water and menu.

Secretariat turned and watched her approach. Dark sunglasses reflected her silvery image and disguised his eyes. The glasses rested on a nose that could kindly be described as aquiline. He removed the glasses and set them on the table.

Not until she was at his table did she realize how big he actually was. Massive shoulders suited his height.

His muscular biceps strained against a short-sleeved shirt stretched taut across a broad chest. She imagined that someone of his build would have difficulty finding clothes that were anything except tight. It was unfortunate that apparently he couldn't afford to have his clothes custom-made.

"Good afternoon," she said as she handed him the menu and set the glass on the red-checked tablecloth. Her heart lodged near her throat as his fingers innocently brushed hers. There was something indefinable about him that was almost intimidating. Not that he frightened her; "intrigued" was more the word.

"Hello." His smile revealed even white teeth. He opened the menu and quickly scanned it. Without looking at her he said, "Don't worry, I don't bite."

"I didn't think you did," she returned, resenting his absolutely incorrect belief that she was easily intimidated.

"I'll have coffee. Nothing more." A scowl made its way across his face.

She wrote down his order, thinking that he didn't look like the type to indulge in delicate French pastries.

As she returned to the counter, she could feel his gaze leveled between her shoulder blades. She was accustomed to the admiring glances of men. She had what her grandmother referred to as the Wainwright coloring, a warm blend of colors that often generated curious stares. Her eyes were the palest blue and her hair a lush shade of golden brown, worn loose so that it curled in natural waves at her shoulders.

"Did you notice the muscles on him?" she muttered

under her breath to Gilly as she laid a spoon to the saucer. "I bet this guy wrestles crocodiles for a living."

Gilly pretended to be wiping down the long counter, her hand rubbing furiously as she stifled a giggle. "I think he's kinda cute."

"Yes, but you're so sweet you'd think boa constrictors were cuddly."

"He's different. I bet he's a real pussycat. Give me five minutes alone with him and I'll prove it."

"No way. He looks dangerous, like he would eat you for breakfast."

"You're teasing, aren't you?"

Elizabeth didn't answer as she delivered the coffee. Before she walked away, she noticed that he drank it quietly, cupping the mug with his massive hands as he stared out the window. A few minutes later, he stood and left a handful of change on the table, then turned to wink at Gilly.

"Goodbye." Gilly waved to him. "Come in again."

"I'd say you've got yourself an admirer," Elizabeth said, glancing from her friend to the retreating male figure.

"Not me," Gilly denied instantly. "He was watching you like a hawk. You're the one who interests him, not me."

"Then I give Tarzan to you," Elizabeth spoke somberly. "Men like him are a bit much for me." She had heard about egotistical males with bodies like his. They spent hours every day building up their muscles so they could stand in front of a mirror and admire themselves.

Just before closing time, Gilly stuck her head around

the door into the kitchen, where Elizabeth was finishing refilling the condiments.

"I bet he works on the docks."

"Who?"

"Don't be obtuse."

"Oh, Tarzan. I suppose," Elizabeth murmured, not overly interested. "I don't think he'll be back."

"He will," Gilly asserted confidently. "And sooner rather than later. There was a look in his eyes. He's attracted to you, Beth. Even I noticed." The implication was that Elizabeth should have recognized it, too.

Gilly was right. The next afternoon he arrived at the same time. Elizabeth was carrying a tray of dirty dishes to the counter when she brushed against his solid male figure.

"Excuse me." The low, almost gravelly tone left no doubt as to who was speaking.

"My fault," she muttered under her breath, disliking the uncomfortable warmth that emanated from the spot where their bodies had touched. Easily six inches taller than she was, Tarzan loomed above her. Most women would have been awed by his closeness. But the sensations she was feeling were more troubling for the way they intrigued her than frightening. He wasn't wearing his reflective glasses today. The color of his eyes, along with his guarded look, was a surprise. Their amber shade resembled burnished gold marked by darker flecks, and he was staring at her as intently as any jungle beast. Again she had the impression that this man could be dangerous. Gilly might view him as a gentle giant, but she herself wasn't nearly as confident.

"What did I tell you?" Gilly whispered in a know-it-all voice.

"I guess you know your ape-men," Elizabeth returned flippantly.

For a second Gilly looked stunned at Elizabeth's cynicism. "How can you look at someone as gorgeous as this guy and call him an ape?" Righteously, she tucked the menu under her arm. "I'm taking his order today," she announced, and she strolled across the floor.

Watching her friend's movements, Elizabeth had to stifle a small laugh. Gilly's walk couldn't be more obvious; she was interested in him, and before the afternoon was over, Tarzan would know it.

"His name's Andrew Breed," Gilly cheerfully informed her as she scooted past Elizabeth on her return. "But he says most everyone calls him Breed." She moved behind the counter before Elizabeth could respond.

Elizabeth was too busy with her own customers to notice much about either Gilly or Andrew Breed. Only once was she aware that he was studying her, his strong mouth quirked crookedly. His attention made her self-conscious. Once she thought he was going to ask her something, but if he was, the question went unasked. As he'd done the day before, he left the money for his coffee on the table and sauntered out of the café, this time before she was even aware he'd gone.

The remainder of the afternoon dragged miserably. The weather was uncharacteristically hot and humid, and she could feel tiny beads of perspiration on her upper lip. A long soak in the bath, a light meal and the

TV were sounding more appealing by the minute. She had spent most of her evenings looking for an apartment. The more she learned about Gilly's plight living at home, the more she wanted to help her friend. She had promised that if she found a place, they could move in together and share the rent, though Gilly need never know the actual figure.

Unfortunately, Elizabeth was quickly learning that Gilly hadn't underestimated the difficulty of finding a reasonably priced apartment in the city. She couldn't very well rent one for 2,000 a month and tell Gilly her share was 500. Her friend, although flighty, was smart enough to figure that out.

Gilly and Elizabeth worked together to close down the café that evening. Elizabeth's thoughts were preoccupied as Gilly chattered away excitedly about one thing or another. The girl's boundless enthusiasm affected everyone she met. She was amazing.

In the small break room behind the kitchen, Elizabeth sat, kicked off her shoes and rubbed her aching feet. Gilly hobbled around, one shoe on and the other off as she opened her purse and dug around for something in the bottom of the large bag. "What's the big hurry?" Elizabeth inquired.

"What's the hurry?" Gilly stammered. "Breed'll be out front any minute. We're going to dinner."

"Breed?" Her heart did a tiny flip-flop. "You mean to say you're going out to dinner with someone you hardly know?"

"What do you think I was telling you?"

Elizabeth straightened and slipped her feet back into

the new practical pumps she'd purchased with Gilly's approval. "I guess I wasn't paying any attention."

"I guess not!" Gilly shook her head and did a quick glance in the small mirror. "Oh dear, I'll never make it on time." Her delicate oval face creased with concern. "Beth, do me a favor. Go out front and tell him I'm running a little late. I'll be there in a few minutes."

"Sure." Her response was clipped and short. She didn't want to date Breed herself, but she wasn't sure how she felt about Gilly seeing him. The thought was so ridiculous that she pinched her mouth closed, irritated with herself.

"You don't mind, do you?" Gilly jerked her head around to study Elizabeth.

"Of course not. It's the least I can do to smooth the course of true love."

"Not about that," Gilly said.

Elizabeth tipped her head to one side in confusion.

"I mean about me going out with Breed."

"Me mind?" Elizabeth asked, giving an indifferent shrug. "Why should I care one way or the other?"

Gilly arched both nicely arched brows. "Because it's really you he's interested in."

"You keep saying that," Elizabeth said, shaking her head in denial. "Either you've got some sixth sense or I'm completely dense."

Without hesitation, Gilly threw back her head, her tight curls bouncing. "You're dense."

Resolutely squaring her shoulders, Elizabeth headed for the front of the café. Evelyn followed her out to lock the door after her, just as Gilly stuck her head around the kitchen door. "He's coming!" she cried. "I can see him across the street." Her round, panic-stricken eyes pleaded with Elizabeth. "Keep him occupied, will you?"

"Don't worry." She smiled at Evelyn on the other side of the glass door as he turned the lock. He looked at her and playfully rolled his eyes.

When Elizabeth turned around, she was only a few inches from Breed. This man had the strangest effect on her. She wasn't sure how she felt about him. His appeal blossomed with every encounter. It hadn't taken her long to realize that her first impression of him as a muscle-bound egomaniac was completely wrong. He seemed almost unaware of the effect he had on women.

"Gilly will be ready in a minute. She's changing clothes now."

The tight corners of Breed's mouth edged upward. "No problem. I'm early."

She folded her arms around her slim waist. "She's looking forward to tonight." Realizing her body language was revealing her state of mind, she quickly dropped her hands to her sides.

"I make you uncomfortable, don't I?"

Color rose from her neck, brightening her cheeks. "It's not that. I... I don't think I've ever known anyone quite like you."

"As big, you mean?"

"No, not that."

His strong, angular chin tilted downward fractionally. "And I don't think I've ever known anyone as beautiful as you." The words were soft, husky.

She sensed immediately that he wished he could

withdraw them. He hadn't intended to say that. She was sure of it.

"My size *is* intimidating," he stated flatly, taking a step in retreat. There was a strong suggestion of impatience in the way he moved, something she hadn't noted in the past. And right now he was angry with himself.

Ignoring his strong, male profile, she turned and looked up at the cloudless blue sky.

They both spoke at once.

"The weather…"

"How long…"

"You first." Breed smiled, and a pleasant warmth invaded her limbs.

"I was going to say that I was enjoying the weather this summer. After all that talk about the California smog and San Francisco's famous fog, I wasn't sure what to expect."

"You're not from California?" He looked surprised.

She didn't know why he should be; her light Boston accent wasn't difficult to decipher. "No, my roots are on the East Coast. Boston."

He nodded.

"Do you work on the wharf?" Conversation was easy with him; something else she hadn't expected. "Gilly and I were trying to guess."

"I'm a longshoreman."

It was her turn to give a polite nod. "It must be hard work." What else would give him muscles like that?

Fresh as a dewy rosebud, Gilly floated out the door in a light-blue summer dress. "Sorry to keep you waiting, Breed."

His amber eyes crinkled at the corners with a warm smile. "It was worth it," he said as he moved to her side, taking her hand in his.

Wiping a bead of perspiration from her forehead, Elizabeth gave Breed and Gilly a feeble smile. "Have fun, you two."

"Would you like to join us?" Gilly said.

Elizabeth took a step backward. As crazy as it sounded, she was half tempted. "I can't tonight. I'm going to look at another apartment."

"Beth, it's hopeless," Gilly said, her voice emphatic.

Breed's eyes surveyed her with open interest. "You're looking for an apartment?"

"Are we ever!" Gilly proclaimed enthusiastically.

"Let me know what happens. I might be able to find something for you. My brother-in-law manages a building, and he told me he has a vacancy coming."

Gilly almost threw herself into his arms. "Really? Can we see it soon? Oh, Beth, what do you think?"

Elizabeth's smile wasn't nearly as enthusiastic. If Breed's brother-in-law showed them the apartment, he was sure to mention the rent, and Elizabeth knew Gilly couldn't afford much.

"Let me check out this ad tonight, and we can talk about it later."

A half-hour later Elizabeth was soaking in a hot tub filled with light-scented bubble bath. With the back of her head resting against the polished enamel, she closed her eyes, regretting that she hadn't gone with Breed and Gilly.

Two

"Oh, Beth!" Gilly exclaimed as she hurriedly stepped from room to room of the two-bedroom apartment in the marina district. "I can hardly believe how lucky you were to find this place. It's perfect."

Elizabeth was rather proud of it herself. The building was an older brick structure that had recently been renovated. She'd been fortunate to find it, even more fortunate to have convinced Gilly and Gilly's parents that the rent was cheaper for the first six months because there was still construction going on in the building. The perfection of the apartment made her deception easier. She could afford to pay three-quarters of the rent without Gilly ever being the wiser.

Polished wooden floors in the entryway led to a large carpeted living room that made liberal use of skylights.

"I still can't believe it," Gilly said as she turned slowly, her head tilted back to view the boundless blue sky through the polished glass ceiling. "I never dreamed you'd find something like this. Did you see that kitchen?" She returned her attention to Elizabeth. "Even my mother doesn't have such new appliances." With a deep sense of awe, she stepped into the kitchen and ran her hand along the marble counter. "I can't believe how well everything is working out for us." Pausing to glance at her wristwatch, she shook her head. "I've got one last load to bring over. I shouldn't be more than an hour."

"Don't worry. I'll hold down the fort," Elizabeth returned absently.

There were several things she wanted to do herself, including grocery shopping. She could fill the cupboards and Gilly would have no way of knowing how much she'd spent. When they divided the bill, Gilly wouldn't realize that she was only paying a fraction of the total. Elizabeth was enjoying the small duplicity. With a growing sense of excitement, she changed her clothes and started to make out an errand list. The Wainwrights were known for their contributions to charity, but this wasn't charity. She felt as though she owed Gilly something. If it hadn't been for Gilly, she was convinced she would still be trapped in the sluggish indifference that had dominated her life these past months. Her mother would have liked Gilly. Elizabeth pulled herself up straight. She hadn't thought about her mother in weeks. Even so, the memory remained sharp, with the power to inflict deep emotional pain. Just then the doorbell chimed. She couldn't imagine who it could be. Her step quickened as she walked to the door and opened it.

"Hello, Breed." Her hand tightened on the glass doorknob.

He handed her a large bouquet of flowers. "Welcome to the neighborhood," he said with a boyish grin.

"You live around here?" Her voice caught in her throat as she accepted the flowers. "Come in, please. I'm not being much of a hostess." She stepped back to allow him to enter and closed the door with her foot. "Gilly isn't here, but you're welcome to come in and tour the place if you like."

A smile glinted from his eyes as he followed her into the kitchen. "I'd like."

Deftly, she arranged the flowers and set them in the middle of the round kitchen table before leading the way through the apartment, glossing over the details.

"You're renting this for how much?"

Her heart dropped to her stomach. Gilly had apparently said something to Breed about their rent. She gave a light, breezy laugh, or what she hoped sounded light and breezy, and repeated what she'd told Gilly.

"Funny, I didn't notice any construction." He stood at the picture window.

"Of course you didn't." She continued the deception while keeping her gaze lowered. "Even carpenters go home in the evening." She was rescued from any further explanation by Gilly, who breathlessly barged through the door carrying a large box.

"Let me help." Immediately Breed took it from her and helped her carry in the remaining boxes.

When they'd finished, Gilly strolled into the kitchen.

"Breed offered to take us out to dinner. You'll come, won't you?"

Elizabeth's gaze flittered past her friend to Breed. She was uncomfortably aware of the unspoken questions he was sending her way.

"Not this time."

Gilly exhaled a heavy breath and pushed the curls away from her face in an exasperated movement. "But you will soon, right?" She glanced from Breed to Elizabeth.

"Another time," Elizabeth agreed, going back to her list.

"Promise?" Gilly prompted.

"Promise," Elizabeth returned, unsure why she felt the way she did. There was something about Breed that troubled her. Not his size, although he was right: that in itself *was* intimidating. His eyes often held a mischievous glint, as if he knew something she didn't. Not that he was laughing at her—far from it. There was understanding, compassion, and sometimes she thought she caught a glimmer of something close to sympathy. He was a complicated man, and she was afraid that if she investigated further, she would like him a lot more than she had a right to.

She should have realized that neither of them would go on accepting her refusal to join them. The following Saturday Gilly was adamant that Elizabeth go with them to the beach.

"You're coming!" she insisted, stuffing an extra beach towel in her bag.

"Gilly…" Elizabeth moaned.

"It's a gorgeous day. How can you even think about sitting at home when you can be lazing on the beach, soaking up the sun?"

"But I don't want to intrude."

"Intrude? Are you nuts? We want you to come."

Gilly had gone out with Breed twice in the last week. They'd asked Elizabeth along both times.

Elizabeth liked Breed. The intensity of her feelings both surprised and alarmed her. Each time Gilly and Breed went out they returned early, and then the three of them sat in the living room and talked while drinking coffee. At every meeting, Elizabeth grew more aware of him. Gilly had reacted naturally to the magnetic appeal of the man, but it had taken Elizabeth longer to recognize his potency.

He was a wonderful conversationalist. His experiences were broad and seemingly unlimited. Several times she had to bite her tongue to keep from revealing too much of herself and her background in response. In some ways she felt there wasn't anything she couldn't share with him.

She didn't know what to make of Gilly's relationship with him. They seemed to enjoy one another's company and had formed an easy friendship. But Gilly was the world's friend. After she and Breed had spent an evening together, Elizabeth would study her roommate closely. Gilly didn't appear to be falling in love, and Elizabeth found that conclusion comforting. Not that she was such an expert on love. There had been several times when she had wondered whether she was in love, but then she'd decided that if she had to wonder, she wasn't.

"Put on your swimsuit!" Gilly shouted from the kitchen now. "And hurry. Breed'll be here in ten minutes."

"You're sure you want me along?" Elizabeth continued to waver.

Gilly turned around and rolled her eyes theatrically. "Yes! You really do have a problem with the obvious, don't you?"

Elizabeth changed into her silky turquoise bikini. On the beaches of the Riviera, the skimpy two-piece had been modest. Now, studying herself in the mirror, she felt naked and more than a little vulnerable.

Gilly gave a low wolf whistle. "Wow! That doesn't look like it came from Best Beach Bargains dot com."

"Is it okay? There's not much to it." Elizabeth's gaze was questioning.

"I know. It's gorgeous—*you're* gorgeous."

"I'm not sure I should wear it…. I've got a sundress that would serve just as well."

"Elizabeth," Gilly insisted, "wear the bikini." She bit into a carrot stick. "Honestly, sometimes I swear you're the most insecure person I've ever met." She took the carrot stick out of her mouth and held it in her fingers like a cigarette. "By the way, where *did* you get that suit? I've never seen anything like it."

Elizabeth hesitated, her mind whirling in a thousand directions. "A little place… I don't remember the name."

"Well, wherever it is you shop, they sure have beautiful clothes."

"Thank you," Elizabeth mumbled as she put on a white cover-up. Quickly she changed the subject. "You're looking great yourself."

Gilly lowered her gaze to her rose-colored one-piece with a deep-veed neckline and halter top. "This old rag?"

"You just got that last week."

"I know, but next to you, it might as well be a rag."

"Gilly, that's not true, and you know it."

"Yes, but look at you. You're perfect. There isn't anything I wouldn't sacrifice for long legs and a figure like yours."

Elizabeth was still laughing when Breed arrived. He paused and gave Gilly an appreciative glance. "I should have suggested the beach sooner. You look fantastic."

She positively sparkled under his appraisal. "Wait until you see Elizabeth's suit. She's the one with the glorious body."

Breed didn't comment, but he exchanged a meaningful glance with Elizabeth that said more than words.

Admittedly, she wanted to impress him. Deep within herself she yearned for his eyes to reveal the approval he had given Gilly. To divert her mind from its disconcerting course, she tightened the sash of her cover-up and added suntan lotion to her beach bag.

"I'm ready if you are," she said to no one in particular. She continued to feel a little uneasy infringing on Gilly's time with Breed, but she was pleased to be spending the day in the sun. In past summers she had prided herself on a luxurious tan. Already it was the third week of June, and she looked as pale as eggwhite.

An hour later they had spread a blanket on a crowded beach at Santa Cruz, sharing the sand with a thousand other sun-worshippers. Breed sat with his knees bent as Gilly smoothed lotion into his broad shoulders.

Mesmerized, Elizabeth couldn't tear her eyes away. Gilly's fingers blended the tanning lotion with the thin sheen of perspiration that slicked his muscular back. She rubbed him with slow, firm strokes until Elizabeth's mouth went dry. The bronze skin rippled with the massaging movements, his flesh supple under Gilly's manipulations. Lean and hard, Breed was excitingly, sensuously, all male.

Elizabeth's breath caught in her throat as Breed turned his head and she felt his gaze. His eyes roamed her face, pausing on the fullness of her lips. They were filled with silent messages meant only for her. They were messages she couldn't decipher, afraid of their meaning. Her cheeks suffused with hot color, and she dragged her eyes from his.

"You probably should put on some lotion, too, Elizabeth," he commented. The slight huskiness of his voice was the only evidence that he was as affected as she by their brief exchange.

"He's right," Gilly agreed. "When I've finished here, I'll do you."

Elizabeth was amused at the look of disappointment he cast her. He'd planned to do it himself, and Gilly had easily thwarted him.

After Gilly's quick application of lotion to her back, Elizabeth slathered her face, arms and stomach, and lay down on her big beach blanket. A forearm over her eyes blocked out the piercing rays of the afternoon sun. Pretending to be asleep, she was only half listening as Breed and Gilly chatted about one thing or another.

"Hey, look!" Gilly cried excitedly. "They've started a game of volleyball. You two want to play?"

"Not me," Elizabeth mumbled.

"You go ahead," Breed insisted.

A spray of sand hit Elizabeth's side as Gilly took off running. Judging by her enthusiasm, no doubt she was good at the game.

"Mind if I share the blanket with you?" Breed asked softly.

"Of course not." Despite her words, her mind was screaming for him to join Gilly at volleyball.

He stretched out beside her, so close their thighs touched. She tensed, her long nails biting into her palms. Her nerves had fired to life at the merest brush of his skin against hers. She attempted to scoot away, but granules of sand dug into her shoulder blade, and she realized she couldn't go any farther.

Never had she been more acutely aware of a man. Every sense was dominated by him. He smelled of spicy musk and fragrant tobacco. Did he smoke? She couldn't remember seeing him smoke. Either way, nothing had ever smelled more tantalizing.

Salty beads of perspiration dotted her upper lip, and she forced her mouth into a tight line. If he were to kiss her she would taste the salty flavor of his... She sat up abruptly, unable to endure any more of these twisted games her mind was playing.

"I think I'll take a swim," she announced breathlessly.

"Running away?" His gaze mocked her.

"Running?" she echoed innocently. "No way. I want to cool down."

"Good idea. I could use a cold water break myself." With an agility she was sure was unusual in a man his size, he got quickly to his feet.

As he brushed the sand from the backs of his legs, she ran toward the ocean. With her long hair flying behind her, she laughed as she heard him shout for her to wait. The water was only a few feet away, and they hit the pounding surf together.

The spray of cold water that splashed against her thighs took Elizabeth's breath away, and she stopped abruptly. Shouldn't the ocean off the California coast be warmer than this?

Breed dived into an oncoming wave and surfaced several feet away. He turned and waited for her to join him.

Following his lead, she swam to him, keeping her head above water as her smooth, even strokes cut into the swelling ocean.

"What's the matter?" he called. "Afraid to get your hair wet?"

"I don't want to look like Jack Sparrow."

He laughed, and she couldn't remember hearing a more exciting sound.

"You should laugh more often."

"Me?" A frown darkened his eyes. "You're the one

who needs a few lessons on having fun." He placed a hand at her waist. "Let's take this wave together."

Without being given an option, she was thrust into the oncoming wall of water. As they went under the giant surge, she panicked, frantically lashing out with her arms and legs.

Breed pulled her to the surface. "Are you all right?"

"No," she managed to say, coughing and choking on her words. Saltwater stung her eyes. Her hair fell in wet tendrils over her face. "You did that on purpose," she accused him angrily.

"Of course I did," he countered. "It's supposed to be fun."

"Fun?" she spat. "Marie Antoinette's walk to the guillotine was more fun than that."

Breed sobered. "Come on. I'll take you back to the blanket."

"I don't want to go back." Another wave hit her, and her body rolled with it, her face going below the surface just as it crested. Again she came up coughing.

He joined her and helped her find her footing. "This is too much for you."

"It isn't," she sputtered. "If this is supposed to be fun, then I'll do it." With both hands she pushed the wet, stringy hair from her face. The feel of his body touching hers was doing crazy things to her equilibrium. The whole world began to sway. It might have been the effect of the ocean, but she doubted it.

"Will you teach me, Breed?" she requested in a husky whisper. She felt his body tense as the movement of the Pacific tide brought him close.

"Hold on," he commanded, just as another wave engulfed them.

She slipped her arms around his neck and held her breath. His arms surrounded her protectively, pressing her into the shelter of his body. Their feet kicked in unison, and they broke the surface together.

"How was that?" he asked.

Her eyes still closed, she nodded. "Better." Why was she kidding herself? This was heaven. Being held by Breed was the most perfect experience she could remember. That took her by surprise. She'd been held more intimately by others.

Slowly she opened her eyes. He pushed the hair from her face. "You're slippery," he murmured, pulling her more tightly into his embrace. His massive hands found their place at the small of her back.

"So are you. It must be the suntan lotion." Her breasts brushed his torso, and shivers of tingling desire raced through her. Such a complete physical response was as pleasant as it was unexpected.

"Watch out!" he called as they took the next wave. With their bodies intertwined, they rode the swell together.

A crooked smile was slanting Breed's mouth as they surfaced. Again his fingers brushed the long strands of wet hair from her face. He tucked them behind her ear, exposing her neck.

Elizabeth could feel the pulse near her throat flutter wildly. He pressed his fingertips to it and raised his eyes to her. In their golden depths she read desire, regret, surprise. He seemed to be as unprepared for this physical attraction as she was.

His mouth gently explored the pounding pulse in her neck. Moaning softly, she rolled her head to one side. His lips teased her skin, sending unanticipated shivers of delight washing over her. When he stopped, his eyes again sought hers.

"You taste salty."

Words refused to form. It was all she could do to nod.

He had come with Gilly. She had no right to be in the ocean with him, wanting him to kiss her so badly that she could feel it in every pore of her body.

"We should go back." She heard the husky throb in her voice.

"Yes," he agreed.

But they didn't move.

His crooked grin returned. "Did you have fun?"

She nodded.

"I'm sorry about your hair."

"Are you trying to tell me I look like Jack Sparrow?"

"No. If you want the truth, I've never seen you look more beautiful."

Her skin chilled, then flushed with warmth. She couldn't believe that his words had the power to affect her body temperature.

"You're being too kind," she murmured, the soft catch in her voice revealing the effect of his words.

They lingered in the water as if they both wanted to delay the return to reality for as long as possible. Then, together, they walked out of the surf, hand in hand.

When they reached their blanket, he retrieved their

towels. "Here." He handed her the thickest one and buried his face in his own.

Sitting on the blanket, Elizabeth dug through her beach bag and came up with a comb. She was running it through her hair when Gilly came rushing up, a tall, blond man beside her.

"Breed and Elizabeth, this is Peter."

"Hi, Peter." Breed rose to his feet, standing several inches taller than the other man. The two of them shook hands. For a second Breed looked from Gilly to Peter, then back again. His brows pulled into a thick frown.

"Peter invited me to stay and play volleyball, then grab some dinner," Gilly explained enthusiastically. "He said he'd take me home later. You two don't mind, do you?"

Elizabeth's eyes widened with shock. Did Gilly honestly believe she should come to the beach with one man and leave with another?

"We don't mind," Breed answered for them both.

"You're sure?" Gilly seemed to want Elizabeth's approval.

"Go ahead," Elizabeth murmured, but her eyes refused to meet Gilly's.

"You guys looked like you were having fun in the water."

A gust of wind whipped Elizabeth's wet hair across her face. She pushed it aside. The action gave her vital moments to compose herself. Obviously Gilly had been watching her. Worse, it could be the reason her roommate had decided to stay there with Peter. She couldn't allow that to happen.

"We had a wonderful time." Breed answered for them both again.

"I'll see you tonight, then," Gilly said, walking backward as she spoke.

Frustrated, Elizabeth called out for Gilly to wait, but her friend ignored her, turned, and took off running. "We can't let her do that," she told Breed.

"What?" A speculative light entered his eyes.

"What's the matter with the two of you? Gilly's going off with a complete stranger. It isn't safe." She tugged the comb through her hair angrily. "Heaven knows what she's walking into. You didn't have to be so willing to agree to her crazy schemes. I'm not going to leave this beach without her." She knew she should say something about her fear that her own behavior with him had led to Gilly's decision, but her courage failed her.

"She's twenty and old enough to take care of herself." Despite his words, his low voice contained a note of vague concern.

"She's too trusting."

Ignoring her, he opened the cooler he'd brought and took out a bucket of chicken. "Want a piece?" he questioned, biting into a leg.

"Breed…" Elizabeth was quickly losing her patience. They were an hour from San Francisco, and he was literally handing Gilly over to a stranger.

"All right." He expelled his breath forcefully and closed the lid on the food. "Gilly knows Peter. I introduced them last week."

"What?" she gasped. None of this was making sense.

"The last time I went out with Gilly, we were really meeting Peter."

"I don't believe this."

"I didn't exactly need an expert to see that it was going to take weeks of coming to the Patisserie before you'd agree to go out with me."

"What's that got to do with anything?"

"Plenty." He didn't sound thrilled to be revealing his motivations. "I don't blame you. I know I can be a little intimidating at first."

She wanted to explain that it wasn't his size that intimidated her, but she didn't know how to account for her reticence. She couldn't very well explain that it was the way his eyes looked in a certain light or something equally vague. "So you dated Gilly instead?"

He nodded. "She knew that first night it was you I was interested in. We planned this today." The tone of his voice relayed his unwillingness to play the game.

No wonder Gilly had been so anxious for her to join them every time she'd gone out with Breed.

"But you looked surprised when Gilly brought Peter over." She recalled the partially concealed question his eyes had shot at Gilly and Peter.

"Those two should be nominated for the Academy Award. They were supposed to have been long-lost friends." His jaw tightened as he turned away from her to look out over the ocean. His profile was strong and masculine.

"You didn't have to tell me." His honesty was a measure of how much he cared.

"No, I didn't. But I felt you had the right to know."

His arms circled his bent knees. "I hope Gilly realizes what a good friend you are."

Lightly, she traced her fingers over the corded muscles of his back. A smile danced at the edges of her mouth as she stretched out on the blanket. "No, I think you've got the facts wrong. It's me who needs to thank Gilly."

He turned just enough so that he could see her lying there, looking up at him.

"How could I have been so stupid?" She whispered the question, staring into the powerful face of this man whose heart was just as big as the rest of him.

He lay on his stomach beside her.

"Have you always been big?"

"Have you always had freckles on your nose?" he asked, turning the tables on her. His index finger brushed the tip of her nose.

Her hand flew to her face. "They're ugly. I've hated them all my life."

"You disguise them rather well."

"Of course I do. What woman wants orange dots glowing from her nose?"

"They're perfect."

"Breed," she said, raising herself up so that she rested her weight on her elbows, "how can you say that?"

"Maybe it's because I find you to be surprisingly delightful. You're refreshingly honest, hard-working, and breathtakingly beautiful."

She recalled all the flattery she'd received from men who had something to gain by paying attention to her. A large inheritance was coming to her someday. That was enough incentive to make her overwhelmingly attractive to any man.

But here she was on a crowded California beach with someone who didn't know her from Eve. And he sincerely found her beautiful. She cast her gaze downward, suddenly finding her deception distasteful. A lone tear found its way to the corner of her eye.

"Elizabeth, what's wrong?"

She didn't know how she could explain. "Nothing," she returned softly. "The wind must have blown sand in my eye." By tilting her chin upward toward the brilliant blue sky, she was able to quell any further emotion.

She lay down again, resuming her sun-soaking position. Breed rolled over, positioning himself so close she felt his skin brush hers.

"Comfortable?" he asked.

"Yes."

His large hand reached for hers, and they just lay there together, fingers entwined. They didn't speak, but the communication between them was stronger than words.

Finally she dozed.

"Elizabeth." A hand at her shoulder shook her lightly. "If you don't put something on, you'll get burned."

Struggling to a sitting position, she discovered Breed kneeling above her, holding out her cover-up. "You'd better wear this."

She put it on. "Is there any of that chicken left?"

"Are you hungry?"

"Starved. I was in such a rush this morning, I didn't eat breakfast."

Opening the cooler, Breed fixed her a plate of food that was enough to feed her for three meals.

She didn't say so, though. She just took a big bite of the chicken. Fabulous. But she couldn't decide if it was the meal or the man.

The sun had sunk into a pink sky when Breed pulled up to the curb outside her apartment.

"You'll come in for coffee, won't you?" Elizabeth spoke the words even though they both knew that coffee had nothing to do with why he was coming inside.

She continued with the pretense, filling the coffeemaker with water and turning it on. She turned to discover his smoldering amber eyes burning into her. Her heart skipped a beat, then accelerated wildly at the promise she read there.

Wordlessly, she walked into his arms. This was the first time he'd held her outside the water, and she was amazed at how perfectly their bodies fitted together. The top of her head was tucked neatly under his chin.

Her smile was provocative as she slipped her arms around his neck and tilted her head back to look up at him.

His eyes were smiling back at her.

"What's so amusing?"

"The glow from your freckles is blinding me."

"If I wasn't so eager for you to kiss me, I'd make you pay for that remark."

Breed lowered his mouth to an inch above hers. "I have a feeling I'm going to pay anyway," he murmured as he tightly wrapped his arms around her.

Being so close to this vibrant man was enough to disturb her senses. She tried to ignore the myriad sensations his touch aroused in her. As silly and crazy as it seemed, she felt like Sleeping Beauty waiting for the kiss that would awaken her after a hundred years.

Tenderly his mouth brushed over her eyelid, causing her lashes to flutter shut. Next he kissed her nose. "I love those freckles," he whispered.

Lastly he kissed her mouth with a masterful possession that was everything she had dreamed a kiss could be. It was a kiss worth waiting a hundred years for. He was gentle yet possessive. Pliant yet hard. Responsive yet restrained.

"Oh, Breed," she whispered achingly.

"I know." He breathed against her temple. "I wasn't expecting this, either."

She closed her eyes and breathed in the mingled scent of spicy musk and saltwater. With her head pressed close to his heart, she could hear the uneven beat and knew he was as overwhelmed as she was at how right everything felt between them.

"I should go," he mumbled into her hair. He didn't need to add that he meant he should leave while he still had the power to pull himself out of her arms. "Can I see you tomorrow?"

Eagerly, she nodded.

He pulled away. "Walk me to the door."

She did as he requested. He kissed her again, but not

with the intensity of the first time. Then, lightly, he ran one finger over her cheek. "Tomorrow," he whispered.

"Tomorrow," she repeated, closing the door after him.

Three

Elizabeth adjusted the strap of her pink linen summer dress as Gilly strolled down the hall and leaned against the doorjamb, studying her. "Hey, you look fantastic."

"Thanks." Elizabeth's smile was uneasy. Breed had been on her mind all day, dominating her thoughts, filling her consciousness. Yesterday at the beach could have been a fluke, the result of too much sun and the attention of an attractive man. Yet she couldn't remember a day she had enjoyed more. Certainly not in the last two years. Breed made her feel alive again. This morning she'd been cooking her breakfast and humming. She couldn't remember the last time she'd felt so content. When she was with him, she wanted to laugh and throw caution to the wind.

Continuing to date him was doing exactly that. She couldn't see herself staying in San Francisco past the summer. When it came time to return to Boston, her heart could be so entangled with Breed that leaving would be intolerable. No, she decided, she had to protect herself...*and* him. He didn't know who she was, and she could end up hurting him. She couldn't allow herself to fall in love with him. She had to guard herself against whatever potential there was to this relationship. She couldn't allow this attraction to develop into anything more than a light flirtation.

"I sure wish I knew where you got your clothes," Gilly continued to chatter. "They're fantastic."

Elizabeth ignored the comment. "Do you think I'll need the jacket?" The matching pink top was casually draped over her index finger as her gaze sought Gilly's.

Gilly gave a careless shrug, crossing her arms and legs as she gave Elizabeth a thorough inspection. "I think I'd probably take it. You can never be certain what the weather's going to do. Besides, Breed may keep you out into the early-morning hours."

"Not when I have to work tomorrow, he won't," Elizabeth returned confidently.

The doorbell chimed just as she finished rolling the lip gloss across the fullness of her bottom lip.

"I'll get it," Gilly called from the kitchen.

Placing her hands against the dresser to steady herself, Elizabeth inhaled, deeply and soothingly, and commanded her pounding heart to be still. The way she reacted to Breed, someone would think she was a sixteen-year-old who had just been asked out by the captain of the football team.

"It's Breed," Gilly said, sauntering into the room.

Elizabeth gave herself one final inspection in the dresser mirror. "I thought it must be." Folding her jacket over her forearm, she walked into the living room, where he was waiting.

"Hi," she said as casually as possible. He looked good. So good. His earthy sensuality was even more evident now than in the dreams her mind had conjured up the previous night. Suddenly she felt tongue-tied and frightened. She could so easily come to love this man.

"Beth didn't say where the two of you were going," Gilly said before biting into a crisp apple.

"I thought we'd take in the outdoor concert at the Sigmund Stern Grove. A cabaret sextet I'm familiar with is scheduled for this afternoon. That is—" he hesitated and caught Elizabeth's eye "—unless you have any objection."

"That sounds great." By some miracle she found her voice. The corded muscles of Breed's massive shoulders relaxed. If she hadn't known better she would have guessed that he was as nervous about this date as she was. He glanced at his watch. "If we plan to get a seat in the stands, then I suggest we leave now."

Gilly followed them to the door. "I won't wait up for you," she whispered, just loud enough for Elizabeth to hear.

"I won't be late," Elizabeth countered with a saccharine-sweet smile, discounting her friend's assumption that she wouldn't be home until the wee hours of the morning.

Breed opened the door to a late-model, mud-splattered, army-green military-style Jeep and glanced up at her quizzically. "I had to bring Hilda today. Do you mind?"

A Jeep! The urge to laugh was so strong that she had

to hold her breath. She'd never ridden in one in her life. "Sure, it looks like fun."

His hand supported the underside of her elbow as she climbed inside the vehicle. A vague disturbance fluttered along her nerve-endings at his touch, as impersonal as it was. He'd placed a blanket over the seat to protect her dress. His thoughtfulness touched her heart. The problem was, almost everything about this man touched her heart.

Once she was seated inside the open Jeep, her eyes were level with his. She turned and smiled as some of the nervous tension flowed from her.

When his warm, possessive mouth claimed her lips, Elizabeth's senses were overwhelmed with a rush of pleasure. The kiss, although brief, was ardent, and left her weak and shaking. Abruptly, Breed stepped back, as though he had surprised himself as much as he did her.

Dazed, she blinked at him. "What was that for?" she asked breathlessly.

He walked around to the other side of the Jeep and climbed inside without effort. He gripped the steering wheel as he turned and grinned at her. "For being such a good sport. To be honest, I thought you'd object to Hilda."

"To a fine lady like Hilda?" she teased. A trace of color returned to her bloodless cheeks. "Never. Why do you call her Hilda?"

"I don't know." He lifted one shoulder in a half-shrug. "Her personality's a lot like a woman's. It seems when I least expect trouble, that's when she decides to break down." The mocking glint of laughter touched his amber eyes. "She's as temperamental as they come."

"Proud, too," Elizabeth commented, but her words were drowned out by the roar of the engine. Hilda coughed, sputtered, and then came to life with a vengeance.

"See what I mean?" he said as he shifted gears and pulled onto the street.

By the time they'd reached the park, her carefully styled hair was a mess. The wind had whipped it from its loose chignon and carelessly tossed it about her neck and face.

"You all right?" he asked with a mischievous look in his eye.

She opened her purse and took out a brush. "Just give me a minute to comb my hair and scrape the bugs from my teeth and I'll be fine."

The pleasant sound of his laughter caused the sensitive muscles of her flat stomach to tighten. "I think Hilda must like you," he said as he climbed out and slammed the door. "I know I do." The words were issued under his breath, as if he hadn't meant for her to hear them.

The park was crowded, the free concerts obviously a popular program of the Parks and Recreation Department. Already the stands looked full, and it didn't seem as if they would find seats together. Other couples had spread blankets on the lush green grass.

With a guiding hand at her elbow, he led her toward the far end of the stands. "I think we might find a seat for you over here."

"Breed." She stopped him and turned slightly. "Couldn't we take the blanket from Hilda and sit on the lawn?"

"You'd want to do that?" He looked shocked.

"Why not?"

His eyes surveyed her dress, lingering momentarily on the jutting swell of her breasts. "But you might ruin your dress."

A flush of heat warmed her face at the bold look he was giving her. "Let me worry about that," she murmured, her voice only slightly affected.

"If you're sure." His eyes sought hers.

"Get the blanket, and I'll find us a place to sit."

A few minutes later they settled onto the grass and waited silently for the music to start. She had sat in the great musical halls of Europe and throughout the United States, but rarely had she anticipated a concert more. When the first melodious strains of a violin echoed through the air, she relaxed and closed her eyes.

The sextet proved to be as versatile as they were talented. The opening selection was a medley of classical numbers that she recognized and loved. Enthusiastic applause showed the audience's approval. Then the leader came to the front and introduced the next numbers, a variety of musical scores from classic films.

She shifted position, the hard ground causing her to fold her legs one way and then another.

"Here," Breed whispered, situating himself so that he was directly behind her, his legs to one side. "Use me for support." His hands ran down her bare arms as he eased her body against his. After a while she didn't know which score was louder, the one the musicians were playing or the one in her heart.

After the hour-long concert, Breed took her to a restaurant that he claimed served the best Mexican food this side of the Rio Grande.

"What did you think?" he asked as they sat across from one another in the open-air restaurant, eating cheese enchiladas and refried beans.

A gentle breeze ruffled her sandy hair about her shoulders as she set her fork aside. "How do I feel about the concert or the food?"

"The concert." He pushed his plate aside, already finished, while she was only half done.

"It was great. The whole afternoon's been wonderful." She cupped a tall glass of iced tea. Breed would be taking her home soon, and already she was dreading it. This day had been more enjoyable than all of the last six months put together, and she didn't want it to end. Every minute they were together was better than the one before. It sounded silly, but she didn't know how else to describe her feelings. Deliberately she took a long sip of her drink and set her fork aside.

"Are you finished already?"

Her gaze skimmed her half-full plate, and she nodded, her appetite gone.

"I suppose we should think about getting you back to the apartment."

Her heart sang at the reluctance in his voice. For one perfect moment their gazes met and locked. She didn't want to go home, and he didn't want to take her.

"How about a walk along the beach?" he suggested with a hint of reluctance.

She wondered why he was wary. Afraid of what she made him feel? No matter. She herself demonstrated no such hesitation. "Yes, I'd like that."

Hilda delivered them safely to an ocean beach about fifteen minutes outside the city. Others apparently had the same idea; several couples were strolling the sand, their arms wrapped around one another's waists.

"Do you need to scrape the bugs from your teeth this time?" Breed asked as he shifted into Park and turned off the engine. A smile was lurking at the edges of his sensuous mouth.

"No," she replied softly. "I've discovered that the secret of riding in Hilda is simply to keep my mouth closed."

His answering smile only served to remind her of the strength and raw virility that were so much a part of him. Her gaze rested admiringly on the smoothly hewn angles of his face as he climbed out of the Jeep and came around to her side. She must have been crazy to ever have thought of him as an ape-man. The thought produced a grimace of anger at herself.

"Is something wrong?" He even seemed sensitive to her thoughts.

"It's nothing," she said, dismissing the question without meeting his gaze.

Again his touch was impersonal as he guided her down a semi-steep embankment. A small, swiftly flowing creek separated them from the main part of the beach.

She hesitated as she searched for the best place to cross.

"What's the matter?" he teased with a vaguely challenging lilt to his voice. "Are you afraid of getting your feet wet?"

"Of course not," she denied instantly. "Well, maybe a little," she amended with a sheepish smile. It wasn't the water as much as the uncertainty of how deep it was.

"Allow me," he said as he swept her into his arms. One arm supported her back and the other her knees. Her hands flew automatically to his neck.

"Breed," she said under her breath, "what are you doing?"

"What any gallant gentleman would do for a lady in distress. I'm escorting you to safety." His amber eyes were dancing with mischief. He took a few steps and teetered, causing her grip on his neck to tighten.

"Breed!" she cried. "I'm too heavy. Put me down."

His chiseled mouth quirked teasingly as he took a few more hurried steps and delivered her safely to the other side. When he set her down, she noticed that his pants legs were soaking wet.

"You *are* a gallant knight, aren't you." Her inflection made the question a statement of fact.

Something so brief that she thought she'd imagined it flickered in his expression. It came and went so quickly she couldn't decipher its meaning, if there was one.

The dry sand immediately filled her sandals, and after only a few steps she paused to take them off. He did the same, removing his shoes and socks, and setting them beside a large rock. She tossed hers to join his.

They didn't say anything for a long time as they strolled, their hands linked. He positioned himself so that he took the brunt of the strong breeze that came off the water.

Elizabeth had no idea how far they'd gone. The sky was a glorious shade of pink. The blinding rays of the sinking sun cast their golden shine over them as they continued to stroll. The sight of the lowering sun brought a breathless sigh of wonder from her lips as they paused to watch it sink beneath the horizon.

Watching the sun set had seemed like such a little thing, and not until this moment, with this man at her side, had she realized how gloriously wondrous it was.

"Would you like to rest for a while before we head back?" he suggested. She agreed with a nod, and he cleared her a space in the dry sand.

With her arms cradling her knees, she looked into a sky that wasn't yet dark. "How long will it be before the stars come out?"

"Not long," Breed answered in a low whisper, as if he were afraid words would diminish the wonder of the evening. Leaning back, he rested his weight on the palms of his hands as he looked toward the pounding waves of the ocean. "What made you decide to come to San Francisco?" he asked unexpectedly.

Elizabeth felt her long hair dance against the back of her neck in the breeze. "My mother. She spent time here the summer before she married my father, and she loved it." Her sideward glance encountered deep, questioning eyes. "Is something wrong?"

He was still. "Are you planning on getting married?"

She wasn't sure she was comfortable with this line of questioning. "Yes," she answered honestly.

He sat up, and she noticed that his mouth had twisted wryly. "I wish you'd said something before now." The steel edge of his voice couldn't be disguised.

"Well, doesn't everyone?"

"Doesn't everyone what?" His fragile control of his temper was clearly stretched taut.

Scooting closer to his side, she pressed her head against his shoulder. "Doesn't everyone think about getting married someday?"

"So is there a Mr. Boston Baked Bean sitting at home waiting for you?"

"Mr. Boston Baked Bean?" She broke into delighted peals of laughter. "Honestly, Breed, there's no one."

"Good." He groaned as he turned and pressed her back against the sand. Her startled cry of protest was smothered by his plundering mouth. Immediately her arms circled his neck as his lips rocked over hers in an exchange of kisses that stirred her to the core of her soul.

Restlessly his hands roamed her spine as he half lifted her from the soft cushion of the sandy beach. She arched against him as he sensually attacked her lower lip, teasing her with biting kisses that promised ecstasy but didn't relieve the building need she felt for him.

"Breed," she moaned as her hands cupped his face, directing his hungry mouth to hers. Anything to satisfy this ache inside her. A deep groan slipped from his throat as she outlined his lips with the tip of her tongue.

Breed tightened his hold, and his mouth feasted on

hers. He couldn't seem to give enough or take enough as he relaxed his grip and pressed her into the sand. Desire ran through her bloodstream, spreading a demanding fire as he explored the sensitive cord of her neck and paused at the scented hollow of her throat.

Her nails dug into his back as she shuddered with longing.

She felt the roughness of his calloused hand as he brushed the hair from her face. "I shouldn't have done that," he whispered. His voice was filled with regret. With a heavy sigh, he eased his weight from her. "Did I hurt you?" He helped her into a sitting position, but his hand remained on the curve of her shoulder, as if he couldn't let go.

"You wouldn't hurt me," she answered in a voice so weak she felt she had to repeat the point. "I'm not the least bit hurt." Lovingly, her finger traced the tight line of his jaw. "What's wrong? You look like you're sorry."

He nestled her into his embrace, holding her as he had at the concert, his arms wrapped around her from behind. His chin brushed against the crown of her head.

"Are you sorry?" She made it a question this time.

"No," he answered after a long time, his voice a whisper, and she wondered if he was telling the truth.

Without either of them being aware of it, darkness had descended around them. "The stars are out," she commented, disliking the finely strung tension their silence produced. "When I was younger I used to lean out my bedroom window and try to count the stars."

"I suppose that was a good excuse to stay up late," he said, his voice thick, rubbing his chin against her hair.

She smiled to herself but didn't comment.

His embrace slackened. "Do you want to go?"

"No." Her response was immediate. "Not yet," she added, her voice losing some of its intensity. She shifted position so that she lay back, her head supported by his lap as she gazed into the brilliant heavens. "It really is a gorgeous night."

"Gorgeous," he repeated, but she noted he was looking down on her when he spoke. "You certainly have a way of going to my head, woman."

"Do I?" She sprang to a sitting position. "Oh, Breed, do I really?"

He took her hand and placed it over his pounding heart. "That should answer you."

She let her hands slide over his chest and around his neck. Twisting, she turned and playfully kissed him.

"But the question remains, do I do the same thing to you?" he asked, his voice only slightly husky.

Elizabeth paused and shifted until she was kneeling at his side. Their eyes met in the gilded glow of the moon. "What does this tell you?" she said, more serious than she had been in her life. Taking his hand, she pressed it against her heart, holding it there as he inhaled a quivering breath.

"It tells me—" he hesitated as if gathering his resolve "—that it's time to go." He surged to his feet, then offered her a hand to help her up.

With a smile, she slipped her fingers into his.

The walk back to the Jeep seemed to take forever. Surely they hadn't gone this far.

"Isn't that Hilda?" she asked, pointing to the highway up ahead.

"Couldn't be." He squinted against the dark. "We haven't gone far enough yet."

"Far enough?" she repeated incredulously. "We couldn't possibly have wandered much farther than this." Their portion of the beach was deserted now, although she noted a few small fires in the distance, proof that there were others around. "Isn't that the rock where we left our shoes?" She pointed at the large boulder directly ahead of them.

"No." He was adamant. "We have at least another half mile to go."

Another half mile? Elizabeth's mind shouted. Already a chill had rushed over her bare arms, and the sand squishing between her toes was decidedly wet. The surf was coming in, driving them farther and farther up the beach.

"I'm sure you're wrong," she told him with more confidence than she was feeling. "That's got to be the rock." She was unable to banish the slight quiver from her voice.

Angrily, he stripped off his shirt and placed it around her bare shoulders. "You're freezing." He made it sound like an accusation. "For heaven's sake, why didn't you say something?"

"Because I knew you'd do something silly like take off your shirt and give it to me," she shot back testily. "That's the rock, I'm sure of it," she reiterated, hurrying ahead. The only light was from the half moon above, and when she knelt down and discovered a sock, she leapt triumphantly to her feet. "Ah, ha!" She dangled it in front of his nose. "What did I tell you!"

"That's not mine," he returned impatiently. "Good grief, Elizabeth, look at the size. That belongs to a child."

"This is the rock," she insisted. "It's got to be."

"Fine." His voice was decidedly amused. "If this is the rock, then our shoes would be here. Right?" He crossed his arms and stared at her with amused tolerance.

Boldly, she met his glare. "Someone could have taken them," she stated evenly, feeling suddenly righteous.

"Elizabeth." He paused and inhaled a calming breath. "Trust me. The rock and Hilda are about a half-mile up the beach. If you'll quit arguing with me and walk a little way, you'll see that I know what I'm talking about."

"No." She knotted her fists at her sides in angry resolve. "I'm tired and I'm cold, and I think you've entirely lost your sense of direction. If you feel this isn't the rock, then go ahead and go. I'll be waiting for you here."

"You're not staying alone."

"I'm not going with you."

His eyes became hard points of steel, then softened. "Come on, it's not far."

"No." She stamped her foot, and splashed grit and sand against her bare leg from an incoming wave.

"You're not staying."

"Breed, listen to reason," she pleaded.

A wave crashed against his leg and he shook his head grimly.

"All right," she suggested. "Let's make a wager. Are you game?"

"Why shouldn't I be? You're wrong." The mood lightened immediately. "What do you want to bet?"

"I'll march the unnecessary half-mile up the beach with you. But once you realize you're wrong, you have to carry me piggyback on the return trip. Agreed?"

"Just a minute here." A smile twitched at the corners of his mouth. "What do I get if I'm right?"

"A personal apology?" she suggested, confident she wouldn't need to make one.

His look was thoughtful. "Not good enough."

She slowly moistened her lips and gently swayed her hips. "Ten slow kisses in the moonlight."

He shook his head. "That's *too* good."

She laughed. "Are you always so hard to please?"

"No," he grumbled. "Come on, we can figure it out as we walk." He draped his arm over her shoulders, pulling her close. She wasn't sure if it was because he was as cold as she was now or if he simply wanted her near his side. She tucked her arm around his waist, enjoying the cool feel of his skin against her.

"It's a good thing you've got those freckles," he said seriously about five minutes later. "Without those lighting the way, we'd be lost for sure."

In spite of herself, she laughed. Breed had the ability to do that to her. If someone else had made a similar comment she would have been angry and hurt. But not when it was Breed.

Ten minutes later they spied another large boulder in the distance.

"What did I tell you?" He oozed confidence.

"Don't be so sure of yourself," she returned, only slightly unnerved.

"If my eyes serve me right, someone was kind enough to place our shoes on top so they wouldn't be swept out with the waves."

Her confidence cracked.

"Listen, Sacajawea. If you ever get lost, promise me you'll stay in one place."

"I get the message," she grumbled.

"Promise me," he said more forcefully. "I swear, you'd argue with Saint Peter."

"Well, you're no saint," she shot back.

His grip tightened as his eyes looked into hers. "Don't remind me," he murmured just before claiming her lips in a hungry kiss that left her weak and breathless. "I think we'll go with those ten kisses after all," he mumbled against her hair. "You still owe me nine."

By the time they made it up to the highway and Hilda, then found an all-night restaurant and had coffee, it was well after one. And it was close to two when Elizabeth peeled back the covers to her bed.

When the alarm went off a few hours later, she was sure the time was wrong. Her eyes burned, and she felt as if she'd hardly slept.

Gilly was up and dressed by the time Elizabeth staggered into the kitchen and poured herself a cup of strong coffee.

"What time did you get in?" Gilly asked cheerfully.

"Two," Elizabeth mumbled almost inaudibly.

"I thought you were the one who insisted it was going

to be an early night," Gilly said in a teasing, know-it-all voice.

"Do you have to be so happy in the morning?" Elizabeth grumbled, taking her first sip of coffee, nearly scalding her mouth.

"When are you seeing Breed again?"

He hadn't said anything the night before about another date. But they *would* be seeing one another again; Elizabeth had never been more sure of anything. A smile flitted across her face at the memory of their heated discussion about the rock. She could feel Gilly's gaze skimming over her.

"Obviously you're seeing him soon," the younger woman announced, heading toward her bedroom.

Breed came into the café later that afternoon at what she'd come to think of as his usual time.

He gave Elizabeth a warm smile and yawned. Almost immediately she yawned back and delivered a cup of coffee to his table.

"How do you feel?" he asked, his hand deliberately brushing hers.

"Tired. How about you?"

"Exhausted. I'm not used to these late nights and early mornings." He continued to hold her hand, his thumb stroking the inside of her wrist.

"And you think *I* am?" she teased.

His eyes widened for an instant. "Can I see you tonight?"

The idea of refusing never even occured to her. "Depends." No need to let him feel overconfident. "What do you have in mind?" She batted her eyelashes at him wickedly.

"Collecting on what's due me. Eight, I believe, is the correct number."

Four

The moon silently smiled down from the starlit heavens, casting its glow over the sandy beach. Breed and Peter had gathered driftwood, and blue tongues of fire flickered out from between the small, dry logs.

Elizabeth sat in the sand beside the fire and leaned against Breed, reveling in his quiet strength. His arms were wrapped around her from behind, enclosing her in his embrace. His breathing was even and undisturbed in the peace of the night. Communicating with words wasn't necessary. They'd been talking all week, often into the early hours of the morning. Now, words seemed unnecessary.

"I love this beach," she murmured, thinking how easy it would be to close her eyes and fall asleep in Breed's arms. "Ever since the first night you brought me here, I've come to think of this beach as ours."

His hold tightened measurably as he rubbed his jaw over the top of her head, mussing her wind-tossed hair all the more. Gently he lowered his head and kissed the side of her neck. "I'd say we're being generous sharing it with the world, wouldn't you?"

She snuggled deeper into his arms. "More than generous," she agreed.

The sound of Gilly's laughter came drifting down the beach. She and Peter had taken off running, playing some kind of teasing game. Elizabeth enjoyed it when the four of them did things together, but she was grateful for this time alone with Breed by the fire.

"Where do they get their energy?" she asked, having difficulty restraining a wide yawn. "I don't know about you, but I can't take another week like this."

"I always mean to get you home earlier," he murmured, his voice faintly tinged with guilt.

They'd gone out every night, and she hadn't once gotten home before midnight. Each time they promised one another they would make it an early night, but they hadn't met that goal once. The earliest she had crawled into bed had been twelve-thirty. Even then, she'd often lain awake and stared at the ceiling, thinking how dangerously close she was to falling in love with Breed.

"I wish I knew more about the constellations," she whispered, disliking the meandering trail of her thoughts. Love confused her. She had never been sure what elusive qualities distinguished love from infatuation. And if she did convince herself she was in love with Breed, would she ever be certain that it wasn't gratitude for the renewed lease on life he had so unwittingly given her? Tonight, in his arms, she could lie back and stare at the stars blazing in the black velvet sky. Only weeks ago she would have stumbled in the dark, unable to look toward the light. He had fixed that for her.

A hundred times she had flirted with the idea of telling him who she was. Each time, she realized that the knowledge would ruin their relationship. As it was, she would be faced with leaving him, Gilly and San Francisco soon enough.

She recognized that it was selfish to steal this brief happiness at the expense of others, but she couldn't help herself. It had been so long since she'd felt this good. Without even knowing it, Breed and Gilly had given her back the most precious gift of all: the ability to laugh and see beyond her grief. Being with them had lifted her from the mire of regret and self-pity. For that she would always be grateful.

"What's wrong?" Breed asked, tenderly brushing the hair from her temple.

His sensitivity to her moods astonished her. "What makes you ask?"

"You went tense on me for a moment."

She twisted so that she could lean back and study his ruggedly powerful face. His eyes were shadowed and unreadable, but she recognized the unrest in his look. Something was troubling him. She could sense it as strongly as she could feel the moisture of the ocean mist on her face. She'd recognized it in his eyes several times this past week. At first she'd thought it was her imagination. A yearning to understand him overcame her. "Things aren't always what they appear," she found herself saying. She hoped that he would trust her enough to tell her what was troubling him. But she wouldn't force his confidence.

Everything seemed to go still. Even the sound of the waves pounding against the beach faded. "What makes you say that?"

She resumed her former position, disappointed and a little hurt. Still, if Breed had secrets, so did she, and she certainly wasn't about to blurt out hers, so in all fairness, she shouldn't expect him to.

"Nothing." Her low voice was filled with resignation.

Slowly, tantalizingly, he ran his hands down her arms. "I have to go out of town next week."

"Oh." The word trembled on her lips with undisguised disappointment.

"I'll be flying out Monday, but I should be back sometime Tuesday," he explained.

"I'll miss you."

He drew her back against the unrestrained strength of his torso. "I wouldn't go if it wasn't necessary. You're right, you know." He spoke so low that she had to strain to hear him. "Things aren't always what they appear."

Later, when Breed had dropped her off at the apartment and she had settled in bed, his enigmatic words echoed in her mind. She couldn't imagine what was troubling him. But whatever it was, she sensed he was planning to settle it while he was out of town. He'd been quiet tonight. At first she had attributed his lack of conversation to how tired they both were. But it was more than that. She didn't know why she was so sure of it, but she was.

When she had first met Breed, she'd seen him only as muscular and handsome, two qualities she had attributed to shallow and self-centered men. But he had proved her wrong. This man was deep and intense. So intense that she often wondered what accounted for the powerful attraction that had brought them together.

A shadowy figure appeared in the doorway. "Are you asleep?" Gilly whispered.

Elizabeth sat up, bunching the pillows behind her back. "Not yet." She gestured toward the end of her bed, inviting her roommate to join her.

Gilly took a long swallow from a glass of milk and walked into the moonlit room, then sat on the edge of the bed. "I don't know what's wrong. I couldn't sleep, either."

"Did you have a good time tonight?" Elizabeth felt compelled to whisper, although there was no one there to disturb.

"I enjoy being with Peter," Gilly confessed with an exaggerated sigh, "but only as a friend."

"Is that a problem?"

Gilly's laugh was light and airy. "Not really, since I'm sure he feels the same way. It makes me wonder if I'll ever fall in love."

Elizabeth bit into her lip to keep from laughing out loud. "Do you realize how funny you sound? First you're happy because you and Peter are happy being just friends. Then you're disappointed because you aren't in love."

Gilly's smile was highlighted by the filtered light of the moon passing through the open window. "Yes, I suppose it does sound a little outrageous. I guess what I'd really like is to have the kind of relationship you and Breed share."

"He's a special man." Elizabeth spoke wistfully. Breed had taught her valuable lessons this past week. Without her long walk in the valley she might not have recognized the thrill of the mountaintop. Breed and Gilly had taught her to laugh and love life again. Life was beautiful in San Francisco. No wonder her mother had loved this city.

"I've seen the way he looks at you," Gilly continued, "and my heart melts. I want a man to feel that way about me."

"But not Peter."

"At this point I'm not choosy. I want to know what it's like to be in love. Really in love, like you and Breed."

"In love? Me and Breed?" Elizabeth tossed back the words in astonished disbelief.

"Yes, you and Breed," Gilly returned indignantly.

"You've got it all wrong." Elizabeth's thoughts were waging a fierce battle with one another. Gilly had to be mistaken. Breed couldn't be in love with her. She could only end up hurting him. The minute he learned about her wealth and position, he would feel betrayed and angry. She couldn't allow that to happen. "We're attracted, but we're not in love," she returned adamantly, nodding once for emphasis.

The sound of Gilly's bemused laugh filled the room. "Honestly, how can anyone be so blind?"

"But Breed and I hardly know one another," Elizabeth argued. "What we feel at this point is infatuation, maybe, but no one falls in love in two weeks."

"Haven't you read *Romeo and Juliet?*" Gilly asked her accusingly. "People don't need a long courtship to know they're in love."

"Breed's a wonderful man, and I'd consider myself fortunate if he loved me." A thickening lump tightened her throat, making it impossible to talk for a moment. "But it's too soon for either of us to know what we really feel. Much too soon," Elizabeth reiterated.

Gilly was uncharacteristically quiet for a long moment. "Maybe I'm way off," she murmured thoughtfully. "But I don't think so. I have the feeling that once you admit what's going on inside your heart and your head, you won't be able to deny it."

"Perhaps not," Elizabeth murmured, troubled by Gilly's words.

"Are you seeing him tomorrow?"

"Not until the afternoon. He decided that after all the sleep I lost this week, I should sleep late tomorrow."

"But you're awake because you're lying here thinking about him. Right?" Gilly asked softly.

"No." Elizabeth yawned loudly, raising her arms high above her head. She hoped her friend would take the not-so-subtle message.

"And not being able to sleep doesn't tell you anything?" Gilly pressed.

"It tells me that I'd have a much easier time if a certain know-it-all wasn't sitting on the end of my bed, bugging the heck out of me." As much as she wanted to deny her friend's assessment, Elizabeth had been impressed more than once with Gilly's insight into people and situations. At twenty, she was wise beyond her years.

"I can take a hint, unlike certain people I know," Gilly said, bounding to her feet. "You wait, Elizabeth Wainwright. When you realize you're in love with Breed, your head's going to spin for a week."

Turning onto her side, Elizabeth scooted down and pulled the covers up to her chin. "Don't count on it," she mumbled into the pillow, forcing her eyes closed.

Standing beside the foot of the bed, Gilly finished the rest of her milk. "I'll see you in the morning," she said as she headed toward the door.

"Gilly." Elizabeth stopped her. "Breed's not really in love with me, is he?"

Staring pointedly at the ceiling, Gilly slowly shook her head in undisguised disgust. "I swear the girl's blind," she said to the light fixture, then turned back to Elizabeth. "Yes, Breed's head over heels in love with you. Only a fool wouldn't have guessed. Good night, fool."

"Good night," Elizabeth murmured with a sinking feeling. She'd been naive to believe that she could nurture this relationship and not pay an emotional price. She had to do something soon, before it was too late. If it wasn't already.

"All right," Breed said, breathing heavily. He tightened his grip on Hilda's steering wheel. "Out with it."

Elizabeth's face paled as she glanced out the side of the Jeep. The afternoon had been a disaster from the start, and all because of her and her ridiculous mood. She had hoped to speak honestly with Breed. She wanted to tell him that she was frightened by what was happening between them. At first she'd thought to suggest that he start seeing someone else, but the thought of him holding another woman had made her stomach tighten painfully. The crazy part was that she'd never thought of herself as the jealous type.

"Are you pouting because I'm going away? Is that the reason for the silent treatment?"

"No," she denied in a choked whisper. "That's not it." She kept her face averted, letting the wind whip her honey curls in every direction. She was so close to tears it was ludicrous.

When he pulled over to the curb and parked so he could face her, her heart sank to her knees. His gentle hand on her shoulder was nearly her undoing. She didn't want him to be gentle and concerned. If he were angry, it would be so much easier to explain her confused thoughts.

"Beth, what is it?"

Like Gilly, Breed had started calling her Beth. But it wasn't what he called her, it was the way he said it, the tender, almost loving way he let it roll from his lips. No name had ever sounded so beautiful.

Miserable, she placed her hand over his and turned around so that she could see his face. Of their own volition, her fingers rose to trace the angular lines of his proud jaw.

He emitted a low groan and took hold of her shoulders, putting some distance between them. "I have enough trouble keeping my hands off you without you doing that."

She dropped her hands, color rushing to her cheeks. "That's what's wrong," she said in a low voice she hardly recognized as her own. "I'm frightened, Breed."

"Of what?"

She swallowed back the uneasiness that filled her. "I'm worried that we're becoming too intense."

He dropped his hands and turned so that he was staring straight ahead. As if he needed something to do with his fingers, he gripped the steering wheel. She could tell that he was angry by the way his knuckles whitened. His look proved he didn't understand what she was saying.

"Things are getting too hot and heavy for you. Is that it?"

It wasn't, but she didn't know how else to explain her feelings. "Yes…yes they are."

"Then what you're saying is that you'd prefer it if we didn't see each other anymore?"

"No!" That thought was intolerable.

"The trouble with you is that you don't know what you want." The icy edge to his tone wrapped its way around her throat, choking off a reply.

He didn't appear to need one. Without hesitating, he turned the ignition key, and Hilda's engine roared to life. Jerking the gearshift, he pulled back onto the street.

"I feel we both need time to think." She practically had to shout to be heard above the noise of the traffic. Breed didn't answer. Before she could think of another way to explain herself, he had pulled up in front of her brick apartment building. He left the engine running.

"I agree," he said, his voice emotionless. "We've been seeing too much of one another."

"You've misunderstood everything I've said," she murmured miserably, wishing she had explained herself better.

"I don't think so," he replied, his jaw tightening. "I'll call you Tuesday, after I get back to town. That is, if you want to hear from me again."

"Of course I do." Frustration rocked her. "I'm sorry I said anything. I don't want you to go away angry."

He hesitated, and although he didn't say anything for several moments, she could feel the resentment fade. The air between them became less oppressive, lighter. "The thing is, you're right," he admitted tightly. "Both of us needed to be reminded of that. Take care of yourself while I'm away."

"I will," she whispered.

"I'll phone you Tuesday."

"Tuesday," she agreed, climbing out of the car. She stood on the sidewalk as he pulled away and merged with the flowing traffic.

A flick of her wrist turned the key that allowed her into the apartment. Gilly was sitting on the sofa, reading a romance novel and munching on a carrot. "How did everything go?" she asked.

"Fine," Elizabeth responded noncommittally. But she felt miserable. Her talk with Breed hadn't settled anything. Instead of clearing the air, it had only raised more questions. Now she was left with three days to sort through her thoughts and decide how she could continue to see him and not complicate their relationship by falling in love.

"If everything's so wonderful, why do you look like you're going to burst into tears?"

Elizabeth tried to smile, but the effort failed miserably. "Because I am."

"I take it you don't want to talk."

It was all Elizabeth could manage to shake her head.

Later that evening, as the sun was sinking low into a lavender sky, Gilly dressed for an evening out. Her cousin was getting married, and her parents expected her to attend the wedding although she never had cared for this particular cousin.

"Are you sure you won't come?" Gilly asked Elizabeth for the sixth time.

"I'm sure," Elizabeth responded from the kitchen table, making an exaggerated stroke along the side of her nail with a file. Fiddling with her fingernails had given the appearance she was busy and untroubled. But she doubted that her smoke screen had fooled Gilly. "I thought you'd conned Peter into going with you?"

"I regret that," Gilly said with frank honesty.

"Why?" Elizabeth glanced down at her collection of nail polish.

"Knowing my dad, he's probably going to make a big deal about my bringing Peter. This whole thing's going to end up embarrassing us both. I hate being forced to attend something just because it's family."

Elizabeth cast her a sympathetic look. She'd suffered

through enough family obligations to empathize with her friend's feelings.

Gilly and Peter left soon afterward, and she finished her nails, wondering if Breed would notice when she saw him next. She watched television for a while, keeping her mind off him. But not for long.

She picked up the paperback Gilly had been reading, and quickly read the first couple of chapters, surprised at how much she was enjoying the book. The next thing she knew, Gilly was shaking her awake and telling her to climb into bed or she would get a crick in her neck.

It was the middle of the morning when she woke again. Feeling out of sorts and cranky, she read the morning paper and did the weekly grocery shopping. When Gilly suggested a drive, she declined. Not until later did she realize that she'd been waiting for Breed to phone, even though he'd said he wouldn't, and was keenly disappointed when he didn't.

Monday evening, when her cell did ring she all but flew across the room in her eagerness to grab it from her purse. She desperately wanted it to be Breed. But it wasn't. Instead, she found herself talking to her disgruntled father.

"I haven't heard from you in a while. Are you okay?"

"Of course I am." Although disappointment coated her voice, she had to admit she was pleased to hear from her father. She was even more grateful that Gilly was taking a shower and wasn't likely to overhear the conversation. "I'm happy, Dad, for the first time since Mom died."

"I was thinking about this job of yours. Are you still

working as a…waitress?" He said the word as though he found it distasteful.

"Yes, and I'm enjoying it."

"I've been talking to some friends of mine," he said in a tone that told her he was anxious about her. "If you feel you need to work, then we could get you on at the embassy. Your French is excellent."

"Dad," she interrupted, "I like it at the Patisserie. Don't worry about me."

"But as a common waitress?" The contemptuous disbelief was back in his voice again. "I want so much more for you, Princess." Her father hadn't called her that since she was thirteen. "When are you coming home? I think it might be a good idea if you were here."

"Dad," she said impatiently, "for the first time in months I'm sleeping every night. I'm eager for each new morning. I'm happy, really happy. Don't ruin that."

She could hear her father's uncertainty, feel his indecision. "Have you met someone special?" he said.

The question was a loaded one, and she wasn't sure how to respond, especially in light of her discussion with Breed. "Yes and no."

"Meaning…?" he pressed.

"I've made some friends. Good friends. What makes you ask?"

"No reason. I just don't want you to do something you'll regret later."

"Like what?" Indignation caused her voice to rise perceptibly.

"I don't know." He paused and exhaled forcefully. "Siggy's phoned for you several times."

Elizabeth released an inward groan. Siegfried Winston Chamberlain III was the most boring stuffed shirt she'd ever known. More than that, she had openly disliked him from the day a small, helpless bird had flown into a freshly washed window and broken its neck. The look in Siggy's eyes revealed that he'd enjoyed witnessing its death. From that time on she'd avoided him. But he had pursued her relentlessly from their teenage years, though she was certain he wasn't in love with her. She wasn't even sure he liked her. What she did recognize was the fact that a union between their two families would be financially expedient to the Chamberlains.

"Tell Siggy the same thing you told him when I was in Paris."

"Siggy loves you."

"Dad…" Elizabeth didn't want to lose her temper, not on the phone, when it would be difficult to settle their differences. "I honestly don't think Siggy knows what love is. I've got to go. I'll phone you next week. Now, don't worry about me. Promise?"

"You'll phone next week? Promise?"

She successfully repressed a sharp reply. Her father had never shown such concern for her welfare. He was acting as though she was working undercover for the CIA.

Honestly, she mused irritably. Would she ever understand her father?

"You miss him, don't you?" Gilly asked her later that evening.

Elizabeth didn't even try to pretend. She knew Gilly

was referring to Breed. She had confided in her friend, and was again grateful for Gilly's insight and understanding. He had been on her mind all weekend. Monday had dragged, and she was counting the hours until she heard from him again. "I do," she admitted readily. "I wish I'd never said anything."

Gilly nodded sympathetically.

But it was more than missing Breed, Elizabeth thought to herself. Much more. For three days it had been as though a vital part of her was missing. The realization frightened her. He had come to mean more to her in a few weeks than anyone she'd known. Gilly, too. As she'd explained to her father, she was making friends. Maybe the first real friends of her life. But Breed was more than a friend, and it had taken this separation to prove it.

Tuesday Elizabeth kept taking out her cell to see if she had missed his call.

"From the look of you, someone might think you're waiting to hear from someone," Gilly teased.

"Am I that obvious?"

"Is the sun bright? Do bees buzz?" Gilly sat on the chair opposite Elizabeth. "Why not call him? Women do that these days, you know."

Elizabeth hesitated long enough to consider the idea. "I don't know."

"Well, it isn't going to hurt anything. His pride's been bruised. Besides, anything's better than having you mope around the apartment another night."

"I do not mope."

Gilly tried unsuccessfully to disguise a smile. "If you say so."

Elizabeth waited until nine for Breed to phone. She could call him, but seeing him in person would be so much better. Maybe Gilly was right and, despite what he'd said about calling her, he was waiting for her to contact him. She wouldn't sleep tonight unless she made the effort to see him. It wouldn't do any good to try to fool herself otherwise.

"I think I'll go for a walk," she announced brightly, knowing she wasn't fooling her friend.

"Tonight's perfect for a stroll," Gilly murmured, not taking her attention from the television, but Elizabeth noticed the way the corners of her eyes crinkled as she struggled not to reveal her amusement. "I don't suppose you want me to wait up for you."

With a bemused smile, Elizabeth closed the door, not bothering to answer.

There were plenty of reasons that could explain why Breed hadn't called. Maybe his trip had been extended. He might not even be home. But as Gilly had pointedly stated, the evening *was* perfect for a stroll. The sun had set below a cloudless horizon and darkness had blanketed the city. The streets were alive with a variety of people. Elizabeth didn't notice much of what was going on around her. Her quick, purpose-filled strides took her the three blocks to Breed's apartment in a matter of a few short minutes. She had never been there, yet the address was burned into her memory.

For all her resolve, when she saw the light under his

door, her heart sank. Breed was home and hadn't contacted her.

Her first light knock went unnoticed, so she pressed the buzzer long and hard.

"Beth!" Breed sounded shocked when he opened the door.

"So you made it back safely after all," she said, aware of the faintly accusatory note in her voice. He must have realized that she would be waiting for his call. "What time did you get back?" The minute the question slipped from her lips, she regretted having asked. Her coming was obvious enough.

"About six." He stepped back, silently and grudgingly issuing the invitation for her to come inside.

She was surprised at how bare the apartment looked. The living area displayed nothing that stamped the apartment with his personality. There were no pictures on the walls, or books and magazines lying around. The place seemed sterile, it was so clean. It looked as if he'd just moved in.

"I thought you said you would phone."

"I wasn't sure you wanted to hear from me."

Without waiting for an invitation, she sat on the sofa and crossed her long legs, hoping to give a casual impression.

He took a chair on the other side of the room and leaned forward, his elbows resting on his knees. There was a coiled alertness about him that he was attempting to disguise. But Elizabeth knew him too well. In the same way that he was sensitive to her, she was aware of him. He seemed to be waiting for her to speak.

"I missed you," she said softly, hoping her words would release the tension in the room. "More than I ever thought I would."

He straightened and looked uncomfortable. "Yes. Well, that's only natural. We've been seeing a lot of each other the last couple of weeks."

Her fingers were laced together so tightly that they began to ache. She unwound them and flexed her hands before standing and moving to the window on the far side of the room. "It's more than that," she announced with her back to him. Deliberately she turned, then leaned back with her hands resting on the windowsill. "Nothing seemed right without you...."

Breed vaulted to his feet. "Beth, listen to me. We're tired. It's been a long day. I think we should both sleep on this." His look was an odd mixture of tenderness and impatience. "Come on, I'll drive you home."

"No." She knew a brush-off when she heard one. He didn't want her here; that much was obvious. He hadn't been himself from the moment she set foot in the door. "I walked here, I'll walk back."

"All right, I'll come with you." The tone of his voice told her he would brook no argument.

She lifted one shoulder in a half-shrug. "It's a free country."

He relaxed the minute he locked the door. There was something inside the apartment he hadn't wanted her to see, she realized. Not a woman hiding in his bedroom; she was sure of that. Amusement drifted across her face and awoke a slow smile.

"What's so funny?" he wanted to know.

"Nothing."

His hand gripped hers. "Come on, and I'll introduce you to BART."

She paused midstride, making him falter slightly. With her hands positioned challengingly on her hips, she glared defiantly at him. "Oh, no, you don't, Andrew Breed. If you don't want to see me again, then fine. But I won't have you introducing me to other men. I can find my own dates, thank you."

A crooked smile slashed his face as he turned toward her, his eyes hooded. "Bay Area Rapid Transit. BART is the subway."

"Oh." She felt ridiculous. The natural color of her cheeks was heightened with embarrassment.

"So you missed me," he said casually as they strolled along the busy sidewalk. "That's nice to know."

She greeted his words with silence. First he had shunned her, and now he was making fun of her. Other than a polite "good night" when they arrived at her building, she didn't have anything to say to him. The whole idea of going to him had been idiotic. Well, she'd learned her lesson.

"The thing is, I discovered I missed you, too."

Again she didn't respond.

"But missing someone is a strange thing," he continued. "There are varying degrees. Like after your mother died, I imagine…"

Elizabeth felt a chill rush over her skin that had nothing to do with the light breeze. "I never told you my mother was dead," she said stiffly.

Five

"You don't mind, do you?" Gilly asked contritely. "I wouldn't have mentioned your mother to Breed if I'd known you objected."

"No, don't worry about it," Elizabeth said gently, shaking her head.

"Even though Breed and I went out several times before you started dating him, I knew from the beginning that he was really only interested in you. From the first date you were all he talked about."

Breed had explained to Elizabeth yesterday that Gilly had told him about her mother. Yet she'd doubted him. Everything about last night remained clouded in her mind. From the moment she'd entered his apartment, she had felt like an unwelcome intruder. None of his actions made sense, and her suspicions had begun to cross the line into outright paranoia.

"Peter and I are going to dinner and a movie," Gilly said, changing the subject.

"I have some shopping I want to do," Elizabeth returned absently.

* * *

Not until later that evening, when she was facing the store detective, did she remember that she couldn't phone Gilly, whose cell would be off in the theater, and have her come. A heaviness pressed against her heart, and she struggled to maintain her composure as the balding man led her toward the department store office.

She walked past the small crowd that had gathered near her and saw a tall, familiar figure on the far side of the floor in the men's department.

"Breed!" she called, thanking heaven that he had chosen this day to shop.

He turned at the sound of her voice, his brows lowering. "Beth, what is it?"

She bit into her bottom lip, more embarrassed than she could ever remember being. "Someone stole my purse. I haven't got any way to get home or a key to the apartment."

Elizabeth's face was buried in her hands when Breed delivered a steaming cup of coffee to the kitchen table where she sat. The manager had let her into the apartment, but she still had so much to deal with to straighten everything out that the feeling was overwhelming.

"Tell me again what happened," Breed said as he straddled a chair beside her.

She shook her head. Everything important was inside her purse. Her money, credit cards, cell phone, identification. Everything. Gone in a matter of seconds. As crazy as it sounded, she felt as if she had been personally violated. She was both stunned and angry.

"I don't want to talk about it," she replied stiffly. What she wanted was for Breed to leave so she could be alone.

"Beth." He said her name so gently that she closed her eyes to the emotion he aroused in her. "Honey, I can't help unless I know what happened."

One tear broke past the thick dam of her lashes and flowed unrestrained down her pale face. Resolutely, she wiped it aside.

"I decided to do a little shopping after work. Peter had picked up Gilly, and they were going out, and I didn't want to go home to an empty house." Breed hadn't mentioned anything last night about getting together, and she didn't want to sit around in an empty apartment missing him.

"Go on," he encouraged. He continued to hold her hand, his thumb stroking the inside of her wrist in a soothing action that at any other time would have been sensuous and provocative.

"I'd only bought a couple of things and decided to stop in the rest room before taking BART home. I set my purse and the packages on the counter while I washed. I turned to dry my hands. When I turned back, my purse, the packages…everything was gone. I was so stunned, I didn't know what to do."

"You must have seen something."

"That's what Detective Beaman thought. But I didn't. I didn't even hear anything." She paused, reliving the short seconds. She could tell them nothing.

Even now, an hour later, sitting in her kitchen, a feeling of disbelief filled her. This couldn't really be happening. This was a bad dream, and when she woke, everything would be fine again. At least that was what she desperately wanted to believe.

"What did they take?"

"Breed, don't. Please. I can't talk about it anymore. I just want to take a bath and pretend this never happened." Later she would have to contact her father. It didn't take much of an imagination to know what his response was going to be. He would insist she leave San Francisco, and then they would argue. She let the unpleasant thoughts fade. She didn't want to think about it.

Breed released her wrist and stood. His hands were positioned on his lean hips, his expression grim and unyielding. "Beth," he insisted in a low, coaxing tone. "Think. There's something you're not remembering. Something small. Close your eyes and go over every minute of the time you were shopping."

She clenched her teeth to keep from yelling. "Don't you think I haven't already?" she said with marked impatience. "Every detail of every minute has been playing back repeatedly in my mind."

He exhaled sharply, letting her know his patience was as limited as her own.

She stared pointedly at the bare surface of the table, which blurred as the welling tears collected in her eyes. She managed to restrain their fall, but she couldn't keep her chin from trembling. Tears were a sign of weakness, and the Wainwrights frowned on signs of weakness.

Breed sighed as he eliminated the distance between them and stood behind her. Gently he comforted her by massaging her shoulders and neck. The demanding pressure of his fingers half lifted her from the chair, forcing her to stand.

She held herself stiffly, angry. "This is your fault," she whispered in a faintly hysterical tone.

"Mine?" He turned her around. His amber eyes narrowed into thin slits.

She didn't need him to tell her how unreasonable she was being, but she couldn't help herself. Her tears blurred his expression as she lashed out at him bitterly. "Why were you so unwelcoming last night? Why didn't you want me at your apartment? Not to mention that you said you'd call and then you didn't." She inhaled shakily. "Don't bother to deny it. I'm not stupid. I know when I'm not wanted. And why...why didn't you come into the café today?" Her accusations were fired as quick as machine gun bullets.

He groaned as his hands cupped her face. Anger flashed across his features, then vanished. "There wasn't a single minute that you weren't on my mind." Self-derisive anger darkened his eyes.

"Then why...?" Her heart fluttered uncertainly, excited and yet afraid.

Motionless, he held her, revealing none of his thoughts. "Because," he admitted as the smoldering light of desire burned in his eyes. His hand slid slowly along the back of her waist, bringing her infinitesimally closer.

When he fitted his mouth to hers, a small, happy sound escaped from her throat. His thick arms around her waist lifted her from the kitchen floor. Her softness was molded to his male length as he kissed her until her lips were swollen and trembling.

"I missed you so much," she admitted, wrapping her arms around his neck. "I was so afraid you didn't want to see me again."

"Not want to see you?" he repeated. His husky tone betrayed his frustration. "You confuse me. I don't know what kind of game you're playing."

Anxiously, she brushed the hair from his face and kissed him, her lips exploring the planes and contours of his angular features with short, teasing kisses. "I'm not playing any game," she whispered.

He loosened his grip so that her feet touched the floor once again. "No games?" Amusement was carved in the lines of his face. "I don't believe that."

Deliberately she directed his mouth to hers and kissed him long and slow, her lips moving sensuously over his.

He broke the contact and held her at arm's length as he took several deep breaths.

"What's wrong?" she whispered. She didn't want him to pull away from her. A chill seeped through her bloodstream as she tried to decipher his attitude. The messages he sent her were confused. He wanted to be with her, but he didn't. He liked coming to her apartment but didn't want her at his. His kisses affected her as much as they affected him, yet he pulled away whenever things became too intense.

The phone rang, and he dropped his hands and stared at it as if it were an intruder. "Do you want me to answer it?" he questioned.

She shook her head and answered it herself. "Hello." She couldn't disguise the soft tremble in her voice. "Yes, yes, this is Elizabeth Wainwright."

Breed brushed his fingers through his hair as he paced the room.

"Yes, yes," she repeated breathlessly. "I did lose my purse." Not until the conversation was half over did the words sink into her consciousness.

"Breed!" she cried excitedly as she replaced the receiver. "They've found my purse!"

"Who did?" He turned her in his arms, his tense features relaxing.

"The store. That was them on the phone. Apparently whoever took it was only after the cash. Someone turned it in to the office only a few minutes ago after finding it in the stairway."

"Your credit cards and identification?"

"There. All they took was the cash."

He hauled her into his arms and released a heavy sigh that revealed his relief. Her own happy sigh joined his. "They said I should come and pick it up. Let's go right away," she said, laughing. "I feel naked without my purse." Giddy with relief, she waltzed around the room until he captured her and swung her in the air as if she weighed no more than a doll.

"Feel better?"

"Oh, yes!" she exclaimed, kissing him lightly. "Can we go now?"

"I think we should." He laced his fingers through hers, then lifted their joined hands to his lips and kissed the back of her hand.

He locked the apartment with the spare key the manager had given her and tucked it into his pocket. Hand in hand, they walked outside.

She patted Hilda's seat cushion as she got in. "You know what I thought last night?" she asked as Breed revved the engine.

He turned and smiled warmly at her. "I can't imagine." His finger lingered longer than necessary as it removed a long strand of silken hair that the wind had blown across her happy face.

"For one fleeting instant I was convinced you were hiding a woman in your bedroom." At the shocked look he gave her, she broke into delighted giggles.

"Beth." Thick lines marred his smooth brow. "Whatever made you suspect something like that?"

Pressing her head against his shoulder, she released a contented sigh. "I don't know." She *did* know, but she wanted to relish this moment. Yesterday's ghosts were buried. Today's happiness shone brightly before her. Her joy was complete. "Forward, Hilda. Take me to my purse."

Breed merged with the heavy flow of traffic. "I suppose you're going to insist on celebrating."

"Absolutely."

"Dinner?"

She sat up and placed her hand on his where it rested on the gearshift. She had to keep touching him to believe that all this was real. "Yes, I'm starved. I don't think I've eaten all day."

"Why not?" He gave her a questioning glance.

She poked his stomach. "You know why."

He reclaimed her hand, and again he kissed her fingers. She had the sensation he felt exactly as she did and couldn't keep his hands off her.

"What did Beaman say?"

"It wasn't Beaman. He said his name, but I can't remember it now."

"What did he say?" Breed glanced briefly in her direction.

"Just that I should come right away."

"That you should come right away." He drawled the words slowly. Then he dropped her hand and tightened his hold on the steering wheel as he glanced in the rearview mirror. The tires screeched as he made a U-turn in the middle of the street. The unexpected action caused Hilda to teeter for an instant.

"Breed!" Elizabeth screamed, holding on to the padded bar on the dash. "What is it? What's wrong?"

He didn't answer her as he weaved in and out of the traffic, blaring his horn impatiently. When they pulled up in front of her apartment again, he looked around and tensed.

She had no idea what had gotten into him. "Breed?" She tried a second time to talk to him. He sat alert and stiff. The look in his eyes was frightening. She had never seen anything more menacing.

"Call the police," he told her as he jumped from the Jeep.

"But, Breed—"

"Now. Hurry."

Confused, she jumped out, too. "What am I supposed

to tell them?" she asked as she followed him onto the sidewalk and reached for his hand.

He pushed her arm away. "That wasn't the store that called," he explained impatiently. "It was whoever took your purse, and they're about to rob you blind."

"How do you know?" Nothing made sense anymore. Breed was like a dangerous stranger. Rage contorted his features until she hardly recognized him.

He grabbed her shoulders, his fingers biting mercilessly into her flesh. "Look." He jerked his head toward a moving van parked in front of the building. "Do as I say and call 9-1-1," he ordered in a threatening voice. "And don't come into the apartment until after the police arrive. Now go."

"Breed..." Panic filled her as he walked toward the door. "Don't go in there!" she shouted frantically, running after him. He was so intent that he didn't hear her. His glance of surprise when she grabbed his arm was quickly replaced with an angry scowl. "Get out of here."

With fear dictating her actions, she ran across the street to the safety of a beauty salon. She was sure the women thought she was crazy when she pulled out her cell, dialed the emergency police number, and reported a robbery in progress, all the while staring out through the large front window.

Like a caged animal, she paced the sidewalk outside her apartment, waiting for the patrol car. She held both hands over her mouth as she looked up and down the street. Everything was taking so long. Each second was an hour, every minute a lifetime. Not until the first police vehicle pulled up did she realize how badly she was trembling.

"In there," she said, and gave them her apartment number. "My boyfriend went up to stop them."

Another police car arrived, and while one officer went into the building on the heels of the first two, the other stayed outside and questioned her. At first she stared at him blankly, her mind refusing to concentrate on her own responses. Her answers were clipped, one-word replies.

Fifteen minutes later, two men and a woman were led out of the building by the police. Breed followed, talking to an officer. He paused long enough to search out Elizabeth in the growing crowd and smile reassuringly.

Her answering smile was shaky, but she felt her heart regain its normal rhythm. Her eyes followed him as he spoke to one officer and then another. When he joined her a few minutes later, he slipped an arm around her waist with familiar ease. Her fears evaporated at his touch.

"Do you recognize any of them?" he asked her.

Lamely, she nodded. "The woman was in the elevator with me, but she didn't go into the rest room."

"But she got off on the same floor?"

She wasn't sure. "I don't remember, but she must have."

"It doesn't matter if you remember or not. There's enough evidence here to lock them up." His arm remained on her waist as he directed her inside.

"How'd you know?" Dazed and almost tongue-tied,

she stared up at him. "What clued you in to what was going on?"

"To be honest, I don't know," he admitted. "Something didn't ring true. First, it wasn't Beaman who phoned, and then there was something about the way you were instructed to come right away. They were probably waiting within sight of the building and watched us leave."

"But how'd they know my address and phone number?" All her identification listed her Boson address. Even her driver's license was from Massachusetts. There hadn't been any reason to obtain a California license, since she didn't have a car and was only planning on staying for the summer.

"Your name, address, and telephone number are printed on your checks."

She groaned. "Of course."

"We need to go to the police station and fill out a few forms. Are you up to that?"

"I'm fine. But I want to know about you. What happened in there?"

"Nothing much." It didn't sound like he wanted to talk about it. "I counted on the element of surprise."

"Yes, but there were three of them." She wasn't about to let the subject drop. "How did you defend yourself?"

His wide shoulders tensed as he hesitated before answering. "I've studied the martial arts."

"Breed!" she exclaimed. "Really? You should have said something." The longer she was with him, the more she realized how little she actually knew about him. She had actually avoided asking too many questions, afraid of revealing too much about herself. But she wouldn't shy away from them anymore.

Gilly and Peter returned to the apartment chatting happily.

Elizabeth glanced up and sighed. "Where were you when I needed you?" she teased her roommate.

"When did you need me?"

"Today. Someone took my purse."

"They did more than that," Breed repeated with a trace of anger.

"What happened?" Peter looked incredulous. "I think you better start at the beginning."

Slowly, shaking her head, Elizabeth sighed. "Let me explain."

An hour later Breed glanced pointedly at his wristwatch and held out his hand to Elizabeth. "Walk me to the door." The quiet firmness of his request and the tender look in his eyes sent her pulse racing.

"Sure," she said, eagerly moving around the sofa to his side.

He waited until they reached the entryway to turn her into his arms. Her back was supported by the panels of the door. His hands were on each side of her head as his gaze roamed slowly over her upturned face. For one heart-stopping second his eyes rested on her parted lips; his look was as potent as a physical touch.

"I want to see you tomorrow."

She released a heavy sigh. "Oh, thank goodness," she said, offering him a brilliant smile. "I was afraid I was going to be forced to ask *you* out."

His look grew dark and serious. "You'd do that?"

"Yes." She didn't trust herself to add an explanation.

He pulled his gaze from hers. "Would you like to go fishing?"

"You mean with poles and hooks and worms?"

"I've got a sailboat. We could leave tomorrow afternoon, once you're off work."

"Can I bring anything?"

"The worms," Breed teased.

"Try again, buddy. How about some sandwiches?" She could have Evelyn make some up for her before she left the Patisserie tomorrow.

"Fine."

Breed's kiss was disappointingly short but immeasurably sweet. Long after he left, she felt his presence linger. Twice she turned and started to say something to him before realizing he'd left for the evening.

Elizabeth felt Gilly's curious stare as she came out of the bedroom the following afternoon.

"Where's Breed taking you, for heaven's sake? You look like you just finished plowing the back forty."

Self-consciously, Elizabeth looked down at her tennis shoes and the faded jeans that were rolled midway up her calf. The shirttails of her red-checkered blouse were tied loosely at her midriff.

"Fishing. I'm not overdressed, am I? I have my swimsuit on underneath."

"You look…" One side of Gilly's mouth quirked upward as she paused, her face furrowed in concentration. "Different," she concluded.

"I'll admit I don't usually dress like this, but—"

"It's not the clothes," Gilly interrupted. "There's a certain aura about you. A look in your eye."

Turning, Elizabeth found a mirror and examined herself closely. "You're crazy. I'm no different than I was last week—or last night, for that matter."

Gilly ignored her and paid excessive attention to the crossword puzzle she was doing.

"No quick reply?" Elizabeth asked teasingly. She was used to doing verbal battle with her roommate.

Gilly bit into the eraser at the end of the pencil. "Not me. I learned a long time ago that it's better not to argue with you." But she rolled her eyes when she thought Elizabeth wasn't looking.

Breed arrived just then, and Elizabeth didn't have the opportunity to banter further with Gilly. If there was something different about her, as her friend believed, then it was because she was happier, more complete.

Outside the building, Elizabeth scanned the curb for Hilda, but the Jeep wasn't parked within sight.

"Here." Breed held open the door to a silver sedan, the same car he'd driven before introducing her to Hilda.

"Where's Hilda?"

"Home." Breed's reply was abrupt.

"Good grief, how many cars have you got?"

The smile that lifted the corners of his mouth looked forced. "One too many," he answered cryptically.

She wanted to question him further, but he closed her door and walked around to the driver's side. He paused and glanced warily at the street before climbing inside the car.

"Are you planning on kidnapping me?" she teased.

For an instant his sword-sharp gaze pinned her against the seat. "What makes you ask something as crazy as that?" Impatience sounded in his crisp voice.

She had meant it as a joke, so she was surprised that he had taken her seriously. She arched one delicately shaped brow at his defensive tone and cocked her head. "What's gotten into you?"

"Nothing."

Releasing her breath slowly, she gazed out the side window, watching as the scenery whipped past. From the minute he had asked her on this outing, she had been looking forward to their time together. She didn't want anything to ruin it.

At the marina, his heavy steps sounded ominously as he led her along the long wooden dock toward his sailboat. But his mood altered once they were slicing through the water, the multicolored spinnaker bloated with wind. Content, she dragged her fingers in the darkish green waters of San Francisco Bay, delighting in the cool feel against her hand, while Breed sat behind her at the tiller.

"This is wonderful!" she shouted. But he couldn't hear her, because a gust of wind carried her voice forward. Laughing, she scooted closer, rose to her knees and spoke directly into his ear, smiling.

His returning smile revealed his own enjoyment. He relaxed against the gunnel, his long legs stretched out and crossed at the ankles. With one hand he managed the tiller as he motioned with the other for Elizabeth to sit at his side.

She did so willingly.

When he reached a spot that apparently met his specifications, he lowered the sails and dropped anchor.

Giving her nothing more than the basic instructions, he baited her hook and handed her a fishing pole.

"Now what?" She sat straight-backed and unsure as he readied his own pole and lowered the line into the deep waters on the opposite side of the boat.

"We wait for a hungry fish to come along and take a nibble."

"What if they're not hungry?"

"Are you always this much trouble?" he asked her, chuckling at her indignant look. "Your freckles are flashing at me again."

Involuntarily she brushed at her nose, as though her fingers could rub the tan flecks away. She was about to make a feisty retort when she felt a slight tug on her line.

"Breed," she whispered frantically. "I... I think I've got one." The pole dipped dramatically, nearly catching her off guard. "What do I do?" she cried, looking back to him, her eyes unsure.

"Reel it in."

"I can't," she said, silently pleading with him to take the pole from her. She should have known better.

"Sure you can," he assured her calmly. To offer her moral support, he reeled in his own line and went over to her, encouraging her as she struggled to bring in the fish.

She couldn't believe how much of a battle one small fish could wage. "What have I caught?" she shouted in her excitement. "A whale?" Perspiration broke out across her forehead as she pulled back on the pole and reeled in the fish inch by inch.

When the line snapped and she staggered backward, Breed caught her at the shoulders. "You all right?"

"No, darn it, I wanted that fish. What happened?"

He looked unconcerned and shrugged. "Any number of things. Want to try again?"

"Of course," she replied indignantly. He seemed to think she was a quitter, and she would like nothing better than to prove him wrong.

With her line back in the bay, Elizabeth leaned against the side, lazily enjoying the sun and wind. "Have you ever stopped to think that after all the times we've gone out, we still hardly know anything about each other?" she asked.

Her statement was met with silence. "What's there to know?"

She was treading on dangerous ground, and she knew it. Her relationship with Breed had progressed to the point where she felt he had a right to know who she was. But fear and indecision prevented her from broaching the subject boldly. "There's lots I'd like to know about you."

"Like what?" There was the slightest pause before his mouth thinned. He didn't seem overly eager to reveal more of himself.

"Well, for one thing...your family." If she led into the subject, then maybe he would ask her about hers, and she could explain bits and pieces of her background until things added up in his mind, since telling him outright was bound to be fatal to their promising relationship.

"Not much to tell you there. I'm the oldest of four boys. My great-grandfather came to California from Germany in search of lumber. He died here and left the land to his son." He paused and glanced at her. "What about you?"

She pressed her lips tightly together. For all her desire for honesty and despite her earlier resolution, when it came time to reveal the truth about her family, she found she couldn't. The bright, healthy color the wind and the sun had given her cheeks was washed swiftly away, leaving her unnaturally pale.

"I've got one older brother, Charlie." She swallowed tightly. "I don't think you'd like him."

"Why not?"

She lifted one petite shoulder. "He's…well, he's something of a stuffed shirt."

"Lawyer type."

She nodded, wanting to change the subject. "How much longer before I lure another fish to my bait?"

"Patience," Breed said, his back to her.

Her eyes fluttered closed. Her heart was pounding so hard she was sure he would notice. Unwittingly, he had given good advice. She had to be patient. Someday soon, when the time was right, she would tell him everything.

Six

The stars were twinkling like diamond chips in an ebony sky. The water lapped lightly against the side of Breed's boat, which, sails lowered, rocked gently in the murky water of San Francisco Bay. Four pairs of eager eyes gazed into the night sky, anticipating the next rocket burst to explode into a thousand shooting stars and briefly light up the heavens.

"I love the Fourth of July," Elizabeth murmured. Breed sat beside her, his arm draped casually over her shoulder. Gilly and Peter sat on the other side of the boat, holding hands. They might not be in love, but as Gilly had explained, they were certainly good friends.

One burst after another brightened the sky. Breed had said something earlier that week about going to Candlestick Park to watch the fireworks, but once the four of them had piled into Breed's sedan, they discovered that the traffic heading for the park was horrendous. He'd suggested that they take his sailboat into the bay and observe the fireworks from there, instead, an idea that had been met with enthusiasm by the others.

For nearly a week Breed had taken Elizabeth out on his boat every night after work. Sometimes they fished, depending on how much time they had and what their plans were afterward. He had led her forward a couple of times to raise and lower the sails. She loved to sail as much as he did, and the time they shared on the water had become the high point of her day. They talked openly, argued over politics, discussed books. He challenged her ideas on conservation and pollution, forcing her to stop and think about things she had previously accepted because of what she'd been told by others. Gently, but firmly, he made her form her own opinions. And she loved him for it.

She hadn't told him that she loved him, of course. The emotion was new to her and frightened her a little. The love she'd experienced in the past for her family and friends had been a mixture of respect and admiration. The only person with whom she had ever shared such a close relationship had been her mother. Of course, she would have grieved if her father had been the one who had suffered the stroke and died. But her mother had been her soulmate.

The love she felt for Breed went beyond friendship. Her love was fiery and intense, and the physical desire was sometimes overwhelming. Yet the joy she felt in his arms exceeded desire. Yes, she wanted him. More than that, she wanted to give herself to him. He must have known that, but he never allowed their lovemaking to go beyond a certain point. She didn't know why he was holding himself back. Not that she minded; that aspect of their relationship was only a small part of her feelings. When they could speak openly and honestly about their feelings and their commitment to one another, then they could deal with the physical aspect of their relationship. Her love went so much deeper. In analyzing her feelings, she thought that they also met on a higher plane, a spiritual one. Perhaps because of that, he felt it was too soon to talk about certain things. In some ways, they didn't need to.

She often wanted to talk to Gilly about her feelings, but she wasn't sure her friend, who was so much younger, would understand. If her mother had been alive, Elizabeth could have spoken to her. But she wasn't, and Elizabeth was forced to keep the inexplicable intensity of this relationship buried deep within her heart.

The only thing that marred her happiness was the sensation that something was troubling Breed. She'd tried to question him once and run up against a granite wall. Lately he'd been brooding and thoughtful. Although he hadn't said anything, she was fairly certain he'd lost his job. His hours had been flexible in the past, but lately he'd been coming into the Patisserie at all hours. Some days he even came in the morning and then again in the afternoon. Another thing she'd noticed was that they rarely ate in restaurants anymore. All the things they did together were inexpensive. Every Sunday they returned to Sigmund Stern Grove for the free concert. They took long walks on the beach and sailed almost daily. His apparent financial problems created others, effectively killing her desire to tell him about her background. How could she talk about her family's money without sounding insensitive? She had no doubt that the information could ruin what they shared.

When she glanced up from her musings she noted that Peter's arm was around Gilly, who had her head pressed against his shoulder. The look in Gilly's eyes seemed troubled, although Elizabeth realized she could have misread it in the reflected moonlight.

"Gilly, are you feeling okay?" she felt obliged to ask.

Gilly straightened. "Of course. Why shouldn't I be?"

"You're so quiet."

"I think we should enjoy the novelty," Peter interjected. "Once ol' motor-mouth gets going, it's hard to shut her up."

"Motor-mouth?" Gilly returned indignantly, poking Peter in his ribs. Peter laughed and the joking resumed, but not before Elizabeth witnessed the pain in her friend's expression.

An hour later, she helped Breed stow the sails after docking. Gilly and Peter carried the picnic basket and blankets to the car.

"Something's bothering Gilly," Elizabeth murmured to Breed the minute their friends were out of hearing distance.

"I noticed that, too," he whispered conspiratorially. "I think she's falling in love with Peter."

"No." She shook her head decisively. "They're just good friends."

"It may have started out like that, but it's not that

way anymore." He sounded completely confident. He hardly paused as he moved forward to store the sails.

Elizabeth followed him. "What makes you so sure Gilly's in love?"

A weary look stole across his features. "She has that look about her." From his tone, she could tell he didn't want to discuss the subject further.

"Apparently you've seen that look in a lot of women's eyes," she stated teasingly, though with a serious undertone.

"A few," he responded noncommittally.

The thought of him loving another woman produced a curious ache in her heart. She paused and straightened. *So this is jealousy*, she mused. This churning sensation in the pit of her stomach, this inexplicable pain in her chest. As crazy as it seemed, she was jealous of some nameless other woman.

Breed's hand at her elbow brought her back to the present. He took her hand as he stepped onto the dock. "Peter and Gilly are waiting."

The silence coming from the backseat of the car where Gilly and Peter were sitting was heavy and unnatural. A storm cloud seemed to have settled in the sedan, the air heavy with electricity. Breed captured Elizabeth's gaze and arched his brows in question.

She motioned weakly with her hand, telling him she had no more idea of what had happened between their friends than he did. Twice she attempted to start a conversation, but her words were met with uninterested grunts.

Breed pulled up and parked in front of the apartment

she and Gilly shared. As he was helping Elizabeth, Gilly practically jumped from the car.

"Night, everyone," she said in a voice that was high-pitched and wobbly.

"Gilly, wait up. I want to talk to you." Peter bolted after her, his eyes filled with frustration. He cast Breed and Elizabeth an apologetic look on his way past.

Breed glanced at Elizabeth and shrugged. "I'd say those two need some time alone."

"I agree."

"Do you want to go for a drive?" he suggested, tucking her hand under his folded arm as he led her back to the sedan.

"How about a walk instead? After sailing all evening, I could use some exercise."

He turned her in his arms. "We could. But I'd rather drive up to Coit Tower and show you the city lights. The view is fabulous."

Spending time alone with Breed was far more appealing than watching the city lights. "I'd like that," she admitted, getting back inside the car.

A long, winding drive through a dense neighborhood led to the observation tower situated high above the city. He parked, and as she stared out the windshield she realized that he hadn't exaggerated the view. She had seen some of the most beautiful landscapes in the world, but sitting with Breed overlooking San Francisco, she couldn't recall one more beautiful. Words couldn't describe the wonder of what lay before her.

"It's late," he murmured against her hair.

She acknowledged his words with a short nod, but she didn't want to leave and didn't suggest it.

"You have to work tomorrow." His voice was rough and soft, more of an aching whisper.

A smile touched her eyes. Breed couldn't decide if they should stay or go. Alone in the dark with nothing to distract them, the temptations were too great.

She tipped her head back. "Let me worry about tomorrow. I'll survive," she assured him. The night shaded his eyes, but she could feel the tension in him. His breathing was faintly irregular. "Why do you want to leave so much?" she asked in a throbbing whisper.

Her question went unanswered. A long moment of silence followed as he gazed down on her. Gently, he brushed the wispy strands of hair from her cheek, then curled his fingers into her hair. Elizabeth was shocked to realize he was trembling.

Slowly his head moved downward and paused an inch above her lips. "You know why we should leave," he growled.

All day she had yearned for him. Not for the first time, she noticed that he had been physically distant today, his touch casual, as though he was struggling to hold himself back. His restraint made her want him all the more.

"Beth." He whispered her name, and something snapped within him. His mouth plundered hers, and all her senses came to life. She rose slightly from the seat to press closer to him.

A tiny moan slipped from her as his lips found her neck and shot wave after wave of sensual delight through her. Her hands roamed his back, then moved forward and unfastened his shirt. Eagerly she let them glide down the smooth flat muscles of his broad chest.

He groaned and straightened, then buried his face in her neck and held her to him. "Beth..." he moaned. She could feel and see the conflict in his eyes.

He rubbed one hand across his face and eyes, but he continued to hold her tightly to him with the other, as though he couldn't bear to release her yet.

His control was almost frightening. The marvel of it silenced her for several seconds.

With her arms linked behind his head, she pressed her forehead to his.

The tension eased from his muscles, and she could hear the uneven thud of his heart slowly return to normal. When his breathing was less ragged, she lightly pressed her lips to his.

"Don't do that," he said harshly, abruptly releasing her. The tension in him was barely suppressed.

She turned away and leaned her head against the back of the seat, staring straight ahead. When tears of anger and frustration filled her eyes, she blinked hurriedly to forestall their flow.

"There's only so much of this a man can take." He, too, stared straight ahead as he savagely rubbed his hand along the back of his neck. "You know as well as I do what's happening between us."

"I can't help it, Breed," she whispered achingly.

"Yes, you can," he returned grimly.

The aching desire to reach across the close confines of the car and touch him was unbearable. But she didn't dare. She couldn't look at him. "Is…is there something wrong with me?" she asked in a tortured whisper. "I mean, do my freckles turn you off…or something?" Out of the corner of her eye, she saw a muscle twitch in his lean jaw.

"That question isn't worthy of an answer." His eyes hardened as he turned the ignition key and revved the engine.

"Maybe we should stop seeing so much of each other." Her pride was hurt, but the ache extended deep into her heart.

"Maybe we should," he said at last.

Elizabeth closed her eyes against the onrush of emotional pain. One tear escaped and made a wet track down her pale face, followed by another and another.

When he pulled up in front of her apartment building, she didn't turn to him to say good-night. She didn't want him to see her tears. That would only humiliate her further.

"Thanks for a lovely day," she whispered, barely able to find her voice; then she hurriedly opened the door and raced into the apartment foyer.

Breed didn't follow her, but he didn't leave either. His car was still parked outside when Elizabeth reached her apartment and, from deep within the living-room shadows, glanced out the window to watch him. The streetlight silhouetted a dejected figure of a man leaning over the steering wheel.

After a moment she realized that soft, whimpering cries were coming from the bedroom. Trapped in her own problems, she had forgotten Gilly's.

Wiping the moisture from her cheeks, she turned and headed down the hall to knock against her friend's open bedroom door.

"Gilly," she whispered, "what's wrong?"

Gilly sat up on her bed and blew noisily into a tissue. "Beth, I am so stupid."

"If you want to talk, I have all the time in the world to listen." She entered the darkened room and sat on the end of the bed. With all the problems she was having, she chastised herself for not recognizing what had been happening to her friend.

Gilly took another tissue and wiped her eyes dry. "Do you remember how I told you that Peter and I are just friends?"

"I remember."

"Well…" Gilly sniffled noisily, "something changed. I don't know when or why, but sometime last week I looked at Peter and I knew I loved him."

Elizabeth patted Gilly's hand. "That's no reason to cry. I'd think you'd be happy."

"I was, for two glorious days. I wanted to tell someone, but I didn't think it was fair to confide in you. I thought Peter should be the first one to know."

Her roommate *had* appeared exceptionally happy lately, Elizabeth recalled. Gilly had been particularly enthusiastic about the four of them spending the holiday together. She hadn't really thought much about it, though, because Gilly was always happy.

"Then I made the mistake of telling him," she continued. "You were helping Breed put the sails away, and

Peter and I were carrying things to the car." She inhaled a quivering breath.

"What happened?" Elizabeth encouraged her roommate softly.

"I guess I should have waited for a more appropriate moment, but I was eager to talk to him. Everything about the day had been perfect, and we were alone for the first time. So, like an idiot, I turned to him and said, 'Peter, I don't know what's happened, but I love you.'"

"And?"

"First he looked shocked. Then embarrassed. He stuttered something about this being a surprise and looked like he wanted to run away, but then you and Breed returned and we all piled into the car."

"What happened when Breed dropped the two of you off here?"

"Nothing. I wouldn't talk to him."

"Gilly!"

"You wouldn't have wanted to talk, either," she insisted, defending her actions. "I was humiliated enough without Peter apologizing to me because he didn't share my feelings."

"I'm sure he's going to want to talk to you." Elizabeth appealed to the more reasonable part of her friend's nature.

"He can forget it. How could I have been so stupid? If I was going to fall in love, why couldn't it be with someone like Breed?"

Elizabeth lowered her gaze to her hands. "There's only one Breed, and he's mine."

"Oh, before I forget…" Gilly sat up and looked

around her, finally handing Elizabeth a piece of paper with a phone number written across the top. "Your brother phoned."

"My brother? From Boston?"

"No, he's here in San Francisco. He's staying at the Saint Francis. I told him I didn't know what time you'd be back, so he said to tell you that he'd expect you tomorrow night for dinner at seven-thirty at his hotel."

Ordering instead of asking. That sounded just like her brother.

"Did he say anything else?" It would be just like Charlie to say something to embarrass her.

Gilly shook her head. "Not really, except..."

"Yes?" Elizabeth stiffened.

"Well, your brother's not like you, is he?"

"How do you mean?" Elizabeth asked.

"I don't know, exactly. But after I hung up, I wondered if I should have curtsied or something."

After a single telephone conversation, the astute Gilly had her brother pegged. "He's like that," Elizabeth admitted.

"Well, anyway, I gave you the message."

"And I'll show up at the hotel and hope I use the right spoon or my dear brother will be outraged."

For the first time that evening, Gilly smiled.

The café hadn't been open for more than five minutes when Breed strolled in and sat at his regular table. Elizabeth caught sight of his broad shoulders the moment he entered. Even after all these weeks her heart stirred at the sight of him, and now it throbbed painfully. One part of her wanted to rush to him, but she resisted.

Carrying the coffeepot, she approached his table slowly. He turned over the ceramic mug for her.

"Morning," she said as unemotionally as possible.

"Morning," he echoed.

Her eyes refused to meet his, but she could feel his gaze concentrating on her. "Would you like a menu?"

"No, just coffee."

She filled his cup.

"We need to talk," he announced casually as his hands folded around the cup.

She blinked uncertainly. "I can't now," she replied nervously. "Mornings are our busiest time."

"I didn't mean now." The words were enunciated slowly, as if his control over his patience had been stretched to the limit. "Tonight would be better, when we're able to discuss things freely, don't you think?"

She shifted her weight from one foot to the other. "I can't," she murmured apologetically. "My brother's in town, and I'm meeting him for dinner."

His level gaze darted to her, his eyes disbelieving.

"It's true," she declared righteously. "We're meeting at the Saint Francis."

"I believe you."

Frustrated, she watched as a hard mask stole over his face. "Go have dinner with your brother, then."

"I wasn't waiting for your approval," Elizabeth remarked angrily.

His amber eyes blazed for a furious second. "I didn't think you were."

Indecision made her hesitate. She wanted to turn and give him a clear view of her back, yet at the same time she wanted to set things right between them. The harmony they'd shared so often over these past weeks was slowly disintegrating before her eyes.

"Would you care to join us?" The question slipped from her naturally, although her mind was screaming for him to refuse.

"Me?" He looked aghast. "You don't mean that."

"I wouldn't have asked you otherwise." What, she wondered, had she been thinking? The entire evening would be a disaster. She could just imagine Charlie's reaction to someone like Breed.

Breed appeared to give her invitation some consideration. "No," he said at last, and she couldn't prevent the low but controlled breath of relief. "Maybe another time."

"Do you want to meet later?" she asked, and her voice thinned to a quavering note. "Dinner shouldn't take long," she said, glancing down at her practical white shoes. "I want to talk to you, too."

"Not tonight." The lines bracketing his mouth deepened with his growing impatience. Although she'd asked him to join her and Charlie, she realized that he knew she didn't want him there. "I'll give you a call later in the week." He stood, and with determined strides left the café.

She watched him go and had the irrational urge to throw his untouched coffee after him. That arrogant male pride of his only fueled her anger.

* * *

That night Elizabeth dressed carefully in a raspberry-colored dress with a delicate white miniprint. A dress that would meet with Charlie's approval, she mused as she examined herself in the mirror. Not until it was time to go did she stop to consider why he was in town. The family had no business holdings on the West Coast. At least none that she knew about. She hoped he hadn't come to persuade her to return to Boston. She'd just about made up her mind to make San Francisco her permanent home. The city was lovely, and the thought of leaving Breed was intolerable. She wouldn't—couldn't—leave the man she loved.

The taxi delivered her to the entrance of the prestigious hotel at precisely seven-twenty. The extra minutes gave her the necessary time to compose herself. She was determined to make this a pleasant evening. A confrontation with her brother was the last thing she wanted.

"Lizzy."

She groaned inwardly. Only one person in the world called her that.

"Hello, Siggy." She forced herself to smile and extended her hand for him to shake. To her acute embarrassment, he pulled her into his arms and kissed her soundly. Her mouth was opened in surprise, and Siggy seemed to assume she was eager for his attention and deepened the kiss.

Without making a scene, Elizabeth was left to endure his despicable touch.

The sound of someone clearing his throat appeared to bring Siggy back to his senses. He broke the con-

tact, and it was all Elizabeth could do not to rub the
feel of his mouth from hers with the back of her hand.
His touch made her skin crawl, and she glared angrily
from him to her brother.

"There are better places for such an intimate greeting," Charlie said, slapping Siggy on the back. "I told
you she'd be happy to see you."

Siggy ignored Charlie and said, "It's good to see
you, Lizzy."

She was unable to restrain her involuntary grimace.
"Don't call me Lizzy," she said between clenched teeth.

Charlie glanced at his slim gold watch. "Our table
should be ready. Names are something I'll leave for you
two to discuss later."

Later. She cringed at the thought. There wasn't going
to be a later with Siggy, though at least now she understood why Charlie had come to San Francisco. He
wanted to foist Siggy on her. She hadn't thought about
it at the time, but Charlie had mentioned Siggy at every
opportunity lately. That was the reason she'd found herself avoiding her brother, who stood to benefit from
any marriage between the two families. His selfishness
made her want to cry.

By some miracle she was able to endure the meal.
She spoke only when a question was directed to her
and smiled politely at appropriate intervals. The knot in
her throat extended all the way to her abdomen and felt
like a rock in the pit of her stomach. The two men discussed her at length, commenting several times on how
good she looked. Charlie insisted that she would make
a radiant bride and declared that their father would be

proud of her, knowing she had chosen so well. He made marriage between her and Siggy sound like a foregone conclusion. Questions buzzed around her head like irritating bees. In the past she'd had her differences with her father, but he wouldn't do this to her. She had to believe that. Yet her father *had* mentioned Siggy during their last few telephone conversations.

Resignedly, she accompanied her brother and Siggy to Charlie's suite for an after-dinner drink.

The small glass of liqueur helped chase the chill from her slender frame. Siggy sat on the plush sofa beside her and draped his arm possessively around her shoulders. She found his touch suffocating and pointedly removed his arm, then scooted to the other end of the sofa. Undaunted, he followed.

"I can see that you two have a lot to discuss," Charlie said, exchanging knowing smiles with the younger man. Without another word, he excused himself and left Elizabeth alone to deal with Siggy. The moment the door clicked closed, Siggy was on her like a starving man after food.

Pinned against the corner of the couch, she jerked her head left and right in an effort to avoid his punishing kiss.

"Siggy!" she gasped, pushing him off her. "Stop it!"

Composing himself, Siggy sat upright and made a pretense of straightening his tie. "I'm sorry, Lizzy. It's just that I love you so much. I've wanted you for years, and now I know you feel the same way."

"What?" she exploded.

Siggy brushed a stray hair from her flushed cheek.

"Charlie told me how you've had a crush on me for years. Why didn't you say something? You must have known how I feel about you. I've never made any secret of that."

A lump of outrage and shocked disbelief grew in her. Charlie had selfishly and maliciously lied to Siggy. Her own brother had sold her for thirty pieces of silver. She was nothing more to Charlie than the means of securing a financial coup that would link two wealthy families.

"Where is my brother?" Elizabeth managed finally. "I'd like to talk to him."

"He'll be back," Siggy said, as he stood, crossed the room and helped himself to another glass of brandy. "He wanted to give us some time alone. Want some, darling?" He held up the brandy and eyed her solicitously.

"No." Irritated, she shook her head. "So what would happen to the two companies if our families were linked?"

Smug and secure, Siggy silently toasted her. "A merger. It will be the financial feat of the year, Charlie says. My family will give him the exclusive distribution contract for our stores. Already we're planning to expand within a three-state area."

Momentarily shocked, Elizabeth felt tears form in her eyes. It was little wonder that Charlie was doing this. A lucrative—and exclusive—contract with Siggy's family's chain of department stores was something the Wainwrights had sought for years. But the price was far too high. Her happiness was not a bargaining chip.

Charlie returned a few minutes later, looking pleased and excited.

"If you'll excuse us a minute, Siggy," Elizabeth said bluntly, "I'd like to talk to my brother. Alone."

"Sure." Siggy glanced from brother to sister before setting his drink aside. "I'll be in the lounge when you're finished."

The second the door clicked closed, Elizabeth whirled on her brother. "How could you?" she demanded.

Charlie knotted his fists at his sides. "Listen, little sister, you're not going to ruin this for me. Not this time."

"Charlie, I'm your only sister. How could you ask me to marry a man I don't love? A man I don't even respect…"

His mouth tightened grimly. "For once in your life, stop thinking of yourself."

"Me?"

"Yes, you." He paced the floor in short, angry strides. "All right, I admit I went about this poorly, but marrying Siggy is what Mother would have wanted for you."

"That's not true." Her mother knew her feelings about Siggy and would never have pressured her into something like this.

"What do you know?" He hurled the words at her furiously. "You only thought of yourself. You never knew what Mother was really thinking. It was your selfishness that killed her."

The blood drained from Elizabeth's face. She and her mother had spent the afternoon shopping, and when they got back her mother, who wasn't feeling well, had gone to lie down before dinner. Within an hour she was dead, the victim of a massive stroke. In the back of her mind, she had always carried the guilt that something she had done that day had caused her death.

"Charlie, please," she whispered frantically. "Don't say that. Please don't say that."

"But it's true!" he shouted. "I was with father when the doctor said that having you drag her from store to store was simply too much. It killed her. *You* killed her."

"Oh, dear God." She felt her knees buckle as she slumped onto the sofa.

"There's only one thing you can do now to make up for that, Elizabeth. Do what Mother would have wanted. Marry Siggy. It would have made her happy."

He was lying. In her soul, she knew he was lying. But her own flesh and blood, her only brother, whom she had loved and adored in her youth, had used the cruellest weapon in his arsenal against her. With hot tears scalding her cheeks, she stood, clenched her purse to her breast and walked out the door.

She didn't stop walking until she found a taxi. Between breathless but controlled sobs, she gave the cabbie her address. Not until he pulled away from the curb did she realize how badly she was shaking.

"Are you all right, lady?" The cabbie looked at her anxiously in the rearview mirror.

She couldn't manage anything more than a nod.

When they arrived in front of her apartment, she handed him a twenty-dollar bill and didn't wait for the change. Though she had calmed down slightly on the ride home, she didn't want Gilly to see her, so she hurried in the door and headed for her bedroom.

"You're back soon." The sound of the television drifted from the living room.

"Yes," Elizabeth mumbled, keeping her head lowered, not wanting her friend to see her tears. She continued walking. "I think I'll take a bath and go to bed."

Gilly must have looked up for the first time. The sound of her surprised gasp was like an assault, and Elizabeth flinched. "Elizabeth! Good grief, what's wrong?"

"Nothing." Elizabeth looked at the wall. "I'm fine. I just need to be alone." She went into the bedroom and closed the door, leaning against it. Reaction set in, and she started to shake uncontrollably again. Fresh tears followed. Tears of anger. Tears of hate. Tears of pain and pride.

Softly Gilly knocked on the closed bedroom door, but Elizabeth ignored her. She didn't want to explain. She couldn't, not when she was crying like this. She fell into bed and curled up in a tight ball in an attempt to control the freezing cold that made her shake so violently.

When she inhaled between sobs, she heard Gilly talking to someone. Her friend's voice was slightly high-pitched and worried. She felt guilty that she was worrying Gilly like this, but she couldn't help it. Later she would make up some excuse. But she couldn't now.

Five minutes later there was another knock on her door. Elizabeth ignored it.

"Beth," a male voice said softly. "Open up. It's me."

"Breed," she sobbed, throwing back the covers. "Oh, Breed." She opened the door and fell into his arms, weeping uncontrollably. Every part of her clung to him as he lifted her into his arms and carried her into the living room.

With an infinite gentleness he set her on the couch and brushed the hair from her face.

One look at her and he stiffened. "Who did this to you?"

Seven

Elizabeth was crying so hard that she couldn't answer. Nor did she know how to explain. She didn't want to tell Breed and Gilly that the brother she loved had betrayed her in the worst possible way.

Breed said something to Gilly, but Elizabeth didn't hear. "Beth," he whispered, leading her to the couch and half lifting her onto his lap. "Tell me what's upset you."

Forcefully, she shook her head and inhaled deep breaths that became quivering sobs as she tried to regain control of herself. Crying like this was only making matters worse.

She knew the terrible, crippling pain of Charlie's betrayal was there in her eyes, and she couldn't do anything to conceal it. A nerve twitched in Breed's hard, lean jaw, his features tense, and pain showed clearly in his eyes. *Her* pain. She was suffering, and that caused him to hurt as well. She couldn't have loved anyone more than she loved him right at that moment. She didn't know what he thought had happened, and she couldn't utter a word to assure him.

"I'm fine. No one hurt me…not physically," she finally said in a trembling voice she barely recognized as her own. "Just hold me." She had trouble trying to control her breathing. Her body continued to shake with every inhalation.

"I'll never let you go," he promised as his lips moved against her hair. She felt some of the tension leave him, felt his relief that things weren't as bad as he'd thought.

Warm blankets were wrapped around her, so warm they must have recently been taken from the dryer. That must be what Breed had asked Gilly to do, Elizabeth realized.

He continued to talk to her in a low, soothing tone until her eyes drifted closed. Caught between sleep and reality, she could feel him gently free himself from her embrace and lay her on the sofa. A pillow cushioned her head, and warm blankets surrounded her. She didn't know how long he knelt beside her, smoothing her hair from her face, his touch so tender she felt secure and protected. Gradually a calmness filled her, and she knew she was on the brink of falling asleep. Breed left her side but she sensed that he hadn't gone far. He had told her he wouldn't leave, and she was comforted just by knowing he was in the same room.

"All I know," Elizabeth heard Gilly whisper, "was that she was meeting her brother for dinner. What could he have done to cause this?"

"You can bet I'm going to find out," Breed stated in a dry, hard voice that was frightening in its intensity.

"No." Elizabeth struggled to a sitting position. "Just drop the whole thing. It's my own affair."

Breed's eyes narrowed.

"Elizabeth," Gilly murmured, her eyes wide and worried, "I've never seen you like this."

"I'm fine, really." She brushed back her tear-dampened hair. "I'm just upset. I apologize for making a scene."

"You didn't make a scene," Gilly returned soothingly.

Breed brought her a damp cloth and, kneeling at her side, gently brushed it over her cheeks. It felt cool and soothing over her hot skin. His jaw was clenched and pale, as if he couldn't stand to have her hurt in any way, physically or emotionally.

Elizabeth stroked the side of his face, then pulled him to her, wrapping her arms around his neck. "Thank you."

"For what? I should have been there for you."

"You couldn't have known." It wasn't right that he should shoulder any blame for what had happened.

He took her hands and gently raised them to his mouth, then kissed her knuckles. "Beth…" His eyes implored hers. "I want you to trust me enough to tell me what happened tonight."

She lowered her gaze and shook her head. "It's done. I don't want to go over it."

The pressure on her fingers was punishing for a quick second. "I'll kill anyone who hurts you like this again."

"That's exactly why I won't talk about it."

The tension between them was so palpable that she could taste it. Their eyes clashed in a test of wills. Unnerved, she lowered hers first. "I need you here," she whispered in a soft plea. "It's over now. I want to forget it ever happened."

Gilly hovered close. "Do you feel like you could drink something? Tea? Coffee? Soda?"

The effort to smile was painful. "All I want is a hot bath and bed." Her muscles ached, and she discovered that when she stood, her legs wobbled unsteadily, so she leaned against Breed for a moment.

Gilly hurried ahead and filled the bathtub with steaming, scented water. Next she brought in fluffy, fresh towels.

"You want me to stay in the bathroom while you soak?" Breed asked, and a crooked smile slanted his mouth, because of course he knew the answer. The humor didn't quite touch his eyes, but Elizabeth appreciated the effort.

"No. If I need anyone, Gilly can help."

"Pity," he grumbled.

The hot water helped relieve the aching tension in her muscles. Even now her body was coiled and alert. The throbbing in her temples diminished, and the pain in her heart began to recede. As she rested against the back of the tub, she kept running over the details of the evening, but she forced the painful images to the back of her mind. She didn't feel strong enough emotionally to deal with things now. Maybe tomorrow.

Gilly stayed with her, more on Breed's insistence than because she felt Elizabeth needed her. Together they emerged from the steam-filled bathroom, Elizabeth wrapped in her thick terry robe. Breed led Elizabeth into her room. The sheets on her bed had been folded back, and her weak smile silently thanked him.

"You won't leave me?" Her eyes pleaded with him as he tucked her under the covers.

"No," he whispered. "I said I wouldn't." His kiss was so tender that fresh tears misted her eyes. "Go to sleep," he whispered encouragingly.

"You'll be here when I wake up?" She needed that reassurance.

"I'll be here."

The dark void was already pulling her into its welcoming arms. As she drifted into sleep, she could hear Breed's low voice quizzing Gilly.

The sound of someone obviously trying to be quiet and not succeeding woke Elizabeth. The room was dark, and she glanced at her clock radio to note that it was just after three. She sat up in bed and blinked. The memory of the events of the evening pressed heavily against her heart. Although she was confident Charlie would never have abandoned her to Siggy if her brother had known what Siggy was capable of doing, the sense of betrayal remained. To try to push her off on Siggy was deplorable enough. Slipping from between the sheets, she put on her silk housecoat and moved into the living room.

"Hello there," she whispered to Breed, keeping quiet so she wouldn't disrupt Gilly's sleep.

"Did I wake you?" He sat up and wiped a hand across his weary face. The sight of him trying to sleep on the couch was ludicrous. His feet dangled far over the end, and he looked all elbows and arms.

"You wake me? Never. I thought an elephant had escaped and was raging through the living room."

His smile was evident in the moonlight. "I got up to use the bathroom and walked into the lamp," he explained with a chagrined look.

"It was selfish of me to ask you to stay," she said, sitting down beside him.

"I would have stayed whether you asked me to or not." He reached for her hand and squeezed it gently. "How do you feel?"

She shrugged and lowered her gaze to her knees. "Like a fool. I don't usually overreact that way."

"I know," he murmured. "That's what concerned me most." He put his arm around her, and she rested her head against his shoulder. "Sometimes the emotional pain can be twice as bad as anything physical." She gave a long, drawn-out yawn. "When you love and trust someone and they hurt you, then the pain goes beyond anything physical." She began explaining the situation to Breed, though carefully tiptoeing around any discussion of her family's wealth. He'd asked her to trust him, and she did, at least with her feelings. It was important that he realize that.

He didn't comment, but she felt him stiffen slightly. When she leaned against his solid support, he pulled her close, holding her to his chest.

Soon the comfort of his arms lured her back to sleep. When she woke again, she discovered that they had both fallen asleep while sitting upright. His arm was still draped around her, and he rested his head against the back of the sofa. His breathing was deep and undisturbed.

Even from a sitting position, waking up in Breed's arms felt right. She pressed her face against the side of his neck and kissed him, enjoying the light taste of salt and musk.

"Are you pretending to be Sleeping Beauty kissing the handsome prince to wake him?" he asked, opening one eye to study her.

She barely allowed his sideways glance to touch her before straightening. "You've got that tale confused. It was the prince who kissed Sleeping Beauty awake."

"Would it hurt you if I did?" The teasing left his voice as he brought her closer within the protective circle of his arms.

Her eyes sought his. "You could never hurt me," she said in a whisper that sounded as solemn as a vow.

"I don't ever want to," he murmured as his lips claimed hers. The kiss was gentle and sweet. His mouth barely touched hers, enhancing the sensuality of the contact. His hands framed her face, and he treated her as if he were handling a rare and exotic orchid.

"You're looking much more chipper this morning," Gilly said, standing in the doorway of her bedroom. She raised her hands high above her head and yawned.

"I feel a whole lot better."

"I'm happy to hear that. I don't mind telling you that you had me worried."

"You?" Breed inhaled harshly. "I don't think I've

ever come closer to wanting to kill a man. It's a good thing you didn't tell who did this last night, Beth. I wouldn't have been responsible for my actions."

Elizabeth lowered her gaze to the hands folded primly in her lap. "I think I already knew that."

"Take the day off," Gilly insisted as she sauntered into the kitchen and started the coffee.

"I can't do that," Elizabeth objected strenuously. "You need me."

"I'll make do," Gilly returned confidently. She opened the refrigerator, took out a pitcher of orange juice and poured herself a small glass. "But only for today."

Elizabeth returned to her bedroom to change clothes. When she studied herself in the mirror she saw no outward mark of what she'd been through, but the mirror couldn't reveal the inner agony of what Charlie had tried to do.

"I don't believe it," she grumbled as she walked into the living room. "Last night I wanted to die, and today I feel like the luckiest woman alive to have you two as my friends."

"We're the lucky ones," Gilly said sincerely.

"But I acted like such a fool. I can't imagine what you thought."

"You were shocked, upset," Breed insisted with a note of confidence. "Shock often exaggerates the messages transmitted to the brain."

"Such a know-it-all," Gilly complained, running a brush through her short, bouncy curls. She looked at

Elizabeth with a mischievous gleam. "Why do you put up with him?"

Elizabeth shrugged and shook her head. "I don't know. But he's kinda cute."

"I amuse you, is that it?" Breed joined in the teasing banter.

"You're amusing, but not always correct," Elizabeth remarked jokingly. "My brain wasn't confused by shock. But I'll admit, you had me going there for a minute."

He had the grace to look faintly embarrassed. "Well, it sounded good at the time."

Gilly paused on her way out the door. "Have a good day, you two. Call if you need anything. And—" she hesitated and lowered her gaze "—don't hold up dinner for me."

"Working late?" Elizabeth quizzed, experiencing a twinge of guilt that her friend would be stuck at the café alone.

Gilly shook her head. "Peter said he'd be coming by, and I don't want to be here when he does."

"Honestly, Gilly, you're acting like a child."

"Maybe." Gilly admitted. "But at least I've got my pride."

Breed murmured something about pride doing little to keep her warm at night, but luckily Gilly was too far away to hear him.

The door clicked, indicating Gilly had left for work.

"Are you hungry?" Breed asked as he walked across the living room, his hands buried deep inside his pants pockets.

She hadn't eaten much of her dinner the previous night, but even so, she discovered she didn't have much of an appetite. "Not really."

"What you need is something scintillating to tempt you."

Wickedly batting her eyelashes, she glanced at him and softly said, "My dear Mr. Breed, what exactly do you have in mind?"

He chose to ignore the comment.

"I think I'll go over to my place to shower and change. When I come back, I'll bring us breakfast."

Her mouth dropped in mute surprise. She couldn't believe he hadn't risen to her bait, and, selfishly, she didn't want him to leave her alone. Not now. "I'll come with you," she suggested eagerly. "And while you're in the shower, I'll cook us breakfast."

His expression revealed his lack of enthusiasm for her suggestion. "Not this time."

She bristled. "Why not?" The memory of her last visit to his apartment remained vivid. She hadn't been imagining things. He really didn't want her there. And yet she couldn't imagine why.

"You need to stay here and rest."

Her eyes widened in bewildered protest.

"I was thinking that while I'm gone you can get an extra hour's sleep."

Sleep? She was dressed and had downed a cup of strong coffee. He didn't honestly expect her to go back to bed, did he?

"I won't be long," he told her, and without a backward glance he hurried out the door.

"Don't worry about breakfast. I'll have something ready when you come back," she called after him. She didn't like this situation, but there wasn't much she could do. The impulse to speak her mind died on her lips. Now wasn't the time to confront Breed with petty suspicions about her cool welcome at his apartment.

With a cookbook resting on the kitchen counter, she skimmed over the recipe for blueberry muffins. For the moment, keeping busy was paramount. When she stopped to think, too many dark images crowded her thoughts. For a time last night she had started to believe Charlie's vindictive words, which fed on the fear that she was somehow responsible for her mother's death, which had haunted her ever since that awful day. When a tear escaped, despite her determination not to cry, she wiped it aside angrily and forced herself to concentrate on the recipe. Rehashing the details of last night only upset her, so she soundly rejected any more introspection on the subject.

As promised, Breed returned less than an hour later.

A hand on each of her shoulders, he kissed her lightly on the cheek. He looked wonderful, his hair still wet from his shower.

"Hmm…something smells good."

"I baked some muffins," she said as she led the way into the kitchen. Her culinary efforts were cooling on a rack on top of the counter. "I don't know how they taste. The cookbook said they were great to take camping."

"Are you thinking of taking me into the woods and ravaging my body?" he joked as he lifted a muffin from the cooling rack. It burned his fingers, and he gingerly tossed it in the air several times until, laughing, she handed him a plate.

"You might have told me they were still hot."

"And miss seeing you juggle? Never." Her mood had lightened to match his. Sitting beside him at the circular table, she peeled an orange and popped a section into her mouth.

"How about a trip to our beach today?" he suggested, and his mouth curved into a sensuous smile.

"Sure." Her glance caught sight of his massive hands. A slight swelling in one of the knuckles captured her attention. Had he been fighting? Showering wouldn't have taken him an hour. Immediately the thought flashed through her mind that he'd gone to see her brother. "Breed…" Her eyes sought his as she swallowed past the thickness lodged in her throat. "Give me your hand."

The teasing glitter didn't leave his eyes, and he didn't seem to notice the serious light in hers. "Is this a proposal of marriage?"

"Let me see your hand," she repeated.

He went completely still. "Why?"

"Because I need to know that you didn't do anything…dumb."

He smiled briefly and pushed his chair away from the table, then stood and walked to the other side of the room, folding his arms across his massive chest. Expelling an explosive breath, he replied, "I didn't, although the temptation was strong. While I live, no man will ever treat you that way again."

"I appreciate the chivalry," she said evenly, "but I wish you hadn't."

"I found it…necessary." The hard set of his features revealed the tight hold he was keeping on both his temper and his emotions.

Her composure cracked. "I'm not defending him…."

"I should hope not." He shook his head grimly.

"But I don't want you involved," she said.

"I'm already involved."

She stood and, with her own arms folded around her narrow waist, paced the kitchen. The room was filled with Breed. His presence loomed in every corner. "Please understand, I don't want to argue with you."

His eyes narrowed as he moved into the other room and sat on the arm of the sofa. "I've never met anyone like you, Beth. Those two deserve to have the stuffing kicked out of them."

"He's my brother!" she cried defensively. "He may not be a very nice guy, but he's the only one I've got."

He moved into the living room, his back to her. When he turned to face her again a moment later, his grim look had vanished. "Are we going to the beach or not?"

Numbly, she nodded.

"Good." With long strides he crossed the distance separating them. Then he took her by the shoulders and sweetly kissed her. "Let's hurry. It's isn't every day that I get you all to myself."

They rode in his silver sedan, and again she wondered why he no longer drove Hilda. Maybe the Jeep needed repairs and he couldn't afford to have them done until his finances improved. She wished there was some way she could take care of things like that for him without his knowing. Offering him money wasn't the answer, only a sure way of crushing his male ego. Even so, what was the use of having money if she couldn't spend it the way she wanted?

The surf rolled gently against their bare feet as they strolled along the smooth beach, their arms entwined.

"Tell my about your childhood," he asked curiously after a lengthy, companionable silence.

Under other circumstances she might have had the courage to reveal her wealth. But not today. She'd faced enough upheaval in the last twenty-four hours to warrant caution. Her mouth tightened with tension before she managed to speak.

"What's there to tell? I was born, grew up, went to school, graduated, went to school some more, dropped out, and traveled a little."

"Nicely condensed, I'd say."

"Have you been to Europe?" she asked, to change the subject.

"No, but I spent six months in New Zealand a few years back." His response told her he knew exactly what she was doing.

"Did you enjoy it?" Relieved, she continued the game.

"I'd say it was the most beautiful country on earth, but I haven't done enough traveling to compare it with the rest of the world."

She recalled her own trip to the South Pacific. Her time in New Zealand had been short, but she'd shared his feelings about the island nation.

"My mother used to love to travel," she commented, mentally recalling the many trips they'd taken together.

"How long has she been gone?" he asked, his hand reaching for hers.

She swallowed with difficulty and forced her chin up in a defensive stance. "She died two years ago," she explained softly. "Even after all this time, I miss her."

He paused, and traced a finger over her jaw and down her neck. "I'm sorry, Beth. You must have loved her very much."

"I did," she whispered on a weak note.

"Did your family ever go camping?" The question came out of the blue and was obviously meant to change the mood.

"No." She had never slept in a tent in her life. Back-to-nature pursuits had never been among her father's interests.

"Would you like to sometime?"

"Us?"

"I was thinking of inviting Gilly along." Gently, his hand closed over hers. "And Peter," he added as an afterthought.

"Peter? You devious little devil."

"Of course, that will take some finagling," he admitted.

"Finagling or downright deception?"

"Deception," he immediately agreed.

"You shock me, Andrew Breed. I wouldn't have guessed that you had a sneaky bone in your body."

His gaze slid past her to the rolling waves that broke against the sand. "I suspect a lot of things about me would shock you," he murmured, and her thoughts echoed his.

* * *

"What really irritates me," Gilly continued her tirade as she hauled another box of cooking utensils out from the kitchen, "is the fact that I bare my heart to Peter and then he—he just disappears. It's been three days since I've heard from him. Count 'em, Beth, three long days."

"Well, you slammed the door in his face last time he came over, and you hang up on him whenever he calls."

"Well, he deserves it."

Hands on hips, Gilly surveyed the living-room floor. Half of the contents of their kitchen had been packed into cardboard boxes in anticipation of the weekend camping trip. "Is that everything?"

"Well, I certainly hope so." Elizabeth couldn't believe that people actually went through all this work just for a couple of days of traipsing around the woods.

When Breed arrived he looked incredulously at the accumulated gear.

"Before you complain, I only packed what was on your list," Elizabeth said as she flashed him an eager smile. She was ready for this new adventure, although she was suffering a few qualms about not telling Gilly that Peter had been invited. In fact, he had left the night before and claimed a space for them in the Samuel P. Taylor State Park, north of the city.

"Well, maybe we packed a few things not on your meager list," Gilly amended. "You left off several things we might need."

"I don't know how Hilda's going to carry all this," Breed mumbled under his breath.

"Hilda," Elizabeth cried happily. "We're taking

Hilda?" Before Breed could stop her, she rushed down the stairs to the outdated Jeep parked at the curb. Gingerly she climbed into the front seat and patted the dashboard. "It's good to see you again," she murmured affectionately.

"Will someone kindly tell me what's going on?" Gilly stood, one hand placed on her hip, staring curiously at her friend.

"It's a long story," Breed murmured, lifting the first box on board.

Admittedly it was a tight squeeze, but they managed to fit everything.

The radio blared, and they were all singing along as they traveled. When the news came on, they paused to listen. From her squashed position in the backseat, Gilly leaned forward. "Hey, Breed, I don't see any tent back here."

"There isn't one," he said with a smile, glancing at Elizabeth.

"I thought we were going camping?"

"We are," he confirmed.

"With no tent?"

Elizabeth didn't want to carry the deception any further. "Peter pitched the tent yesterday."

"Peter!" Gilly exploded. "You didn't say anything about Peter coming on this trip."

Elizabeth turned and faced her friend. "Are you mad?"

Gilly's gaze raked Elizabeth's worried face. Folding her arms, she resolutely stared out the window. "Why should I be mad? My best friend in the world has just turned traitor."

"If I'm your best friend, then you have to believe I wouldn't do anything to hurt you," Elizabeth returned with quiet logic.

"I'm not answering that."

"Because I'm right," Elizabeth argued irrefutably.

"Peter loves you," Breed inserted, matching Gilly's clipped tones. "And if it means kidnapping you so that he has the chance to explain himself, then I don't consider that much of a crime."

"I suppose you think that someday I'll thank you for this."

"I want to be maid of honor," Elizabeth said with a romantic sigh.

Gilly ignored her and sat in stony silence until Breed turned off the highway and entered the campgrounds. Peter had left word of his location at the ranger station, and within a matter of minutes they were at the campsite.

"I hope you realize that I don't appreciate this one bit," Gilly said through clenched teeth.

"I believe we got the picture." Breed's mouth curved in a humorous smile.

"Really, Gilly, it won't be so bad. All we want is for you to give the poor guy a chance."

Gilly ignored her friend and turned her attention to Breed. "Did you know Beth once called you Tarzan?" she informed him saucily.

"Tarzan?" Breed's large eyes rounded indignantly,

and he turned to Elizabeth with a feigned look of outrage. "Beth, you didn't."

She forced herself to smile and nodded regretfully.

"In that case, will you be my Jane?"

"Love to," she returned happily, placing her hand in his.

Peter had the tent pitched and a small fire going when they arrived. Breed and Elizabeth climbed out of the front seat and stretched. Gilly remained inside, her arms folded as she stared defiantly ahead.

"Hi, Gilly," Peter said as he strolled up to the Jeep, his hands buried in his pockets.

Silence.

Peter continued, "I've always been one to lay my cards on the table, so you're going to listen to me. There's no place to run now."

More silence.

He went on, "You once told me that you loved me, but I'm beginning to have my doubts about that." He levered himself so that he was in the driver's seat and turned to face her. "I was so shocked at your announcement that I must have said and done the worst possible things." He hesitated slightly. "The thing was, I had no idea how you felt."

"Your reaction told me that." Gilly spoke for the first time, her words tight and low.

"You see, I'd realized earlier how much you'd come to mean to me. I'd been trying to work up enough nerve to tell you my feelings had changed."

"Don't you dare lie to me, Peter."

"I'm not," he returned harshly. "For too long I've had

doors shut in my face, phones slammed in my ear. I've about had it, Gillian Haggith. I want you to marry me, and I want your answer right now."

Feeling like an intruder, Elizabeth leaned against the picnic table with Breed at her side. Fascinated, she watched as Gilly's mouth opened and closed incredulously. For the first time in recent history, her friend was utterly speechless.

"Maybe this will help you decide," Peter mumbled, withdrawing a small diamond ring from his jeans pocket.

"Oh, Peter!" Gilly cried, and she threw her arms around him as she burst into happy tears.

Eight

"Shall we give the lovebirds some time alone?" Breed whispered in Elizabeth's ear.

Her nod was indulgent. "How about giving me a grand tour of the grounds."

"Love to."

"I'm especially interested in the modern technological advances."

His thoughtful gaze swept over her face. "Beth, we're in the woods. There are no technological wonders out here."

"I was thinking of things that go flush in the night."

"Ahh, those." The corners of his mouth twitched briefly upward. "Allow me to lead the way."

He set a comfortable pace as they wandered around the campgrounds, taking their time. The sky couldn't have been any bluer, and the air was filled with the scent of pine and evergreen. A creek bubbled cheerfully down its meandering course, and they paused for a few quiet moments of peaceful introspection. Elizabeth's thoughts drifted to her father. Their showcase home in Boston, with all its splendor, couldn't compare to the tranquil beauty of this forest. If he could see this place, she was confident, he would experience the serenity that had touched her in so brief a time.

Gilly had lunch cooking by the time Breed and Elizabeth returned. The two of them smiled conspiratorially, having agreed to pretend ignorance of the conversation they'd overheard earlier. With an efficiency Elizabeth hardly recognized in her friend, Gilly set out the paper plates, a pan of hot beans, freshly made potato salad, and grilled hot dogs with toasted buns.

"I'll do the dishes," Elizabeth joked as she filled her paper plate. Gilly sat beside Elizabeth at the picnic table.

"I'm sorry about what I said earlier," Gilly murmured as telltale color crept up her neck. "It was childish and immature of me to tell Breed that you once referred to him as Tarzan." She released her breath with a thin edge of exasperation. "Actually, it was probably the stupidest thing I've ever done in my entire life. How petty can I get?"

"You had a right to be angry." Even so, Elizabeth appreciated her friend's apology. "Not telling you that Peter was coming here was underhanded and conniving."

Breed lifted his index finger. "And my idea. I take credit."

Elizabeth's eyes captured his, and her gaze wavered slightly under his potent spell. "But if it had backfired, the blame would have been mine. I'm learning a lot about the workings of the male mind."

"Do you have to sit across the table from me, woman?" Peter complained as he settled next to Breed.

"I'll be sitting next to you for the rest of my life," Gilly returned with a happy note. "Besides, at this angle you can feast upon my unspoiled beauty."

The diamond ring on her finger sparkled almost as brightly as the happiness in her eyes. Things couldn't have worked out better. Elizabeth realized how miserable her friend had been the last few days and felt oddly guilty that she had been so involved in her own problems.

"Do you two have an announcement to make?" Breed asked as he stared pointedly at Gilly's left hand.

"Gilly and I are getting married," Peter informed them cheerfully.

"We haven't set a date yet," Gilly inserted. "Peter thought we should talk to my parents first. And my church has a counseling class for engaged couples. I thought we should take it. Plus, knowing my mother, she'll want a big wedding, which will take a while to plan. So the earliest we could set the date would be autumn. Maybe early November."

"I was hoping for a quiet wedding on the beach just before dawn with our parents and close friends. Preferably next month sometime," Peter said.

"Next month?" Gilly choked. "We can't do that. My mother would never forgive me."

"I thought it was me you were marrying, not your mother," grumbled Peter.

Setting the palms of her hands on the tabletop, Gilly half rose from her seat and glared jokingly at Peter. "Are you trying to pick a fight already?" she asked with a saucy grin.

"It's my wedding, too," Peter challenged. "I think, in the interest of fairness to your future husband, you should consider my ideas."

Gilly mumbled something under her breath, and reached for the potato salad.

Holding back a smile, Elizabeth glanced at Breed, who seemed to be enjoying the moment. She felt as if she could read his thoughts, and she agreed. Gilly and Peter fought much more now that they were in love.

They finished their meal, then got serious about setting up camp.

"I'll unload Hilda," Breed said as he stood.

"I'll help," Peter offered, pointing to Gilly. "The wedding will be next month, on the beach at sunrise."

"Thanks for the invitation, big shot. I hope I can make it."

"I'm doing the dishes," Elizabeth reminded them, and she hurriedly swallowed the last bite of her meal. Everyone was suddenly busy, and she didn't want to sit idle.

The paper plates were easily disposed of in a garbage container. She placed the potato salad and other leftovers in the cooler. The only items left were the plastic forks and a single saucepan.

With a dish towel draped around her neck, and the plasticware, liquid soap and rag dumped inside the saucepan, she headed toward the creek she'd discovered with Breed.

"Hey, where are you going?" Gilly called out as Elizabeth left.

"To wash these." She held up the pan. "I'll be right back. Breed said something about taking a hike."

Gilly's smile was crooked. "Yes, but I think he was referring to me and Peter. If we don't quit fighting, I have the feeling we may have to walk home."

Elizabeth located the stream without a problem and knelt on the soft earth beside the water, humming as she rubbed the rag along the inside of the aluminum pan. A flash of color caught her attention, and she glanced upward. A deer was poised in a meadow on the other side of the water. Mesmerized, she watched the wild creature with a powerful sense of awe and appreciation.

Slowly, she straightened, afraid her movements would frighten off the lovely animal. But the doe merely raised its regal head, and she stared into its beautiful dark eyes. The animal didn't appear to be frightened by her presence.

Wondering how close she could get, she crossed the burbling water, stepping carefully from one stone to another. When she reached the other side, the doe was gone. Disappointed, she walked to the spot where the animal had been standing and saw that it had gone farther into the forest, and now was barely visible. She decided to follow it, thinking she might be able to catch a glimpse of a fawn. She wished she'd thought to bring her camera. But she hadn't expected to see anything like this.

Keeping a safe distance, she followed the deer, rather proud of her ability to track it. She realized that the animal wasn't trying to escape or she wouldn't have had a chance of following it this far.

The lovely creature paused, and she took the opportunity to rest on a felled tree while keeping an eye on the deer. A glance at her watch told her that she'd been away from camp almost an hour. She didn't want to worry anyone, so even though the chase was fun, she felt forced to abandon it. With bittersweet regret, she stood and gave a waving salute to her beautiful friend.

An hour later, she owned up to the fact that she was lost. The taste of panic filled her mouth, and she took several deep breaths to calm herself.

"Help!" she screamed, as loudly as she could. Her voice echoed through the otherwise silent forest. "I'm here!" she cried out, a frantic edge to her words. Hurrying now, she half ran through the thick woods until she stumbled and caught herself against a bush. A thorny limb caught on the flesh of her upper arm and lightly gouged her skin.

Elizabeth yelped with pain and grabbed at her wound. When her fingers came away sticky with blood, a sickening sensation attacked her stomach.

"Calm down," she told herself out loud, thinking the sound of her own voice would have a soothing effect. It didn't, and she paused again to force herself to breathe evenly.

"Breed, oh, Breed," she whispered as she moved through the dense cover, holding her arm. "Please find me. Please, please find me."

Her legs felt weak, and her lungs burned with the

effort to push on. Every step cost her more than the previous one.

She tried to force the terror from her mind and concentrate on happy thoughts. The memory of her mother's laughter took the edge of exertion from her steps. The long walks with Breed along the beach. She recalled their first argument and how she'd insisted that she could find the way back. Without him, she would have been lost then, too. His words from that night echoed in her tired mind. *If you ever get lost, promise me you'll stay in one place.* She stumbled to an abrupt halt and looked around her. Nothing was familiar. She could be going in the opposite direction from the campground for all she knew. She was dreadfully tired and growing weaker every minute, the level of her remaining endurance dropping with each step.

If she was going to stop, she decided, she would find a place where she could sit and rest. She found a patch of moss that grew beside a tree and lowered herself to a sitting position. Her breath was uneven and ragged, but she suspected it was more from fear than anything.

Someone would find her soon, she told herself. Soon. The word repeated in her mind a thousand times, offering hope.

Every minute seemed an hour and every hour a month as she sat and waited. When the sun began to set, she realized she would probably be spending the night in the woods. The thought couldn't frighten her any more than she was already. At least not until darkness settled over the forest.

Not once did she doze or even try to sleep, afraid she

would miss a light or the sound of a voice. Tears filled her eyes at the darkest part of the night that preceded dawn and she realized she could die out here. At least, she was convinced, her mother was waiting for her on the other side of life.

Of course, she had regrets—lots of them. Things she had wanted to do in her lifetime. But her biggest regret was that she had never told Breed how much she loved him.

She stood up gratefully when the sun came over the horizon, its golden rays bathing the earth with its warmth. She was so cold. For a time she had been convinced she would freeze. Her teeth had chattered, and she'd huddled into a tight ball, believing this night would be her last.

Her stomach growled, and her tongue had grown thick with the need for water. For a long time she debated whether she should strike out again and look for something to drink or stay where she was. Every muscle protested when she decided to search out water, and she quickly sat back down, amazed at how weak she had become.

She tried to call out, but her voice refused to cooperate, and even the attempt to shout took more energy than she could muster.

With her eyes closed, her back supported by the tree trunk, she strained her ears for the slightest sound. The day before, while walking with Breed, she had thought the woods were quiet and serene. Now she was astonished at the cacophony that surrounded her. The loud squawk of birds and the rustle of branches in the breeze filled the forest. And then there were the other noises she couldn't identify.

"Beth." Her name echoed from faraway, barely audible.

With a reserve of energy she hadn't known she possessed, Elizabeth leaped to her feet and screamed back. "Here… I'm here!" Certain they would never hear her, she ran frantically toward the sound of the voice, crying as she pushed branches out of her way. They would search in another area if she couldn't make herself heard. She couldn't bear it if she had come so close to being found only to be left behind.

"Here!" she cried again and again, until her voice was hardly more than a whisper.

Breed saw her before she saw him. "Thank God," he said, and the sound of it reached her. She turned and saw the torment leave his face as he covered the distance between them with giant strides.

Fiercely, she was hauled into his arms as he buried his face in her neck. A shudder ran through him as she wrapped her arms around him and started to weep with relief. Huge tears of happiness rolled down her face, making wet tracks in the dust that had settled on her cheeks. She was so relieved that she didn't notice the other men with Breed until he released her.

Some of the previous agony returned to Breed's eyes as he ran his finger down the dried blood that had crusted on her upper arm.

A forest ranger handed her a canteen of water and told her to take small sips. Another man spoke into a walkie-talkie, advising the members of the search party that she had been found and was safe.

The trip back to camp was hazy in Elizabeth's memory. Questions came at her from every direction. She answered them as best she could and apologized profusely for all the trouble she had caused.

The only thing that stood out in her mind was how far she had wandered. It seemed hours before they reached the campground. Breed took over at that point, taking her in his arms and carrying her into the tent.

The next thing she knew, she was awake and darkness surrounded her. She sat up and glanced around. Gilly lay sleeping on one side of her, Breed on the other. Peter was beside Gilly.

Breed's eyes opened, and he sat up with her. "How do you feel?" he whispered.

"A whole lot better. Is there anything to eat? I'm starved."

He took her hand and helped her out of the sleeping bag. Sitting her at the picnic table, he rummaged around and returned with a plate heaped with food.

He took a seat across the table from her—to gaze upon her unspoiled beauty, he told her, laughing. A lantern that hung from a tree dimly lit the area surrounding the tent and table. His features were bloodless, so pale that she felt a surge of guilt at her thoughtlessness.

She set her fork aside. "Breed, I'm so sorry. Can you forgive me?"

He wiped a hand across his face and didn't answer immediately. "I've never been so happy to see freckles in my life."

"You look terrible."

He answered her with a weak smile. "You're a brave woman, Beth. A lot of people would have panicked."

"Don't think I didn't," she told him with a shaky laugh. "There were a few hours there last night when I was sure that I'd die in those woods." She glanced lovingly at him. "The craziest part of it was that I kept thinking of all the things I regret not having done in my life."

"I suppose that's only natural."

"Do you want to know what I regretted the most?"

"What?" he asked with a tired sigh, supporting his forehead with the palms of his hands, not looking at her.

"I kept thinking how sorry I was that I'd never told you how much I love you."

Slowly, Breed raised his gaze to hers. The look in his tired amber eyes became brilliant as he studied her.

"Well, say something," she pleaded, rubbing a hand across her forehead. "I probably would have told you long ago except that I was afraid the same thing would happen to me as happened to Gilly." She paused and inhaled a deep, wobbly breath. "I know you love me in your own way, but I—"

"In my own way?" Breed returned harshly. "I love you so much that if we hadn't found you in those woods I would have stayed out there until I died, looking for you." He got up from the picnic table and walked around to her. "You asked me if I can forgive you. The answer is yes. But I don't think my heart has recovered yet. We're bound to have one crazy married life together,

I can tell you that. I don't think I can take many more of your adventures."

"Married life…?" she repeated achingly.

Breed didn't answer her with words, only hauled her into his arms and held on to her as if he couldn't bear to let her go.

"If this is a dream, don't wake me," she said.

"My love is no fantasy. This is reality."

"Oh, Breed," she whispered as tears of happiness clouded her eyes. She slipped her arms around his neck and pressed her face into his strong, muscular chest.

"Are we going to argue like Peter and Gilly? Or can we have a quiet ceremony with family and a few friends?"

She brushed his lips with a feather-light kiss. "Anything you say."

"Aren't you agreeable!"

She curled tighter in his embrace. "Just promise to love me no matter what." She was thinking of what his reaction would be to her family's wealth and social position. He had a right to know, but telling him now would ruin the magic of the moment. As for not having said anything in the past, she was pleased that she hadn't. Breed loved her for herself. Money and all that it could buy hadn't influenced his feelings. Maybe she was anticipating trouble for no reason.

His smile broadened. The radiant light in his amber eyes kindled a soft glow of happiness in her. His fingers explored her neck and shoulders, holding her so close that for a moment it was impossible to breathe normally. When he moved to kiss her, she slid her hands over his muscular chest and linked them behind his neck. He allowed her only small gasps of air before a new shiver of excitement stole her breath completely.

Her parted lips were trembling and swollen from Breed's plundering kisses when he finally groaned, pulled himself away and sat up straight. "I think the sooner we arrange the wedding, the better." He sighed. "I'd prefer a tent built for two." He ran a hand over his eyes. "And this may be old-fashioned, but I'd like to be married when we start our family."

Elizabeth knew the music in her heart would never fade. Not with this man. He didn't sound old-fashioned to her but refreshingly wonderful.

"I'm so glad you want children." Her voice throbbed with the beat of her heart.

"A houseful, at least." His husky voice betrayed the tight rein he held on his needs. "But for now I'd be content to start with a wedding ring."

"Soon," she promised.

"Tomorrow we'll go down and get the license."

"Tomorrow?" The immediacy frightened her. She wanted to get married, but she couldn't see the necessity of rushing into it quite *that* quickly.

"Maybe we should pack up and drive to Reno and get married immediately."

"No." Elizabeth didn't know why she felt so strongly about that. "I want to stand before God to make my vows, not the Last Chance Hitching Post."

She could see Breed's smile. "You're sure you want to marry me?" he said.

In response, she leaned over and teased him with her

lips. "You'll never need to doubt my love," she said, and playfully nipped at his earlobe.

"Who would have believed you'd get lost in the woods?" Gilly commented late the next night as they unpacked the camping gear in the apartment kitchen.

"Who would have believed we'd both become engaged in one weekend?"

"Elizabeth, I can't tell you how frantic we all were," Gilly said tightly. "Breed was like a man possessed. When you didn't come back, he went to find you. When he didn't return, Peter and I went to look for you both."

Color heated Elizabeth's face. "I was so stupid." Her inexperience had ruined their trip. After a good night's sleep, they'd packed up and headed straight back to San Francisco.

"Don't be so hard on yourself. This was your first time camping. You didn't know."

"But I feel so terrible for being such an idiot."

Gilly straightened and brushed the hair off her forehead. "Thank God you're safe," she said, staring into the distance. "I don't know what would have happened to Breed if we hadn't found you. Beth, he was like a madman. I don't think there was anyone who didn't realize that Breed would have died in the attempt to find you."

Leaning against the counter, Elizabeth expelled a painful sigh. "On the bright side of things, getting lost has done a lot for Breed and me. I wonder how long it would have been otherwise before we admitted how we felt."

"It's taken too long as it is. I knew almost from the beginning that you two were meant for each other."

Elizabeth attempted to disguise a smile. "We don't all have your insight, I guess."

Gilly seemed unaware of the teasing glint in her roommate's eye. "Peter's coming to get me in a few minutes. We're going to go talk to my parents. Will you be safe all by yourself, or should I phone Breed?"

"He's coming over in a while. I'm cooking dinner."

Breed arrived five minutes after Gilly left with Peter. He kissed her lightly on the cheek. "How do you feel?"

"Hungry," she said with a warm smile. "Let's get this show on the road."

"I thought you were cooking me dinner."

"I am. But we left the food in Hilda, which means it's at your place. If I'm going to share my life with you, then the least you can do is introduce me to your kitchen."

That uneasy look came over his features again. "We could go out just as well."

"Breed," Elizabeth intoned dramatically, "how many times do we have to argue about this apartment of yours? It's so obvious you don't want me there."

His mouth tightened grimly. "Let's go. I don't want another argument."

"Well, that's encouraging."

The brisk walk took them about fifteen minutes. His apartment was exactly as she remembered it. No pictures or knickknacks that marked the place as his. That continued to confuse her, but she couldn't believe that he would hide anything from her.

There wasn't much to work with left from their trip, and his cupboards were bare, but she assumed this was because he ate most of his meals out.

"Spaghetti's my specialty," she told him as she tied a towel around her waist.

"That sounds good."

He hovered at her elbow as she sautéed the meat and stood at her side while she chopped the vegetables. He shadowed her every action, and when she couldn't tolerate his brand of "togetherness" another second, she turned and ushered him into the living room.

"Read the paper or something, will you? You're driving me crazy."

His eyes showed his indecision. He glanced back into the kitchen, then nodded as he reached for the newspaper.

Singing softly as she worked, Elizabeth mentally reviewed her cooking lessons from school. The sauce was simmering and the pasta was boiling. She decided to set the table. A few loose papers and mail littered the countertop. Humming cheerfully, she moved them to his desk on the far side of the kitchen. The top of the desk was cluttered with more papers. As she set down his mail, she noticed a legal-looking piece of paper. She continued to hum as idly she glanced at it and realized it was a gun permit. *Breed carried a gun.* A chill shot up her spine. The song died on her lips. Breed and firearms seemed as incongruous as mixing oil and water. She would ask him about it later.

"Anything I can do?" he volunteered, seeming to have relaxed now.

"Open the wine."

"Wine?"

"You mean you don't have any?" she asked as she stirred the pasta. "The flavors in my sauce will be incomplete without the complement of wine."

"I take it you want me to buy us a bottle."

"You got it."

"Okay, let's go." He stood and tucked in his shirttails.

"Me? I can't go now. I've got to drain the pasta and finish setting the table."

He hesitated.

"Honestly, Breed, there's a grocery just down the street. You don't need me to hold your hand."

He didn't look pleased about it, but he turned and walked out.

The minute the door was closed, Elizabeth returned to his desk. She knew she was snooping, but the gun permit puzzled her, and she wanted to look it over. The permit listed a different address, confirming her suspicions that he hadn't been in this apartment long. The paper felt like it was burning her fingers, and she set it aside, hating the way her curiosity had gotten in the way of her better judgment.

She could ask him, of course, but she felt uneasy about that. Where would he keep a lethal weapon in this bare place? She wondered about the kind of gun he carried. With her index finger she pulled out the top desk drawer. It wasn't in sight, but a notebook with her full name written across the top caught her gaze. Fascinated, she pulled it from the drawer and flipped it open. Page after page of meticulous notes detailed her comings and goings, her habits and her friends. *Breed had been following her since she arrived!* But whatever for? This was bizarre.

Coiled tightness gripped her throat as she pulled open another drawer. Hurt and anger and a thousand terrifying emotions she had never thought to experience with regard to Breed filled her senses. The drawer was filled with correspondence with her father. Andrew Breed had been hired by her family as her bodyguard.

Nine

Elizabeth backed away from the drawer. Her hand was pressed against her breast as the blood drained from her face. Her heart was pounding wildly in her ears, and for several seconds she was unable to breathe. So many inconsistencies about Breed fell into place. She was amazed that she could have been so blind, so utterly stupid. His cover had been perfect. Dating her had simplified his job immeasurably.

Her stomach rolled, and she knew she was going to be sick. She closed the drawer and staggered into the bathroom. It was there that Breed found her.

"Beth." His voice was filled with concern. "You look terrible."

She didn't meet his eyes. "I'm… I'm all right. I just need a moment."

He placed his arm across her back, and the touch, although light, seemed to burn through the material of her shirt, branding her. Leading her into the living room, he sat her down on the sofa and brought in a cool rag.

"I was afraid something like this might happen," he murmured solicitously. "You're probably having a delayed reaction to the trauma of this weekend."

She closed her eyes and nodded, still unable to look at him. "I want to go home." Somehow the words managed to slip past the stranglehold she felt around her throat.

Not until they were ready to leave did she glance out Breed's window and realize that, thanks to the city's hills, her apartment could be seen from his. No wonder he was able to document her whereabouts so accurately. Mr. Andrew Breed was a clever man, deceptive and more devious than she could have dreamed. And he excelled at his job. She didn't try to fool herself. She was a job to him and little or nothing more than that.

It was no small wonder he'd suggested they go to Reno and get married right away. He wanted the deed accomplished before they confronted her father. He knew what her family would say if she were to marry a bodyguard. Her emotions when her purse had been taken had been a small-scale version of what she felt now. A part of her inner self had been violated. But the pain went far deeper. Deep enough to sear her soul. She doubted that she would ever be the same again.

Concerned, Breed helped her on with her sweater and gripped her elbow. Several times during the short drive to her apartment he glanced her way, a worried look marring his handsome face. After he had unlocked her apartment and helped her into her room, she changed clothes, took a sleeping pill and climbed into bed. But the pill didn't work. She lay awake with a lump the size of a grapefruit blocking her throat. Every swallow hurt. Crying might have helped, but no tears would come.

She didn't know how long she lay staring at the shadows on the ceiling. The front door clicked open, and she heard Breed whisper to Gilly. She was mildly surprised that he'd stayed, then grinned sarcastically. Of course he would; he'd been paid to baby-sit her. And knowing her father, the fee had been generous.

The front door clicked again, and she heard Gilly assure Breed that she would take care of Elizabeth. The words were almost ludicrous. These two people whom she'd come to love this summer had given her so much. But they had taken away even more. No, she thought. She didn't blame Gilly. She was grateful to have had her as a friend. Gilly might have been in on this scheme, but she doubted it.

Finally Elizabeth heard Gilly go into her bedroom. An hour later, convinced her friend would be asleep, she silently pushed back the covers and climbed out of bed. Dragging her suitcases from the closet, she quickly and quietly emptied her drawers and hangers. She only took what she had brought with her from Boston. Everything else she was leaving for her roommate.

The apartment key and a note to Gilly were left propped against a vase on the kitchen table. A sad smile touched Elizabeth's pale features as she set a second note, addressed to Breed, beside the first. She picked it up and read over the simple message again. It read: *The game's over. You lose.*

The taxi ride to the airport seemed to take hours. Elizabeth kept looking over her shoulder, afraid Breed was following. She didn't want to think of how many times this summer he had done exactly that. The thought made her more determined than ever to get away.

There wasn't a plane scheduled to leave for Boston until the next morning, so she took the red-eye to New York. Luckily, the wait was less than two hours. Her greatest fear was that Gilly would wake up and go to check on her. Finding her gone, she would be sure to contact Breed.

Restlessly, Elizabeth walked around the airport. She knew that she would never forget this city. The cable cars, the sounds and smells of Fisherman's Wharf, sailing, the beach... Her musings did a buzzing tailspin. No, thoughts of San Francisco would always be irrevocably tied to Breed. She wanted to hate him, but she couldn't. He'd given her happy memories, and she would struggle to keep those untainted by the mud of his deception.

The flight was uneventful. The first-class section had only one other traveler, a businessman who worked out of his briefcase the entire time.

Even though it was only 10:00 a.m. when her plane landed, New York was sweltering in an August heat wave. The limousine delivered her to the St. Moritz, a fashionable uptown hotel that was situated across the street from Central Park South.

Exhausted, she took a hot shower and fell asleep almost immediately afterward in the air-conditioned room.

When she awoke, it was nearly dinnertime. Although

she hadn't eaten anything in twenty-four hours, she wasn't hungry.

A walk in Central Park lifted her from the well of overwhelming self-pity. She bought a pretzel and squirted thick yellow mustard over it. As she lazily strolled beside the pond, goldfish the size of trout came to the water's edge, anticipating a share of her meal. Not wanting to disappoint them, she broke off a piece of the doughy pretzel and tossed it into the huge pond.

A young bearded man, strumming a ballad on his guitar, sat on a green bench looking for handouts. She placed a five-dollar bill in the open guitar case.

"Thanks, lady," he sang, and returned her wave with a bob of his dark head.

Most of the park benches were occupied by a wide range of people from all walks of life. She had taken a two-day trip to the Big Apple the previous year and stayed at the St. Moritz, but she hadn't gone into Central Park. The thought hadn't entered her mind.

Today she strolled around the pond, hoping that the sights and sounds of the vibrant city would ease the heaviness in her heart. Unfamiliar settings filled with anonymous faces were no longer intimidating. San Francisco had done that for her.

An hour later she stepped into the cool hotel room and sighed. Reaching for the phone, she dialed Boston.

"Hello, Dad," she said when he picked up, her voice devoid of emotion.

"Elizabeth, where are you?" he demanded instantly.

"New York."

"Why in heaven's name did you run off like that?"

His question drew a faint smile. "I think you already know why," she answered softly, resignedly. "How often have you hired men to watch me in the past?"

"Did he tell you?" her father responded brusquely.

"No. I found out on my own."

"The fool," he issued harshly under his breath.

She disagreed. The only fool in this situation had been herself, for falling in love with Breed.

A strained silence stretched along the wires.

"How often, Dad?" she finally asked.

"Only a few," he answered after a long moment.

"But why?" she asked, exhaling forcefully. The pain of the knowledge was physical as well as mental. Her stomach ached, and she lowered herself into the upholstered wing chair in her suite and leaned forward to rest her elbows on her knees.

"That's a subject we shouldn't discuss over the phone. I want you at home."

"There are a lot of things *I* want, too," she returned in a shallow whisper.

"Elizabeth, please. Be reasonable."

"Give me a few days," she insisted. "I need time to think."

Her father began to argue. She closed her eyes and listened for a few moments. Then she whispered, "Goodbye, Dad," and hung up.

The next morning she checked out of the hotel, rented a car and headed north. Setting a leisurely pace, she stopped along the way to enjoy the beauty of the Atlantic Ocean. It took her three days to drive home.

She recognized that her father would consider her

actions immature, but for her, this time alone with her thoughts had been vital. The long drive, the magnificent coastline, the solitude, gave her the necessary time to come to terms with her father's actions. Decisions were made. Although her father hadn't asked for it, she gave him her forgiveness. He had only been doing what he thought was best.

The thing that shocked her most had been her own stupidity. How could she have been so gullible? All the evidence of Breed's deceit had been there, but she had been blinded by her love. But no more. Never again. Loving someone only caused emotional pain. She had been naive and incredibly foolish.

She wouldn't allow her father to interfere in her life that way again. Once she got home, she would make arrangements to find a place of her own. Breaking away had been long overdue. This summer she'd proved to her father and herself that she was capable of holding a job. And that was what she decided to do: get a job. She spoke fluent French, and enough German and Italian to make her last visit to Europe trouble-free. Surely there was something she could do with those skills.

Not once during the drive home did she allow bitterness to tarnish her memories of Breed. Ultimately, the special relationship they'd shared led to heartache. But she was grateful to him for the precious gift that he'd so unwittingly given her.

One thing she couldn't accept was his calculated deception. Maybe forgiveness would come later, but right now the pain cut so deep that she knew it would take a long time, and maybe it would never come.

It was midafternoon when she pulled up in front of the huge family home.

The white-haired butler opened the door and gave her a stiff but genuine smile.

"Welcome home, Miss Elizabeth." His head dipped slightly as he spoke.

"Hello, Bently."

"Your father's been expecting you, miss. You're to go directly to the library."

Although he hadn't said as much, she knew he was warning her that her father wasn't pleased.

"I'll see to your luggage," he continued.

"Thank you, Bently."

Her elderly ally inclined his head in silent understanding.

Elizabeth stood in the great entry hall and looked around with new eyes. The house was magnificent, a showpiece, but it felt cold and unwelcoming. The heart of this home had died with her mother.

Knocking politely against the polished mahogany door that reached from the ceiling to the floor, Elizabeth waited with calm deliberation.

Charles Wainwright's reply was curt and impatient. "Come in."

"Hello, Father," she said as she walked through the door.

"Elizabeth." He raised himself out of his chair. Relief relaxed the tightness in his weathered brow and he gave her a brief, perfunctory hug. "Now, what's all this nonsense of needing time away?"

She was saved from having to reply by the arrival

of Helene. The maid seemed to appear noiselessly, carrying a silver tray with a coffeepot and two delicate china cups.

Both Elizabeth and her father waited to resume their conversation until Helene had left the room.

"I have a few unanswered questions of my own," she said as she stood and dutifully filled the first cup. She handed it to her father. Charles Wainwright's hair was completely white now, she noted as he accepted the steaming cup from her hand. Once, a long time past, her father's hair had been the same sandy shade as her own. The famous Wainwright blond good looks. Charlie was dark like her mother. But other than her coloring, Elizabeth felt as if she had nothing in common with this man. He wasn't affectionate. She couldn't ever recall him bouncing her on his knee or telling her stories when she was a child. The only time she recalled seeing deep emotion from him had been after her mother's funeral.

Her reverie was interrupted by coffee that dripped from the spout of the silver service and scalded her fingertips. She managed to set the pot aside before giving an involuntary gasp of surprise. Tears filled her eyes, but not from physical pain.

"Elizabeth." Charles Wainwright leapt to his feet. "You've burned yourself." He turned aside. "Helene!" he shouted. Elizabeth couldn't remember hearing that much emotion in his voice for a long time. "Bring the first-aid kit."

"I'm fine," she struggled to reassure him between sudden sobs. She hadn't wept when she learned of Breed's deceit. Nor had she revealed her grief at her mother's funeral. After all, she was a Wainwright, and tears were a sign of weakness. Now she was home, with possibly the only person alive who loved her for herself, and they sat like polite acquaintances, sharing coffee and shielding their hearts. A dam within her burst, and she began to sob uncontrollably.

She could see by the concerned look on his face that her father didn't know how to react. He raised and lowered his hands, impotently unsure of himself. Finally he circled his arms around her and patted her gently on the back as if he were afraid she was a fragile porcelain doll that would break.

"Princess," he whispered, "what is it?"

Helene burst in the door, and Charles dismissed her with a wave of his hand.

"Who's hurt you?"

Between a fresh wave of sobs, she shook her head.

Her father handed her his starched and pressed linen handkerchief, and she held it to her eyes.

"My dear," he said, smoothing her back. "You have the look of a woman in love."

"No." She pulled free of his loose embrace and violently shook her head. "I can't love him after what he's done," she choked out between sobs.

"And what did he do?"

She sniffled. "Nothing. I…can't talk about it. Not now," she whispered in painful denial. "I apologize for acting like an idiot. I'll go upstairs and lie down for an hour or so, and I'll be fine."

"Princess, are you sure you won't tell me?"

Fresh tears squeezed through her damp lashes. "Not

now." She turned toward the great hall. "Dad," she said with her back to him, "I'll probably be leaving for Europe within the week."

Her father was silent for a moment. "Running away won't solve anything." His haunting voice, gentle with wisdom, followed her as she left the library.

One suitcase was packed and another half-filled. She'd realized after one night that she couldn't remain in this house. Once the tears had come, the aching loneliness in her heart had throbbed with its intensity. Her father was right when he told her running away wouldn't heal the void. But escaping came naturally; she had been doing it for so long. Last night she hadn't gone down to dinner, and she'd been shocked when her father brought her a tray later in the evening. She had pretended to be asleep. She regretted that now, and decided to go downstairs and say goodbye to him.

Tucking her passport in her purse, she examined the contents of her suitcases one last time before securing the locks and leaving them outside her door. The reservations for her flight had been made earlier that morning, and plenty of time remained before she needed to leave for the airport. But already she was restless. Forcing a smile on her pale features, she descended the stairs.

She was only halfway down the staircase when she heard Bently engaged in a heated argument with someone at the front door. The other voice was achingly familiar. Breed.

That he was angry and impatient was apparent as his

raised voice echoed through the hall. She took another step, and then her father appeared in the foyer.

"That'll be all, Bently," her father said with calm authority. "I'll see Mr. Breed."

She restrained a gasp and drew closer to the banister. Clearly neither man was aware of her presence.

Breed stepped into the house. His deeply tanned features were set in hard lines as he approached her father.

"I appreciate the fact that you're seeing me." His voice was laced with heavy sarcasm. "But I can assure you that I was prepared to wait as long as it took."

"After four days of pounding down my door, I can believe that's a fair assumption," her father retorted stiffly. "But now that you have my attention, what is it you want?"

"Elizabeth," Breed said without hesitation. "Where is she?"

"Your job of protecting my daughter was terminated when she left San Francisco. I believe you've received your check."

She watched, fascinated and shocked, as Breed took an envelope from his pocket and ripped it in two. "I don't want a dime of this money. I told you that before, and I'm telling you again."

"You earned it."

Every damn penny, Elizabeth wanted to shout at him.

"I kept my word, Wainwright," Breed explained forcefully. "I didn't tell Beth a thing. But I hated every minute of this assignment, and you knew it."

"Why? I thought this type of work was your specialty. You came highly recommended," her father said quietly.

Breed rubbed a hand across his eyes, and she knew the torment she saw in his features was mirrored in her own. When he lowered his hand, he must have caught a glimpse of her from out of the corner of his eye. He hesitated and turned toward her.

"Beth." He said her name softly, as though he was afraid she would disappear again. He moved to the foot of the stairs. The tightness eased from his face as he stared up at her.

"Mr. Wainwright," Breed said, and the anger was gone from his voice as he glanced briefly at her father, "I love your daughter."

"No," Elizabeth said in agitation. "You don't know the meaning of the word. I was nothing more than a lucrative business proposition."

Breed pulled another envelope from his shirt and handed it to her father. His eyes left her only briefly. "While we're on the subject of money…"

Her gaze wavered under the blazing force of his.

"This paper proves that I'm not a poor man. I own a thousand acres of prime California timberland. The land has been in my family for a hundred years," Breed stated evenly, then turned toward her father. "I have no need of the Wainwright money. From the first day I met your daughter, it's stood between us like a brick wall."

He turned back to the stairs, and his look grew gentle. "I love you, Beth Wainwright. I've loved you from the moment we went swimming and I saw you for the wonderful woman you are."

Her heart was crying out for her to run to Breed. But the feelings of betrayal and hurt kept her rooted to the stairs. Her hand curved around the polished banister until she was sure her fingernails would dent the wood.

At her silence, he returned his attention to her father. "Mr. Wainwright, I'm asking for your permission to marry your daughter—"

"I won't marry you," she interrupted in angry protest. "You lied to me. All those weeks you—"

"You weren't exactly honest with me," he returned levelly. "And there was ample opportunity for you to explain everything. You have no right to be mad at me." He paused, and the hardness left his chiseled features. "I'll say it again. I love you, Beth. I want you to share my life."

Indecision played across her face, and her gaze met her father's. Breed's eyes followed hers, and a proud look stole over them.

"I'm asking for your permission, Wainwright," Breed said coolly. "But I'll be honest. I plan to marry your daughter with or without it."

A hint of mirth brightened her father's face. "That's a brash statement, young man."

"Daddy!" Elizabeth called, knowing what her father would say to someone like Breed. Her heart and her pride waged a desperate battle.

Charles Wainwright ignored his daughter. "As it is, I realize that Elizabeth loves you. I may be a crusty old man, but I'm not too blind to see that you'll make her happy. You have my permission, Andrew Breed. Fill this house with grandchildren and bring some laughter into its halls again."

Breed appeared as stunned as Elizabeth.

"Go on." Charles Wainwright flicked his wrist in the direction of his daughter. "And don't take no for an answer."

"I have no intention of doing so," Breed said as he climbed the stairs two at a time.

Elizabeth felt the crazy desire to turn and run, but she stayed where she was, her body motionless with indecision. She bit into her trembling bottom lip as her pride surrendered the first battle.

"Your money will go into a trust fund for our children, Beth," Breed began with a frown. "I don't want a penny of what's yours. There's only one thing I'm after."

"What's that?" she asked in a quiet murmur, battling with the potency of his nearness.

He slid his hands around her waist and pulled her into the circle of his arms. "A wife."

Her breath came in small flutters as he lowered his mouth and paused a scant inch above hers. Their breath merged. She swayed against him, her hands moving over his chest. The entire time her pride urged her to break free and walk away. But her heart held her steadfast.

"Don't fight me so hard," he whispered, claiming her lips in a kiss so tender that she melted against him.

"Together we'll build a lumber kingdom," he whispered into her hair.

"I don't know," she faltered. "I need time to think.

I'm confused." She wanted him so much. It was her pride speaking, not her heart.

"Elizabeth," her father called from the hall. "I think it's only fair to tell you that your Andrew came to me a few weeks back and asked to be relieved of this case. Naturally, I declined and demanded that he maintain his anonymity."

Her eyes met Breed's. "Your business trip?"

He nodded and placed his hands on her shoulders. "Is it really so difficult to decide?" he asked in a husky whisper.

She stared at the familiar features and saw the pain carved in them. "No, not at all."

For a breathless moment they looked at one another.

Then Elizabeth's pride surrendered to her heart as she pressed her mouth to his.

* * * * *

THE TROUBLE WITH CAASI

One

The majestic beauty of white-capped Mount Hood was unobstructed from the twentieth floor of the Empress Hotel in downtown Portland. Caasi Crane stood in front of the huge floor-to-ceiling window, her arms hugging her slim waist. Blake Sherrill's letter of resignation was clenched tightly in one hand.

Blake was the best general manager she'd ever hope to find. His resignation had caught her off guard. As far as Caasi knew he had been perfectly content. His employee file was open on her computer, and Caasi moved across the plush office to study the information.

His salary was generous, she noted, but Caasi believed in paying her employees what they were worth. And Blake earned every cent. Maybe he'd reconsider if she offered him a raise. But according to the file, he'd received a healthy increase only three months earlier.

Scrolling down through the information Caasi paused to read over the original employment application that included his photograph. He was six three and at her guess around a hundred and eighty pounds. Dark hair and brown eyes. None of that had changed. She knew him to be single and thirty. Certainly she would know if he'd married. He hadn't she was sure of that. Had Blake been with Crane Enterprises that long? Funny she didn't remember that.

Caasi pushed the wide-rimmed glasses up from the tip of her nose and sat in the cushioned white leather chair.

Her assistant buzzed, interrupting her thoughts. "Mr. Sherrill's here to see you."

Caasi released the intercom lever. "Please send him in." Mentally she prepared herself. Her father had groomed her well for this position. If Blake was displeased about something, she'd soon discover what it was. Employee performance and customer satisfaction were the name of the game. But an employee, even one as good as Blake, couldn't perform if he was unhappy. If so, Caasi wanted to know the reason. She pretended an interest in his computer file when the door opened. Looking up, she smiled brightly. "Sit down, Blake." Her hand indicated a chair on the other side of her desk.

He wasn't a handsome man. His features were rough and rugged, too craggy to be considered attractive. His chin projected stubbornly and the shadow of his beard was heavy. Caasi didn't doubt that he had to shave twice a day. He wore a dark business suit and silk tie, and his hair was coal dark. Could he be Italian with a name like Sherrill? Funny how she'd never really noticed Blake. At least, not the toughness in the lean, hard figure that stood in front of her.

"If you don't mind, I'd rather stand." With feet braced slightly apart, he joined his hands.

"Honestly," Caasi admonished with a soft smile, "you look like a recruit standing at attention."

"Sometimes I feel that way." The words were hardly above a whisper.

"Pardon?" Caasi looked up again.

"Nothing." The small lines about his eyes and mouth creased in a mirthless smile. "You're right. I'll sit down."

"How long have you been with us, now, Blake?"

"Eight years, six months, and five days," he replied drily

"You counted the days?"

He shrugged. "Maybe I was hoping to gain your attention."

Caasi gave him a troubled look. Clearly something was troubling him? Not in the five years since she'd taken over the company had Blake behaved like this.

"You have my attention now." She held up the resignation letter. "What's the problem?"

He looked away. "There's no problem. The time has come to move on, that's all."

"Is it the money?"

"No."

"Have you got another job offer?" That was the scenario that made the most sense.

"Not yet." This wasn't going well and she was fast losing her grip on the situation.

"All right, Blake, tell me what's up."

"Do you want a full report submitted? There's one due at the end of the month as usual."

"I don't mean that and you know it." Angrily she glared at him

"I thought you read every report," he muttered with an edge of sarcasm.

Caasi paused. "I've never known you to be cynical," Caasi cut in.

"But then, you've never known me, have you?"

Caasi didn't know how to answer him. Maybe if she'd dated more often she'd be able to deal with men more effectively. That was one area in which her father had failed to instruct her. Sometimes she felt like a bungling teenager, and just as naive.

"Take the rest of the week off, Blake. I would like you to reconsider this letter."

"I'm not going to change my mind." There was a determined look about him, unyielding and confident.

She didn't want to lose Blake. "Take it anyway, and let's talk again the first of the week."

He gave her a mocking salute. "As you wish."

Blake's resignation weighed heavily on Caasi the rest of the day. By the time her assistant left, she was in a rotten mood. It was due to far more than Blake, she recognized that. That night was the monthly get-together with Edie and June, her two BFFs.

The months passed so quickly that sometimes it seemed that they were meeting much too often—and at other times it wasn't nearly enough. Yet the two were her best friends…her *only* friends, Caasi admitted grudgingly as she slid the key into the lock of her apartment door.

The penthouse suite on the twenty-first floor had been Caasi's home for as long as she could remember. She must have been eight before she realized that milk came from a cow and not the busboy who delivered all of the family's meals.

Daddy's little girl from the beginning, Caasi had known from the time she could walk that someday she would be president of Crane Enterprises and the string of hotels that ran down Oregon's coast and into California. Isaac Crane had tutored her for the position until his death five years earlier.

Daddy's little girl... The thought ran through her mind as Caasi opened her closet and took out a striped dress of teal, plum, and black. Everything about her reflected her father. A thousand times in her twenty-eight years Caasi had explained that her name hadn't been misspelled but was Isaac spelled backwards.

Soaking in a bubble bath a few minutes later, Caasi lifted the sponge and drained the soothing water over her full breasts and flat stomach. Her big toe idly played with the faucet spout. Her medium-length chestnut hair was piled on top of her head as she lay back and let the hot water refresh her.

Steam swirled around the huge bathroom as Caasi wrapped a thick cotton towel around herself and moved into her bedroom. She didn't feel like going out tonight. A quiet dinner and television would be more to her liking, but she knew Edie and June well enough to realize they wouldn't easily let her forgo their monthly dinner.

An hour later, Caasi entered Brasserie Montmartre, a French restaurant Edie had raved about the previous month. Caasi didn't mind checking out the competition. The Empress's own small French restaurant served—in her opinion—some of the best food in town.

Edie waved when she saw Caasi. June apparently hadn't arrived yet, and Caasi wondered if she would, since June's baby was due any time.

"Greetings, fair one," the pert brunette said as Caasi pulled out a chair and sat down. It was a standard joke between them that, of the three, Caasi was the most attractive. She accepted their good-natured teasing as part of the give and take in any friendship. They were her friends, and heaven knew she had few enough of those these days.

"You look pleased about something," Caasi said. Edie was grinning from ear to ear.

"I am." Edie took a sip of champagne and giggled like a sixteen-year-old. "I should probably wait until June's here, but if I don't tell someone soon, I think I'll bust."

"Come on, give," Caasi urged and nodded at the waiter, who promptly delivered another glass and poured for her. Good service, she mused.

"I'm pregnant!"

Caasi nearly choked on the bubbly liquid. "Pregnant!" she spat back. Not both friends at the same time. It was too much!

"I don't think I've ever seen Freddy more excited."

"But you're the one who said—"

"I know, but I changed my mind. It's crazy, but I'm

really happy about it. The doctor said there's no reason for me to lose my figure, and he's already put me on a high-protein diet. Freddy's agreed to the natural child-birth classes. From what we've read it's the best way for the baby. June's taking them now, and I'm hoping she can let me sit in on one of her sessions. And then there's the nursery to do. I think Freddy may make the cradle."

"Slow down," Caasi said with a light laugh. "My head's spinning already."

"What do you think?" Edie scooted back her chair and arched her shoulders.

"Think about what?" Caasi shook her head.

"Do I show?"

"Show? For heaven's sake, Edie, you can't be more than a couple of months along!"

"You're right." She giggled, her dark eyes dancing. "And no more than a sip of champagne for me. I'm com-pletely off alcohol and caffeine. I was just hoping…"

"Hoping what?" A tall blonde waddled up behind them. June's protruding stomach left little conjecture as to her condition. One hand rested against her rib cage as she lowered herself into the third chair. "Champagne?" Round blue eyes sought those of the others. "What are we celebrating?"

"Babies, in the plural," Edie supplied with a wide grin that lit up her whole face.

June looked blank for a minute.

"It seems our Edie has found herself with child," Caasi informed her.

"Edie?" June whispered disbelievingly. "Not the

same Edie who marched in a rally for zero population growth when we were in high school?"

"One and the same." Edie laughed and motioned for the waiter, who produced a third glass.

"We're talking about the girl who was afraid to eat lettuce because it could ruin her perfect figure."

"Not the one who said 'Lips that touch chocolate shall never touch mine'?" June's eyes rounded with shock.

"'Fraid so," Caasi said with an exaggerated sigh.

"Would you two quit talking about me as if I wasn't here?" Edie demanded.

"A baby." Caasi looked from one to the other and shook her head. "Both of you. Wasn't it yesterday that I was your maid of honor, June? And, Edie, remember how we argued over who got which bed our freshman year?"

"I always thought you'd be the first one to marry," June said to her in a somber tone. "Caasi the beauty. Gray eyes that were to die for and a figure that was the envy of every girl in school."

"The fair one," Edie added.

"The aunt-to-be," Caasi murmured in a poor attempt at humor. "Always the bridesmaid, never the bride."

"I find it more than just ironic," Edie said with conviction. "It's high time you came down from the lofty twentieth floor and joined us mortals."

"Edie!" June snapped. "What a terrible thing to say!"

"It's the champagne," Caasi said, excusing her friend.

"In this instance it's a case of loose lips sinking ships."

"Ships?" Edie inquired.

"Friendships!"

"To friendship." Edie raised her glass and their former good mood was restored.

"To friendship." June and Caasi gently clicked their delicate crystal glasses against Edie's.

"By the way, who's paying for this?" June questioned.

"I don't know," Caasi joked, "but I'm only paying one fifth, since both of you are drinking for two."

They all laughed and picked up their menus.

As Edie had promised, the food was superb. With observant eyes, Caasi noted the texture and quality of the food and the service. Such scrutiny had been ingrained in her since childhood. Caasi doubted that she could dine anywhere and not do a comparison.

"What about next month?" Caasi eyed June's stomach.

"No problem. Doc says I've got a good five weeks."

"Five weeks?" Edie looked shocked. "If I get that big, I'll die."

"You know, Edie, if your shoes are a little too tight, don't worry," Caasi teased.

"My shoes?" Edie looked up with a blank stare.

"After being in your mouth all night, they should fit fine."

Edie giggled and stared pointedly across the table. "I swear, the girl's a real wit tonight."

They divided up the check three ways. Although Caasi wanted to treat her friends, June and Edie wouldn't hear of it.

Sitting back, she watched as the waiter took their checks. No matter what her mood at the beginning of these gatherings, Caasi always felt better afterward. Even Edie's remark had flowed off her like water from an oily surface. These two were like sisters. She accepted their faults and loved them none the less.

Large drops of rain pounded against the street as the three emerged from the restaurant.

"How about an after-dinner dessert?" Edie suggested. "I'm in the mood for something sweet."

June and Caasi eyed one another and attempted to disguise a smile.

"Not me." June bowed out. "Burt's at home, anxiously awaiting my return. He worries if I'm out of his sight more than five minutes."

Edie raised both brows, seeking Caasi's response.

Caasi shrugged. "My feet hurt."

"I thought I was the one with tight shoes," Edie teased, looping her arm through Caasi's. "Come on, be a sport. If you're extra nice I'll even let you take me up to your penthouse suite."

Caasi sighed. "I suppose something light and sweet would do wonders toward making me forget my problems."

"What about you, June? Come on, change your mind."

June shook her head and patted her rounded stomach. "Not tonight."

The hotel lobby at the Empress was peacefully quiet when Edie and Caasi came through the wide glass doors. The doorman tipped his hat politely, and Caasi gave him a bright smile. Old Aldo had been a grand-father when the hotel hired him twenty years before. Other employers would have retired him by now, but Caasi hadn't. The white-haired man had a way of greeting people that made them feel welcome. That quality wouldn't easily be replaced.

The sweet, soulful sounds of a ballad drifted from the lounge, and Edie paused to hum the tune as they waited for the elevator.

"Nice," she commented.

"The piano player's new this week. Would you rather we have our dessert down here?"

Edie's nod was eager. "I think I would. I'm in the mood for romance and music."

Caasi's laugh was sweet and light. "From the look of things, I'd say it's been a regular occurrence lately." Her eyes rested on her friend's still smooth abdomen. They chose to sit in the lounge in order to listen to the music.

The hostess seated them and saw to their order personally. The crowd was a good one. Caasi looked around and noted a few regulars, mostly salesmen who stayed at the hotel on a biweekly basis. The after-work crowd had thinned, but there were a few die-hards.

The middle-aged man at the piano was good. A portion of the bar was built around the piano, and Caasi watched as he interacted with the customers, took requests and cracked a few jokes. She'd make sure he was invited back again.

Edie's spoon dipped into the glass of lemon sorbet while Caasi sampled hers. They didn't talk. They didn't need to. The piano music filled the room. A young couple at the bar started to sing and were joined by several others.

Edie's hand squeezed Caasi's forearm. "I'm sorry about what I said earlier."

"No need to apologize." Edie's gaze faltered slightly under Caasi's direct look. "I understand."

"I worry about you sometimes, Caasi."

"Worry about me? Whatever for?"

"I love you. You're more like a sister to me than my own. I don't know how you can be happy living the way you do. It's not natural."

"What's not natural?" Caasi realized she was beginning to sound like a worn echo.

"Your life."

Mildly disconcerted, Caasi looked away. "It's the only way I've ever known."

"That doesn't make it right. Haven't you ever yearned for someone to share your life? A man to cuddle up against on a cold night?"

Caasi's laugh was forced. "I've got my electric blanket."

"What about children?"

Although content with her lifestyle, Caasi had to admit that seeing both June and Edie pregnant was having a peculiar effect on her. She'd never thought much about being a mother, but, strangely, she found the idea appealing. "I… I think I'd like that, but I'm not so keen on a husband."

"If it's a baby you want, then find yourself a man. You don't need a wedding ring and a march down the aisle to have a baby. Not these days."

Caasi tugged a strand of hair behind her ear, a nervous habit she rarely indulged. "I can't believe we're having this conversation."

"I mean it," Edie said with a serious look.

"What am I suppose to do? Find a good-looking man, saunter up, and suggest children?"

Edie's full laugh attracted the attention of others. "No, silly, don't say a word. Just let things happen naturally."

How could Caasi explain that she wasn't into casual affairs? Had never had a fling, and at twenty-eight remained a virgin? Edie would be sick laughing. Lack of experience wasn't the only thing holding her back; when would Caasi find the time for relationships and/ or motherhood? Every waking minute was centered around Crane Enterprises. Even if she did find herself attracted to a man, she'd have to squeeze him in between meetings and conferences. Few men would be willing to accept that kind of relationship. And what man wouldn't be intimidated by her wealth? No, the die had been cast and she...

"Caasi." Edie's hushed whisper broke into Caasi's thoughts. "What you need is a man like the one who just walked in."

Caasi's gray eyes searched the crowd for the newcomer. "Where?" she murmured.

"There, by the piano. He just sat down."

The blood exploded in Caasi's cheeks, rushing up from her neck until she felt her face shining like a lighthouse on a foggy night. Blake Sherrill was the man Edie had pointed out. Pressing a tentative hand to her face, Caasi wondered at her reaction.

"Now, *that's* blatant masculinity if ever I've seen it."

"He's not that good-looking," Caasi felt obliged to say, grateful that Edie hadn't noticed the way the color had invaded her face.

"Of course not. His type never is. There's a lean hardness to him, an inborn arrogance that attracts women like flies to honey."

"Oh, honestly."

"Notice his mouth," Edie continued.

Caasi already had. Blake looked troubled about something, a surprising occurrence, since he'd always presented a controlled aura when he met with her. She watched as he ordered a drink, then emptied the shot glass in one gulp. That wasn't like Blake either. As far as she knew, he stayed away from liquor.

"See how his lips are pressed together? The tight, chiseled effect. Women go for that."

There was a slight tremor in Caasi's hands as her friend spoke. "Maybe some women. But not me."

"Caasi." Edie groaned. "You can't be *that* oblivious. You're staring at an unqualified hunk. Good grief, my blood's hot just looking at him."

"He's not my type," Caasi muttered under her breath, at the same time thinking she'd never really seen Blake. For years they'd worked together, and not once had she ever thought of him except as an exceptionally good general manager.

"That man is every woman's type. I've seen women threaten to kill for less."

Caasi knew her friend was teasing and offered a half-hearted smile. "Maybe he is my type, I don't know."

"Maybe?" Edie shot back disbelievingly. "Go over and introduce yourself. It can't hurt, and it may do you a lot of good."

"Do you think I should?"

"I wouldn't have said so if I didn't."

"This is crazy." Caasi shoved back her chair. Really, what did she hope to accomplish? Blake *was* more man than she'd ever recognized before, but the idea of a casual affair with him was crazy. More than crazy, it was ludicrous.

"Hurry up before he leaves," Edie whispered encouragingly.

Caasi didn't know why she didn't want her friend to know she was already well acquainted with Blake.

Edie stood with her.

"Are you coming too?" Caasi cast her a challenging glare.

"Not this time, although I'm tempted. I just noticed the time. Freddy will be worried. I'll call you tomorrow."

"Fine." Caasi's spirits lifted. She could leave without saying a word to Blake and Edie need never know.

"I'll just wait by the door to see how you do. Once you've made the contact, I'll just slip away."

Caasi's spirits plummeted.

The stool beside Blake was vacant. Caasi strolled across the room, her heart pounding so loudly it drowned out the piano man. As casually as possible she perched herself atop the tall stool.

Blake looked over at her, surprise widening his eyes momentarily. He turned back without a greeting.

"Evening," she muttered, shocked at how strange her voice sounded. "I thought you were taking the rest of the week off."

"Something came up."

Caasi straightened. "What?"

"It's taken care of—don't worry about it."

"Blake." Her tone was crisp and businesslike.

Pointedly he turned his wrist and looked at his watch. "I was off duty hours ago. If you don't mind, I'd like to leave the office behind and enjoy some good scotch." He raised his shot glass in a mocking toast.

Caasi's throat constricted. "I've had one of those days myself." She didn't mention that his letter had brought it on, but that understanding hung oppressively in the air between them.

The bartender strolled past and braced both hands against the bar. "Can I get you anything?" He directed the question at Caasi.

Obviously he didn't know who she was, which was just as well; she could observe him at work. "I'll have the same as the gentleman."

Blake arched both brows. "It must have been a harder day than I thought."

"It was."

His lips came together in a severe line. "Drink it slowly," he cautioned.

"I can hold my liquor as well as any man," she said, surprised by how defensive she sounded? She didn't want to be. What she wanted was an honest, frank discussion of the reason or reasons he'd decided to leave Crane Enterprises.

"As you say." The corners of his mouth curved upward in challenge.

When Caasi's drink arrived she raised it tentatively to her lips and took an experimental sip. To her horror, she started coughing and choking.

"You all right?" he questioned with a rare smile.

As if she wasn't embarrassed enough, his hand pounded vigorously against her back.

"Stop it," she insisted, her eyes watering.

"I thought you said you could handle your scotch."

"I can!" she choked out between gasps of air. "It just went down wrong, that's all."

Blake rotated the stool so that she was given a profile of his compelling features. She turned back around, aware that half the lounge was watching her. "I'm fine, I'm fine," she felt obliged to say.

"So you are," Blake murmured.

"Aren't you worried about leaving your job?" she asked, even though he'd basically said he didn't want to discuss business. He turned to her then, his eyes dark and glittering as his taut gaze ran over her. "No, as a matter of fact, I'm not."

"Why not?" she queried, her hand curling around the small glass. "At least you owe me the courtesy of telling me why after all these years you want out."

"It's not a marriage, Cupcake."

Caasi bristled. "Don't call me that. Don't ever call me that." Cupcake had been her father's pet name for her. Only Isaac Crane had ever called her that. "I'm not a little girl anymore."

His laugh was short and derisive. "That you're not."

She took another sip of her drink. It burned all the way down her throat and seared a path through her stomach. But she didn't cough and felt pleased with herself.

"What do you want from me?" he asked as he shoved the empty scotch glass aside.

Feeling slightly tipsy and more than a little reckless, she placed her hand gently over the crook in his elbow. "I want to dance."

His head jerked up, and the color seemed to flow from his face. "Not with me."

"Yes, with you," she said softly, surprised at how angry he sounded. Who else did he think she meant? The piano player?

"No."

The word was issued with such force that Caasi felt as if he'd physically struck her. How embarrassing and humiliating. All at once Caasi knew she had to get out of there before disgracing herself further. "Thanks anyway."

Her hands trembled as she slid off the stool. Wordlessly she turned and walked out of the lounge. She made it as far as the elevator before she felt her entire body start to shake.

The penthouse was dark. Very dark. Even the million lights of the city couldn't illuminate the room. Leaning against the door, Caasi heaved her shoulders in a long shuddering sigh. She'd had too much to drink that night, far more than normal. That was what was wrong. Not Edie. Not Blake. Not even her. Only the alcohol.

Undressing, she pulled the long nylon gown over her head. Accidentally, her hand hit against her abdomen and she paused, inhaling deeply. Lightly her fingers traced her breasts, then fell lifelessly to her sides as she hung her head in defeat.

"I am a woman," she whispered. "I am a woman," she repeated, and fell across the bed.

Two

Caasi's head throbbed the next morning when the alarm rang. She rolled over and moaned. She'd made a complete idiot of herself the night before. She couldn't believe that she'd actually suggested that Blake dance with her. Heavens, she hadn't been on a dance floor since her college days. The temptation was to bury her head under a pillow and go back to sleep, but the meeting with Pacific Contractors was scheduled for that morning, plus a labor relations conference for that afternoon.

Laurie, the paragon of virtue who served as Caasi's secretary, was already at her desk when Caasi arrived.

"'Morning," Caasi greeted her crisply.

"Schuster's been on the phone twice. He said it's important." Laurie held out several pink message slips.

Caasi groaned inwardly. Every time Schuster phoned it was important. She didn't want to deal with him. Not today. Not ever, if she could help it.

"Is Mr. Sherrill in yet?" Caasi would give the pesky

troublemaker to Blake to handle. He'd deal with Schuster quickly and efficiently. Caasi almost groaned out loud when she remembered that she'd given Blake the rest of the week off.

"He's been in and out," Laurie announced, following Caasi into the inner office. "He left something on your desk."

A silver tray with a large pot and cup rested on the clean surface of her desk. Beside the cup was a large bottle of aspirin. Caasi managed just a hint of a smile.

"Thanks, Laurie," she murmured and waited until the short, plump woman left the office.

A folded piece of paper lay on the tray beside the aspirin. Slowly, Caasi picked it up, her heart hammering wildly. A single note and her heart was reacting more to that than any profit-and-loss statement.

The large, bold handwriting matched the man. How often had she read his messages and not noticed that his penmanship personified him? The note read: *Thought you could use these this morning. B.*

Caasi realized that she could. Snapping the cap off the bottle, she shook two tablets into the palm of her hand and poured the steaming coffee into the cup. She lifted her hand to touch the chestnut hair gathered primly at the base of her neck as she lazily walked across the carpet.

Everything last night hadn't been a fluke. Edie had raised questions that Caasi had long refused to voice. She was a woman, with a woman's desires and a woman's needs. Home, husband, children—these were things she had conveniently shelved. Seeing June and

Edie happily married, in love and expecting children, was bringing all these feelings to an eruptive head. Her father hadn't counted on that. Caasi was the only child, the last of the Cranes, who were now an endangered species. With Isaac gone, there was only Caasi. Alone. Against the world.

Caasi wanted to be protected and loved, cherished and worried about. Like Edie and June. But at the same time, she wanted to be proud, independent, strong... everything her father had worked so hard to ingrain in her. Sometimes she felt as though a tug-of-war were going on inside her, with her heart at stake. Some days she looked in the mirror only to discover that a stranger was staring back at her.

The phone buzzed, interrupting her musings. Another day was about to begin, and her doubts would be pushed aside and shelved again.

Saturday morning Caasi woke, sat up in bed, and sighed heavily. The past two days, she'd crawled out of bed more tired than she'd been the night before, as if she hadn't slept at all. Now her eyes burned and she felt as if the problems of the world were pressing against her shoulders.

The company copter was flying in that day, and Caasi was scheduled to officiate at a ground-breaking ceremony at Seaside. Another Empress Hotel, the tenth, was about to be launched. She should be feeling a sense of pride and accomplishment, yet all she felt was tired and miserable. The day would be filled with false smiles and promotional hype.

She dressed in a navy-blue linen suit, double-breasted. Her father would approve.

Her breakfast tray was waiting for her, but she pushed it aside. The silver pot of coffee reminded her of Blake. Absent two days and she missed him like crazy. He was scheduled to have gone with her on this little jaunt. Somehow, having Blake along would have made the outing far more endurable.

Caasi was back at her suite by four. Exhausted, she kicked off her shoes and pulled the pins from her hair. The weather was marvelous, a glorious, sunny April afternoon. How could she have felt anything but exhilarated by the crisp ocean breeze? Everything had run smoothly—thanks to Blake, who had been responsible for setting up the ceremony.

The instant his name floated through her mind, the heaviness she'd experienced that morning returned. For years she'd taken him for granted. In rethinking the situation, Caasi realized that he had cause to resign. But he was invaluable to her. He couldn't leave; she wouldn't let him. The sooner he understood her feelings, the better.

Slouching against the deep, cushioned couch, Caasi propped her feet on the shining surface of the glass coffee table. She'd talk to him. Explain Crane Enterprises' position. And the sooner, the better. Now. Why not?

After changing into a three-piece pant suit, Caasi sailed into her office to look through his personnel file. They'd worked together for years and she didn't even know where he lived. There were so many things she didn't know about Blake.

She scanned the computer file until she located the Gresham address, several miles outside of Portland.

Her silver Mercedes had been a gift from her father. Caasi had little need to drive it. Usually she made a point of taking it for a spin once a month. It had been longer than that since she'd last driven it, but the maintenance men kept it tuned and the battery charged for her.

It took almost thirty minutes to find the address. She drove down a long, winding road that seemed to lead nowhere. Although there were several houses around, they were separated by wide spaces. Blake…in the country. The mental image of him tilling the fields flitted into her mind. The picture fit.

She stopped at the side of the road and, before pulling into Blake's driveway, checked the nearest house number against the one she'd scribbled down in her office. The house was an older two-story with a wide front porch, the kind Caasi would picture having an old-fashioned swing. A large weeping willow tree dominated one side of the front yard. Caasi had always loved weeping willows.

By the time she opened the car door and climbed out, Blake had come out of the garage, wiping his hands on an oily rag.

"Caasi." His voice was deep and irritated.

"Afternoon," she replied, sounding falsely cheerful. "This is beautiful country out here."

"I like it." He came to a halt, keeping several feet distant from her.

"Everything went fine today."

"I knew it would."

Caasi untied the lemon-colored chiffon scarf from her throat and stuffed it in her purse. "Can we talk?"

His gaze traveled over her before he lifted one shoulder. "If you like."

Caasi felt some of the tension ease out of her. At least he was willing to discuss things.

"Go in the house; I'll wash up and be there in a minute."

"Okay," she agreed.

"The back door's unlocked," he called to her as he returned to the garage.

Caasi let herself into the rear of the house. An enclosed porch and pantry contained a thick braided rug, on which she wiped her feet. The door off the porch led into a huge kitchen decorated with checkered red-and-white curtains on its large windows.

The glass coffeepot resting on the stove was half full, and Caasi poured herself a mug, hugging it to keep her hands occupied.

Her purse clutched under her arm, she wandered out of the kitchen. A large formal dining room contained built-in china cabinets. An array of photographs filled the open wall space. Caasi stopped to examine each one. They left her wondering if Blake had once been married. A small frown of nervous apprehension creased her brow. Several pictures of children who vaguely resembled Blake dominated the grouping. Another of an older couple, dark and earthy, captured her attention. Caasi lifted the wooden frame to examine the two faces more closely. These must be his parents. They both had round, dark eyes—wonderful eyes that said so much.

Warm, good people. If Caasi ever had the opportunity to meet them, she knew she would enjoy knowing them. They were the salt of the earth.

Another picture rested behind the others; this one was of a large family gathering outside what appeared to be the very house she was in. The willow tree was there, only smaller. The two adults were shown with six children. Blake's family. He stood out prominently, obviously the eldest.

"My parents," he explained from behind her.

Caasi hadn't heard him come in and gave a startled gasp, feeling much like a child caught looking at something she shouldn't. Her hand shook slightly as she replaced the photograph.

"The children?" she asked hesitatingly.

"My nieces and nephews."

"You've never married?"

Blake's mouth thinned slightly. "No." He ran a hand through his dark hair. "You said you wanted to talk?"

"Yes." Her head bobbed. "Yes, I do."

"Sit down." His open palm gestured toward the living room.

Caasi moved into the long, narrow living room. A huge fireplace took up an entire wall, and she paused momentarily to admire the oil painting above the mantel. Mount Hood was richly displayed in gray, white, and a forest of green, against a backdrop of blue, blue sky.

"Wonderful painting," she commented casually, looking for the artist's name and finding none.

"Thanks."

Caasi sat in a chair where she could continue to study

the mountain scene. On closer inspection she found minute details that weren't readily visible on casual notice. "I really like it. Who's the artist?"

The small lines about Blake's mouth hardened. "Me."

"You!" Caasi gasped. "I didn't know you did anything like this. Blake, it's marvelous."

He dismissed the compliment with a short shake of his head. "There's a lot you don't know about me."

"I'm beginning to find that out," she said on a sober note.

His eyes pinned her to the chair.

Uncomfortable, she cleared her throat before continuing. "As I mentioned, the trip to Seaside went without a hitch. But it didn't seem right, not having you there."

"You'll get used to it."

"I don't want to have to do that."

Blake propelled himself out of the overstuffed chair he had sunk into and stalked to the far side of the room. "My decision's been made."

"Change it."

"No."

"Blake, listen." She set her coffee aside and stood. "Today I realized how inconsiderate I've been the last few years. Putting it simply, I've taken you for granted. You were Dad's right-hand man. Now you're mine. I don't know that I can do the job without you."

His laugh was sarcastic, almost cruel. "I have no doubts regarding your ability. More than once I've been amazed at your insight and discernment. You're a magnificent businesswoman, and don't let anyone tell you different."

"If I'm so wonderful, why am I losing you?"

He didn't answer her.

"I'm prepared to double your salary."

"You overpay me as it is."

She clenched her fist at her side and stared at the oil painting, searching for some clue to the man she once thought she knew. "Then it isn't the money."

"I told you it wasn't."

"Then clearly someone else has made you a better offer. Holiday Inn? Hilton?"

"No." His voice was loud and abrupt.

Don't yell at me, she wanted to shout back but held her tongue. They'd never argued. For months on end they'd worked together without saying more than a few necessary words to one another. And suddenly everything has changed.

"Caasi." Her name was issued on a soft groan. "I wouldn't do that to you. I don't know what I'm planning yet, but I won't go to work for the competition."

"What is it you want?" Angrily she hugged her stomach with both arms and whirled around. "I've never known you to be unreasonable."

He was silent for so long, she didn't know whether he intended answering her.

"You can't give me what I want."

"Try me." She turned back to him, almost desperate. Blake was right; she could manage without him. A replacement could come in, be trained, and suffice, but she wanted him. Trusted him.

His dark gaze fell to her mouth. They stood so close that Caasi could see the flecks of gold in his dark irises. A strange hurt she didn't understood seemed to show in them. A desire welled in her to ease that pain, but she didn't know how. Wasn't that a woman's job, to comfort? But then, she was a complete failure as a woman.

He reached out and gently touched the side of her face. A warmth radiated from his light caress. "I was planning to take the summer off. Do some hiking. I've always wanted to climb mountains, especially Rainier."

Sadly, Caasi nodded, her eyes captured by his. "I've never hiked." She laughed nervously. "Or climbed."

"There are lots of things you haven't done, aren't there?" His soft voice contained a note of tenderness. He dropped his hand.

Caasi forced her eyes away. Blake didn't know the half of it. Her gaze fell on the rows of family pictures. "Do...do you like children?" What a ridiculous question and yet it was one she'd asked of him.

"Very much."

"Why haven't you married and raised a houseful? You've got the room for it here."

"The same reason you haven't, Cupcake."

Caasi bit her tongue to keep from reminding him not to call her that. The name itself didn't bother her. Nor did she care if he reminded her of her father. What she didn't like was Blake thinking of her as a child.

"For the last several years," he elaborated, "the two of us have been married to Crane Enterprises."

"But you could have a family and still work for me." She was grasping at straws and knew it.

"I'm a little too old to start now."

"Old," she scoffed. "At thirty-six?"

Blake looked surprised that she knew his age.

"I don't want to lose you."

His expression hardened as if her words had displeased him. "I'll walk you to your car."

Perplexed, she watched him move across the room and pull open the front door.

"You're angry, aren't you?"

He forced a long breath. "Yes."

"But why? What did I do?"

"You wouldn't understand."

Her hand sliced through the air. "You keep saying that. I'm well above the age of reason. I have even been known to exhibit some intelligence."

"And in other ways you're incredibly stupid," he interrupted. "Now go before I say something I'll regret."

Caasi sucked in her breath. Her shoes made a clicking rattle against the wooden steps as she hurried to her car. She couldn't get away from Blake fast enough.

Thirty minues later still angry and upset, Caasi let herself into the penthouse suite and threw her purse on the bed. Her shoes went next, first the right and then the left. She felt like shouting with frustration.

Dinner arrived and she stared at it with no appetite. No breakfast, a meager lunch, and now dinner held no appeal. She should be starved. Steak, potato and baby white asparagus, eaten alone, might as well be overbaked, dried-out macaroni and cheese. Eating alone hadn't bothered her until that night. Why it should now remained a mystery?

The portrait of Blake's parents came into her mind. How easy it was to picture his mother standing in the kitchen with fresh bread dough rising on the counter. Kids eating breakfast and laughing. How could something she'd never known bother her so much? *Children. Family. Home.* Each word was as foreign to her as the moon. Yet she felt a terrible, gnawing loss.

Determinedly she took the crusty French roll and bit into it. Hard on the outside, tender inside, exactly right. It was the only thing in her life that was exactly right.

The phone buzzed, which usually meant trouble. Caasi heaved an irritated sigh and lifted the receiver.

"Mr. Sherrill's on his way up," the hotel receptionist informed her cheerfully.

"Thank you," Caasi answered in a shaky voice. Blake coming here? He'd never been to her private quarters. Maybe when her father was alive, but not since she'd taken over.

Hurriedly she rushed into the bathroom and ran a brush through her hair. Halfway out the door, she whirled around and added a fresh layer of light pink gloss to her lips. Her hands shook, she was rushing so much. She unscrewed the cap from a perfume bottle and added a touch of the expensive French fragrance behind each ear and to the pulse points at her wrists.

Caasi started at the sound of his knock. Pausing to take in a deep, calming breath, she sauntered to the door.

"Why, Blake, what a pleasant surprise," she said sweetly.

He didn't look pleased. In fact, he looked much the same as he had when she'd left him earlier.

The feeling of happy surprise drained out of her.

"Go on, change."

"Change?" She stared at him blankly as he walked inside.

"Clothes," he supplied.

"You're not making any sense."

"Yes I am," he refuted. "What you had on last night will do."

"Do for what?" His attitude was beginning to spark her anger.

"Dancing. That's what you said you wanted."

Hot color extended all the way down her neck. "That was after several drinks."

"You don't want to dance? Fine." He lowered himself onto the long couch. "We can sit and drink."

The dark scowl intimidated her. She'd stood up to angry union leaders, pesky reporters, and a thousand unpleasant situations. Yet one dark glower from Blake and she felt as though she could cry. Her gaze was centered on the carpet, and she noted that in her rush she'd forgotten to put on shoes.

"Caasi?" His voice pounded around the room like thunder.

"I don't know how to dance," she shouted. "And don't yell at me. Understand?" she said. "The last time I went to a dance I was a college sophomore. Things…have… changed."

She moved to the window and pretended an interest in the city lights.

Blake moved behind her and gently laid a hand on her shoulder. "What you need is a few lessons."

"Lessons?" she repeated softly. The image that came to her mind was of the times the hotel had booked the ballroom for the students of several local dance studios.

"I'll be your teacher." The words were husky and low-pitched. The gentle pressure of his hand turned her toward him.

Submissively, Caasi's arms dangled at her sides. "What about music?"

"We'll make our own." He began to hum softly, a gentle ballad that the piano man had played the night before. "First, place your arms around my neck." Lightly his hands rested on the curve of her hip just below her waist.

Caasi linked her fingers behind his neck. "Like this?"

Their eyes met and he nodded slowly—very slowly, as if the simple action had cost him a great deal. The grooves at the sides of his mouth deepened and he drew her close. His hands slid around to the small of her back, his touch feather-light.

Caasi had to stand on the tips of her toes to fit her body to his. When she eased her weight against him he went rigid.

"Did I do something wrong?" she asked in a whisper.

"No." His breath stirred her hair. "You're doing fine."

"Why aren't we moving?"

"Because it feels good just to hold you," he said in a strange, husky voice.

A flood of warmth filled every pore, and when she

raised her eyes she saw that his angry look had been replaced by a gaze so warm and sensuous that she went completely still. She didn't breathe. She didn't move. She didn't blink.

He moved his hand up her back in a slow, rotating action that brought her even closer, more intimately, against him.

"Blake?" Her voice was treacherously low.

His other hand slid behind her neck, and he wove his fingers into her hair. "Yes?" Slowly, Blake lowered his mouth, claiming the trembling softness of hers.

His lips were undemanding, the pressure light and deliciously seductive. But soon the pressure deepened, as if the gentle caress wasn't enough to satisfy him.

Caasi's body surged with a warm, glowing excitement. She'd been kissed before, but never had she experienced such a deep, overwhelming response. Her arms locked around his neck.

"Caasi…" He ground out her name on a husky breath. He kissed her again, and she parted her lips in eager welcome. Their mouths strained against one another, seeking a deeper contact.

Blake tore his mouth away and buried his face in her soft throat.

Caasi sighed softly. "My goodness," she whispered breathlessly, "that's some dance step."

Blake shuddered lightly and broke the contact. "Go change, or we'll be late."

"Be late?" she asked, and blinked.

His fingers traced the questioning creases in her brow, then slid lightly down the side of her cheek and under her chin. "My cousin's wedding is tonight. If we hurry we'll make it to the dance."

"Will I meet your family?" Somehow that seemed important.

"Everyone. Even a few I'd rather you didn't know."

"Oh, Blake, I'd like that," she cried excitedly. "I'd like that very much."

Blake smiled, one of those rare smiles that came from the eyes. He had beautiful eyes, like his parents, and Caasi couldn't move. His look held her softly against him.

"Hurry," he urged in a half groan.

Reluctantly she let him go and took a step in retreat. "Are you sure what I wore last night will be all right? I have plenty of more formal outfits."

"It's fine. But whatever you wear, make sure it has a high neckline."

"Why?" she asked with a light laugh.

"Because I don't want any of my relatives ogling you." He sounded half angry.

Hands on her hips, her mood gay and excited, Caasi laughed. "Honestly, there isn't that much to ogle at."

Boldly, his gaze dropped to the rounded fullness as he studied her with silent amusement. "You have ten minutes. If you haven't appeared by that time, I'll come in and personally see to your dress."

The threat was tempting, and with a happy sigh, Caasi hurried out of the room.

Sorting through her wardrobe, she took out a pink-and-green skirt and top. The blouse had a button front, so the option of how much cleavage to reveal was left strictly to her. Purposely she left the top three buttons unfastened, blatantly revealing the hollow between her breasts. Caasi realized she was openly flirting with Blake, but she hadn't flirted with anyone in so long. The desire to do so overrode her usual modesty.

Blake was standing at the window looking out when she appeared. He turned and froze, his gaze meeting hers.

"Will I do?" Suddenly she felt uncertain. Idly her fingers played with the buttons of her blouse, fastening the most provocative one.

"Dear sweet heaven, you're beautiful."

Caasi felt a throb of excitement pulsate through her. "So are you."

The intensity of his look deepened, and he glanced at his watch. Caasi had the impression he couldn't have told her the time if she'd asked.

"We'd better go."

"I'll get a jacket." Cassie returned to her bedroom and took a velvet jacket from the hanger.

Blake took it out of her hand and held it open, gliding the soft material up her arms. His hands cupped her shoulders and brought her back against him. His breath stirred the hair at the crown of her head.

The sensations Blake was causing were new. So new that Caasi hadn't time to properly examine them. Not then. Not when his hand held her close to his side as they took her private elevator to the parking garage. Not when he opened the passenger door of the '57 T-Bird with the convertible top down. Not when he leaned over and lightly brushed his mouth across hers.

The dance was held in a V.F.W. hall off Sandy Boulevard. The lot was full of cars, the doors to the huge building open while loud music poured into the night.

"Once you meet my relatives you might consider yourself fortunate to be getting rid of me."

Caasi wished he hadn't mentioned his resignation but forced herself to smile in response. "Do you think I could find your replacement here?"

Either he didn't hear the question or chose to ignore it.

"Hey, Blake, who's the pretty lady?" A couple of youths strolled toward them. Caasi could remember trying to walk in the same "cool" manner.

The boy who had spoken was chewing a mouthful of gum.

"You toucha' my lady and I breaka' your head." Blake's teasing voice carried a thread of warning.

Caasi doubted that either boy took him seriously.

"These two are my baby cousins."

"Baby cousins." The boys groaned. "Hey, man, give us a break."

"You taking your lady to Rocky Butte?" The second youth was walking backward in front of Blake and Caasi, his arms swinging at his sides.

"Rocky Butte?" Caasi glanced up at Blake.

"The local necking place." His hand found hers, and Caasi enjoyed the sensation of being linked to this powerful man. "You game?"

"No," she said, teasing. "I want more dancing lessons first."

His chuckle brought an exchange of curious glances between the youths.

"You're not going to dance, are you, Blake? That's for sissies."

"Wait a few years," he advised. "It has its advantages."

They paused in the open doorway. The polished wooden floor was crowded with dancing couples. A five-piece band was playing from a stage to the far right-hand side of the hall. Long tables containing food were against another wall, and several younger children were helping themselves to the trays of sweets. Older couples sat talking in rows of folding chairs.

A sense of wonder filled Caasi. This was a part of Blake. A part of life she had never experienced. "Are you related to all these people?"

"Most of them."

"But you know everyone here?"

"Everyone." He looked down at her and smiled. "Come on, I want you to meet my parents."

As soon as people were aware that Blake had arrived, there were shouts of welcome and raised hands. He responded with his own shouts, then gave Caasi a whispered explanation as to various identities.

"How many uncles do you have?" she asked, astonished.

"Ten uncles and twice as many aunts. I gave up counting cousins."

"It's marvelous. I love it." Her face beamed with excitement and the laughter flowed from her, warm and easy.

Blake stopped once and turned her around, placing a hand on each shoulder. "I don't think I've ever heard you laugh. Really laugh."

She smiled up at him. "I don't know that I have. Not in a long time."

The bride, in a long, white, flowing gown, the train wrapped around her forearm, giggled and hurried to Blake. "I didn't think you'd ever get here," she admonished and stood on tiptoes to kiss his cheek. "Now you have to dance with me."

Blake laughed and cast a questioning glance at Caasi. "Do you mind?"

"No, of course not." She stepped aside as Blake took the young woman in his arms. A wide path was cleared as the couple approached the dance floor. People began to clap their hands in time to the music.

Someone bumped against Caasi, and she turned to apologize. "Sorry," she murmured.

The dark eyes that met hers were cold and unfriendly. The lack of welcome surprised Caasi.

"So *you're* the one who's ruined my brother's life!"

Three

"Ruined your brother's life?" Caasi repeated incredulously. "I'm Caasi Crane." The girl obviously had her confused with someone else. A curious sensation attacked the pit of Caasi's stomach at the thought of Blake with another woman.

"I know who you are," the woman continued in angry, hissing tones. "And I know what you've done."

What she'd done? Caasi's mind repeated. Those same wonderful eyes that had mesmerized her when she had studied the photo of Blake's parents were narrowed and hard in the tall woman beside her. Blake's own eyes darkened with the same deep intensity when he was angry.

"Are you sure you're talking to the right woman?"

"Oh, yes, there's no doubt. I'd know you…"

Loud applause prevented Caasi from hearing the rest of what the woman was saying.

Caasi watched as the young bride, laughing and breathless, hugged Blake. His eyes were full of amusement, but when his gaze found Caasi and saw who was with her, the humor quickly vanished. He kissed the bride, handed her to the waiting groom, and hurried across the crowded dance floor to Caasi's side.

"I see Gina has introduced herself to you," Blake said as he folded an arm around Caasi's shoulders. He smiled down at her, but there was a guarded quality in his gaze.

The eyes of the two women clashed. Something unreadable flickered in Gina's. Surprise? Warning? Caasi didn't know.

"We didn't get around to exchanging names," Caasi said as she held out her hand to Blake's sister. It was important to clear away the misconception Gina had about her.

The hesitation was only minimal before Gina took her hand and shook it lightly.

"If you'll excuse us," Blake said, directing his comment to his sister, "I want to introduce Caasi to Mom and Dad."

"Sure," Gina said, her voice husky. She cleared her throat and shook her head as if to dispel the picture before her. Her look was confused as she glanced from her brother to Caasi. "I'm sure they'd like that."

"I know I would." Caasi didn't need to be a psychic to feel the finely honed tension between brother and sister. That Gina adored him was obvious just by the way she looked at him. That same reverence had been in the eyes of the young bride. Blake was an integral part of this family, loved and respected. Caasi, on the other hand, belonged to no one; her life had never appeared so empty—just a shell. She'd give everything she owned—the hotels, her money, anything—to be a part of something like this, to experience that marvelous feeling of belonging.

Blake was watching her, his look curious. "You look a hundred miles away."

"Sorry," she answered with a feeble smile.

He escorted her to a row of folding chairs. Several older women were gathered in a circle and were leaning forward, chatting busily.

"Mother." Blake tapped one of the women gently on the shoulder and kissed her cheek affectionately.

"Blake!" his mother cried in a burst of enthusiasm as she stood and embraced her son. "You did come! I knew you wouldn't disappoint Kathleen."

The gray-haired woman had changed little from the photo Caasi had seen. Although several years older and plumper, Blake's mother was almost exactly the same. Warmth, love, and acceptance radiated from every part of her. Caasi had recognized those wonderful qualities in the photo; in person they became even more evident.

"Mother." Blake broke the embrace. "I'd like you to meet Caasi Crane." He turned to Caasi. "My mother, Anne Sherrill."

"Miss Crane." Two large hands eagerly enveloped Caasi's. "We've heard so much about you. Meeting you is a long-overdue pleasure."

"Thank you," Caasi replied with a wide smile. "I feel the same way." She couldn't take her eyes from the older woman. "You're very like your photo."

Anne Sherrill looked blank.

"I should explain," Caasi inserted quickly. "I was at Blake's house this afternoon."

"Where's Dad?" Blake's arm continued to hold Caasi to his side. She enjoyed the feeling of being coupled with him, the sense of belonging.

Anne Sherrill clucked with mock displeasure. "In the parking lot with two of your uncles."

Fleetingly Caasi wondered what they were doing in the parking lot but didn't ask.

Blake's rich laughter followed. "Do you want me to check on him for you?"

"And have you abandon Miss Crane?" Mrs. Sherrill sounded outraged.

"Please, call me Caasi," was Caasi's gentle request. "I don't mind." The latter comment was directed at Blake. "I'll stay here and visit with your mother. I wouldn't mind in the least."

"I'll only be a few minutes," Blake promised. "Mom, keep Caasi company, and for heaven's sake, don't let anyone walk away with her." He kissed his mother on the cheek and whispered something about lambs and wolves. With a knowing smile, his mother nodded.

Caasi had to bite her tongue to keep from asking what the comment had been about.

"Have you eaten?" Anne wanted to know. "With that son of mine, you probably haven't had a chance to breathe since you walked in the door. "Let's fix you a plate. Not fancy food, mind you."

Caasi started to protest but realized she *was* hungry. No, starved. "I'd like that," she said as she followed Blake's mother to the row of tables against the wall.

The variety of food was amazing, and all home-cooked, from the look of the dishes. It was probably a pot-luck supper, with each family contributing. Thick slices of ham, sausage, and turkey and a dozen huge salads were set out, along with several dishes Caasi didn't recognize.

Anne handed Caasi a plate and poured herself a cup of punch.

"This looks fantastic," Caasi murmured as she surveyed the long tables. She helped herself to a slice of ham and a couple of small sausage links. The German-style potato salad was thick with bacon and onions, and Caasi spooned a small serving of it alongside the ham. "This should be plenty."

"Take as much as you like. There's always food left over, and I hate having to take anything home with me."

"No, no, this is fine. Thank you."

They sat down again. Caasi balanced her plate on her knees and took a bite of the potato salad. "This is really delicious." The delicate blend of flavors wasn't like anything she'd ever tasted.

"Anne's German potato salad is the best this side of heaven," the middle-aged woman on the other side of Caasi commented.

"You made this?" Caasi looked at Anne.

Anne nodded with a pleased grin. "It's an old family recipe. My mother taught me, and now I've handed it down to my daughters."

Anne Sherrill's heritage to her daughters included warmth, love, and recipes. Caasi's was a famous father and a string of hotels, but given the chance she'd gladly have traded.

"No one makes German-style potato salad like Anne," the other woman continued. When she paused, Anne introduced the woman as Blake's cousin's wife.

"What's in it?" Caasi questioned before she lifted the fork to her mouth. Her interest was genuine.

Anne ran down a list of ingredients with specific instructions. Nothing was listed in teaspoons; it was all in dashes and sprinkles. Caasi doubted that the family recipe had ever been written down. Caasi had never known her own mother and at times when growing up had felt a deep sense of loss—but never more than right now. Her father had tutored her so thoroughly in the ways of business and finance. It was only at times like this that Caasi realized how much she missed a mother's loving influence.

"It's best to let the flavors blend overnight."

Caasi picked up on the last bit of information and nodded absently, her thoughts a million miles away.

"You must come to dinner some Sunday."

"I'd like that," Caasi said. "I'd like it very much."

"This is the first time Blake's brought a woman to a family get-together, isn't it?" The cousin's comment came in the form of a question. "Handsome devil, Blake Sherrill. I've seen the way women chase after him. Yet he's never married."

"No, Blake's my independent one."

Caasi paid an inordinate amount of attention to cutting the ham slice. "Why hasn't he married?"

The hesitation was slight. "I'm not really sure," Anne supplied thoughtfully. "He loves children. I think he'd like a wife and family, but he just hadn't found the right woman, that's all."

Caasi nodded and lifted a bite of meat to her mouth.

"Is tomorrow too soon?" Anne questioned and at Caasi's blank look continued, "For dinner, I mean."

Mentally Caasi went over Sunday's schedule. It didn't matter; she could change whatever had been planned. "I'd enjoy nothing more. What time would you like me?"

Anne wrote the address and time on the back of one of Caasi's business cards. She wasn't sure why Blake's mother had invited her, but it didn't matter—she was going. Being with his family, Caasi couldn't help but learn more about the enigmatic man who was leaving her just when she was beginning to know him.

"I think I see Blake coming now," Anne murmured with a tender smile. "With his father in tow."

Caasi studied the gentle look on the older woman's face before scanning the room for Blake. She could barely make out his figure through the crowd of dancers. The faint stirrings of awareness he awakened within her surprised Caasi. She was proud to be with Blake, to meet his family, to be included in this celebration.

Their eyes sought one another when he stepped into full view. Hers were soft and welcoming; his, slightly guarded.

"Dad, this is Caasi."

Blake's father reached down and took Caasi's hand, his dark eyes twinkling. "Pretty thing." The comment was made to no one directly.

"Thank you," Caasi murmured and blushed.

"Fine bone structure, but a little on the thin side. Always did like high foreheads. It's a sign of intelligence."

"Dad." Blake's low voice contained a thin note of warning.

"George." Anne slipped an arm around her husband's waist. "His tongue gets loose after a beer or two," Blake's mother explained to Caasi.

"Would you like to dance?" A corner of Blake's mouth tilted upward. He looked as if dancing was the last thing he wanted.

"If you like." Caasi would have preferred to stay and talk more with his parents, but she recognized the wisdom of following Blake onto the polished floor.

The band was playing a polka, and with a quick turn, Blake pulled her into his arms.

Caasi let out a small cry of alarm. She didn't know how to dance, especially the polka.

"Just follow me," he instructed. "And for heaven's sake, don't step on my toes with those high heels."

"Blake," she pleaded breathlessly. "I can't dance. I don't know how to do this."

"You're doing fine." He whirled her around again and again until she was dizzy, her head spinning with the man and the music.

They stopped after the first dance, and Blake brought her a glass of punch. Caasi took one sip and widened her eyes at the potency of the drink.

"Rum?" she quizzed.

"And probably a dab of this and that."

"Old family recipe," she said with a teasing smile.

"I'm getting in on several of those tonight. Oh, Blake, I like your family."

"They're an unusual breed, I'll say that." His voice was lazy and deep.

"Is Sherrill a German name?"

"No. Dad's English, or once was. Mom's the one with the German heritage."

The band started playing a slow waltz, and Caasi's eyes were drawn to the dance floor again.

Blake took the cup from her and set it aside. "Shall we?" His eyes met hers, the laughter gone, as he skillfully turned her into his arms.

A confused mixture of emotions whirled in her mind as he slid his arms around her waist, the gentle pressure at the small of her back guiding her movements.

A warmth flowed through her, beginning at his touch and fanning out until she could no longer resist and closed her eyes to its potency.

Caasi placed her head on his shoulder, her face against his neck. The scent of his aftershave attacked her senses. She was filled with the feel and the smell of Blake. It seemed the most natural thing in the world for her tongue to make a lazy foray against his neck, to taste him.

"Caasi." He groaned. "You don't know what you're doing to me."

"I do," she said with a deep sigh. "And I like it. Don't make me stop."

He brought her closer to him, the intimate feel of his body sensuously moving with hers enough to steal her breath.

"This is insane," Blake ground out hoarsely, as if her touch was causing him acute pain.

Gently his mouth nibbled at her earlobe, and red-hot sensations shot through her like a bolt of lightning. "Blake," she pleaded. "Oh, Blake, this feels so good."

Abruptly he broke the contact and led her off the dance floor. "Just how much have you had to drink?" he demanded roughly.

Caasi was too stunned to answer. She opened her mouth but found herself speechless. Angrily she clamped it closed. The embarrassment that filled her face only served to anger her more.

"Apparently not nearly enough." She didn't know why Blake was acting like this. She didn't know how he could turn from a gentle lover to a tormenting in-quisitor in a matter of seconds either.

They stood only a few feet apart, glaring at one another. Neither spoke.

"Hey, Blake, when are you going to introduce me to your lady?" A low masculine voice broke into the pal-pable silence that stretched between them.

A tall, good-looking man with a thick mustache over a wide smile came into view. He was about Blake's age and good-looking in a stylish sports coat. His tie had been loosened, revealing curling black hairs at the base of his throat.

"Johnnie—Caasi. Caasi—Johnnie. My cousin."

Johnnie chuckled, his eyes roaming over Caasi with obvious interest. "You don't sound so thrilled that we're cousins." The comment was directed at Blake, but his eyes openly assessed Caasi.

"I'm not," Blake stated bluntly. "Now, if you don't mind, Caasi and I are having a serious discussion."

"We are?" she interrupted sweetly. "I thought we were through. I was just saying how thirsty I am and how delicious the punch is."

Johnnie cocked his head in gentlemanly fashion. "In which case, allow me to escort you to the punch bowl."

"I'd like that."

"Caasi." Blake's low voice was filled with challenge. "I wouldn't."

"Excuse me a minute, Blake," she returned, ignoring his dark, narrowed look. She placed her arm through Johnnie's offered elbow and strolled away. She didn't need to turn around to see that Blake's eyes were boring holes into her back.

"Like to live dangerously, don't you?" Johnnie quizzed with a good-natured grin.

Caasi's lower lip was quivering, and she drew in a shaky breath. "Not really."

"Then I'd say you enjoy placing others in terminal danger. My life wouldn't be worth a plugged nickel if Blake could find a way of getting hold of me without causing a scene."

The thought was so outrageous that Caasi felt her mouth curve with amusement. "Then why are you smiling?" she asked. Johnnie was obviously a charmer, and she found that she liked him.

"I have to admit," he said with a low chuckle, "it feels good to do one up on Blake. He's the family hero. Everyone looks up to him. Frankly, I'm jealous." Johnnie said it with such devilish charm that Caasi couldn't prevent a small laugh.

"Are you thirsty, or was that an excuse to put Blake in his place?" he queried.

"An excuse," she murmured wickedly.

"Then let's dance."

Caasi hesitated; dancing with Johnnie was another matter altogether. "I'm not sure."

"Come on," he said encouragingly. "Let's give Blake a real taste of the green-eyed monster."

By this time Caasi was beginning to regret her behavior. She was acting like a spoiled child, which undoubtedly confirmed what Blake thought of her.

"I don't think so. Another time."

"Don't look now," Johnnie whispered, "but Blake's making his way over here, and he doesn't look pleased. No," he amended, "he looks downright violent."

Caasi shifted restlessly. The sound of Blake's footsteps seemed to be magnified a thousand times until it was all she could do not to cover her ears.

"Excuse us," Blake said to Johnnie and gripped Caasi's upper arm in a punishing hold, "but this dance is ours."

Caasi glanced at him nervously, resisting the temptation to bite into her bottom lip as he half dragged her onto the dance floor.

When he placed his arms around her the delicious sensations didn't warm her, nor did she feel that special communication that had existed between them only a few minutes previously.

Caasi slid her arms around his neck, her body moving instinctively with his to the rhythm of the slow beat. She studied him through a screen of thick lashes. His mouth was pinched. The dark eyes were as intense as she'd ever seen them, and his clenched jaw seemed to be carved in stone.

Swallowing her pride, Caasi murmured, "I've only had the one glass of punch. I apologize for going off with your cousin. That was a childish thing to do."

Blake said nothing, but she felt some of the anger flow out of him. His arm tightened around her back. "One drink?" he retorted, his mouth moving disturbingly close to her ear.

"Honest."

"You were playing with fire, touching me like that. The way your body was moving against mine…" He paused. "If you aren't drunk, then explain the seduction scene." The harshness in his voice brought her head up and their eyes met, his gaze trapping hers.

"Seduction scene?"

"Come on, Caasi, you can't be that naive," he muttered drily. "The looks you were giving me were meant for the bedroom, not the dance floor."

Her eyes fell and she lost her rhythm, faltering slightly. "Let me assure you," she whispered hotly, hating the telltale color that suffused her face, "that was not my intention."

"Exactly," Blake retorted. "You don't need to explain, because I know you."

"You know me?" she repeated in a disbelieving whisper.

"That's right. You're a cool, suave, sophisticated

businesswoman. Primed from an early age to take over Crane Enterprises. It's all you know. That isn't red blood that flows in your veins—it's ink from profit-and-loss statements."

They stopped the pretense of dancing. Caasi had never felt so cold. A myriad of emotions came at her from every direction.

Wordlessly she dropped her hands and took a few steps in retreat. Her knees were trembling so badly she was afraid to move. The silence between them was charged like the still air before a storm. It was all she could do to turn away and disguise her reaction to his cruel words. Blindly she walked off the dance floor.

Somehow she made her way into the ladies' room. Her reflection in the mirror was deathly pale, her blue-gray eyes haunted.

Her hands trembled as she turned on the faucet and filled the sink with cold water. A wet paper towel pressed to her cheeks seemed to help.

Blake was right. She should have recognized as much herself. She wasn't a woman, she was a machine, an effectively programmed, well-oiled machine. Her father had repeatedly warned her against mixing business with pleasure. He'd said it often enough for her to know better than to become involved with Blake. Even now she wasn't sure why had she agreed to accompany Blake. She had to ask herself where the common sense her father had instilled in her was. Furthermore she wanted to know why the truth in Blake's accusations hurt so much. The sound of someone coming into the room caused Caasi to straighten and make a pretense of washing her hands. She didn't turn around, not wanting to talk to anyone.

"I'm glad I found you." The soft, apologetic voice spoke from behind.

Caasi raised her head and her eyes met Gina's in the mirror. The dark-haired girl looked embarrassed and disturbed. Caasi looked away; she wasn't up to another confrontation.

"I'd like to apologize for what I said earlier," Blake's sister said softly. "It was unforgivable."

Caasi nodded, having difficulty finding her voice. "I understand. It's forgotten." She forced a wan smile.

"Mom said you're coming to dinner tomorrow."

Caasi's eyes widened; she'd forgotten the invitation. "Yes, I'm looking forward to it."

"I hope we can be friends. Maybe we'll get a chance to visit more tomorrow." Gina offered her a genuine smile as Caasi dried her hands.

With most of her poise restored, Caasi returned to the crowded hall. She saw Blake almost immediately. He stood by the exit. Caasi made her way across the room to Blake's mother. Anne looked up and a frown marred her brow.

"I enjoyed meeting you, Mrs. Sherrill."

"Anne," the woman corrected softly. "Call me Anne."

"I'd be honored."

"Is something wrong, Caasi?"

Caasi had always prided herself on her ability to disguise her emotions. Yet this woman had intuitively known there was something troubling her.

"I'm fine, thanks. I'll be at your home tomorrow if the invitation's still open."

"Of course it is."

"Say good-night to your husband for me, won't you?"

Anne's eyes were bright with concern. "You do look pale, dear. I hope you're not coming down with something."

Caasi dismissed the older woman's concern with a weak shake of her head. "I'm fine."

Blake had straightened by the time she came to the front door.

"You're ready to go?" he asked, his tone curt.

"Yes," she said primly. "I'm more than ready."

He led the way to his car, opened her door, and promptly walked around the front and climbed into the driver's side. The engine roared to life even before Caasi could strap her seat belt into place.

The night had grown cold, and Caasi wrapped her arms around herself to ward off the unexpected chill. Maybe it wasn't the night, Caasi mused, but the result of sitting next to Blake. If this cold war continued, she'd soon get frostbite.

They hadn't said a word since they'd left the reception. Caasi couldn't bear to look at him and closed her eyes, resting her head against the seat back.

The wind whipped through her hair and buffeted her face, but she didn't mind—and wouldn't have complained if she had.

The car slowed and Caasi straightened, looking around her. They were traveling in the opposite direction from the Empress. The road was narrow and curving.

"Where are we going?" she asked stiffly.

"To Rocky Butte."

"Rocky Butte?" she shot back incredulously. "Are you crazy?"

"Yes," he ground out angrily. "I've been crazy for eight years, and just as stupid."

Caasi watched as his eyes narrowed on the road. "You're taking me to the local necking place? Have you lost your senses?"

Blake ignored her.

"Why are you bringing me here?" she demanded in frustration. "Do you want to make fun of me again? Is that how you get your thrills? Belittling me?"

Blake pulled off to the side of the road and shoved the gears into Park. The challenge in his chiseled jaw couldn't be ignored.

"Remember me?" she said bravely. "I'm the girl without emotions. The company robot. I don't have blood, that's ink flowing through me," she informed him as unemotionally as possible. To her horror, her voice cracked. She jerked around and folded her arms across her breast, refusing to look at him.

Blake got out of the car and walked around to the front, apparently admiring the view of the flickering lights of Portland. Caasi stayed exactly where she was, her arms the only defense against the chill of the late night.

Blake opened her car door. "Come on."

Caasi ignored him, staring straight ahead.

"Have it your way," he said tightly, slamming the door and walking away.

Stunned, Caasi didn't move. Not for a full ten seconds. He wouldn't just leave her, would he?

"Blake?" She threw open the door and hurried after him. Running in her heels was nearly impossible.

He paused and waited for her.

"Where are you going?" she asked once she reached him.

"To the park. Come with me, Caasi." The invitation was strangely entreating. Would she ever understand this man? She should be screaming in outrage at the things he'd said to her and the way he'd acted.

A hand at her elbow guided her up two flights of hewn rock steps to a castlelike fortress. The area was small and enclosed by a parapet. There were no picnic tables, and Caasi wondered how anyone could refer to this as a park. Even the ground had only a few patchy areas of grass.

The light of the full moon illuminated the Columbia River Gorge far below.

"It's beautiful, isn't it?" Caasi whispered, not really sure why she felt the need to keep her voice low.

"I love this place," Blake murmured. "It was too dark for you to notice the rock embankment on the way up here. Each piece fits into the hillside perfectly without a hair's space between the rocks. That old-world craftsmanship is a lost art. There are only a few masons who know how to do that kind of stonework today."

"When was it built?" Caasi questioned.

"Sometime during the Depression, when President Roosevelt implemented the public-work projects."

Despite her best efforts, her voice trembled slightly. "Why did you bring me here…especially tonight?"

He shot her a disturbing look, as if unaware he'd said as much. "I don't know." He spoke softly, his smoldering gaze resting on her slightly parted lips. He turned toward her, his eyes holding her captive. "I suppose I should take you home."

Caasi's heartbeat soared at the reluctance in his voice. She didn't want to go back to the empty apartment, the empty shell of her life. Blake was here and now and she wanted him more than she'd ever wanted anything in her life.

"Blake…" His name came as a tormented whisper.

A breathless, timeless silence followed as he slipped his arms around her. Ever so tenderly, with a gentleness she hadn't expected from him, Blake fit his mouth over hers. Again and again, his mouth sought hers until Caasi was heady with the taste of him.

He moaned when her tongue outlined the curve of his mouth, and his grip tightened. Caasi melted against him as his hands slid down her hips, holding her intimately to his hard body.

Her hands were pressed against the firm wall of his chest and his heartbeat drummed against her open palm, telling her that he was just as affected as she. He felt warm and strong, and Caasi wanted to cry with the wonder of it.

Reluctantly, he tilted his head back, and his warm gaze caressed her almost as effectively as his lips had.

"Shall we go?"

Caasi fought the catch in her voice by shaking her head. If it was up to her they'd stay right there, exactly as they were, for the rest of their lives.

His hand at her waist led her back to the parked car. He lingered a moment longer than necessary after opening her door and helping her inside.

Blake dropped her off in front of the Empress. "I won't see you inside," he stated flatly.

"Why?" She tried to disguise the disappointment in her voice.

His fingers bit into the steering wheel. "Because the way I feel right now, I wouldn't be leaving until the morning. Does that shock you, Caasi?"

Four

Caasi checked the house number written on the back of her business card with the one on the red brick above the front door. Several cars were in the driveway as well as along the tree-lined street. Caasi pulled her silver Mercedes to the curb, uneasily aware that her vehicle looked incongruous beside the Fords and Volkswagens.

This was a family neighborhood, with the wide sidewalks for bicycle riding and gnarled trees meant for climbing. Caasi looked around her with a sense of unfamiliarity. Her childhood sidewalks had been the elevators at the Empress.

Children were playing a game of tag in the front yard; they stopped to watch her curiously as Caasi rang the doorbell, her arms loaded with a huge floral bouquet.

"Hi," a small boy called out. His two front teeth were missing and he had a thick thatch of dark hair and round brown eyes.

"Hi," Caasi said with a wide smile.

"I'm Todd Sherrill."

"I'm Caasi."

"Are you coming to visit my grandma?"

"I sure am."

The door opened and Gina called into the kitchen, "Mom, it's Caasi." Gina held open the screen door for her. "Come on in, we've been waiting for you."

"I'm not late, am I?" Caasi glanced at her watch.

"No, no."

Anne Sherrill came into the living room from the large kitchen in the back of the house. She was wiping her hands on a flowered terrycloth apron. "Caasi, we're so pleased you could come."

"Here." Caasi handed her the flowers. "I wanted you to have these."

Anne looked impressed at the huge variety of flowers. "They're beautiful. Thank you."

For all the cars parked in the front of the house, the living room was empty. Caasi glanced around as Anne took down a vase from the fireplace mantel. The decor was surprisingly modern, with a sofa and matching love seat. The polished oak coffee table was littered with several magazines.

"Come back and meet everyone," Anne said encouragingly. "The men are involved in their card game and the women are visiting."

"Which is a polite way of saying we're gossiping," Gina inserted with a small laugh.

Caasi followed both women into the kitchen, immediately adjacent to which was a family room filled to capacity. Children were playing a game of Monopoly on the floor while the men were seated at a table absorbed in a game of cards.

A flurry of introductions followed. Caasi didn't have trouble remembering names or faces; she dealt with so many people in a hundred capacities that she'd acquired the skill for such things.

Five of the six Sherrill children were present. Only Blake was missing. Caasi talked briefly with each one and after a few questions learned who was married to whom and which child belonged to which set of parents. Blake and Gina were the two unmarried Sherrill children. But Gina proudly displayed an engagement ring. Caasi's eyes met Gina's. Whatever animosity had existed between them in the beginning was gone. Several grandchildren crowded around Anne and Caasi, following them as Anne led the way outside so that she could show off her prize garden.

"Roses," Gina supplied. "My mother and her roses. Sometimes I swear she cares as much about them as she does about us kids."

"Portland is the City of Roses," Anne said as she strolled through the grounds pointing out each bush and variety of rose as if these, too, were her children.

The bigger grandchildren followed them, while Gina carried a two-year-old on her hip. Young Tommy had just gotten up from his nap and was hiding his sleepy face against his aunt's shoulder.

Todd, the eight-year-old who had introduced himself at the front of the house, linked his hand with Caasi's.

"You're pretty," he commented, watching her closely. "Are you my aunt?"

"Does this mean only pretty girls are your aunts?" Caasi teased him, enjoying the feeling of being a part of this gathering.

Todd looked flustered. "Aunt Gina's pretty, and Aunt Barbara's pretty."

"Then you can call me Aunt if you want to," Caasi told him tenderly. "But I'll have to be a special aunt."

"Okay," he agreed readily. They heard another boy calling him, wanting Todd to play. Todd looked uncertain.

"It's all right, you can go," Caasi assured him. "I'll stay with your grandma, and you can come see me later."

The brown eyes brightened. "You'll be here for dinner?"

"Yup."

"Will you play a game of Yahtzee with me afterwards?"

"If you like."

"'Bye, Aunt Caasi."

Todd's words sent a warm feeling through her. She watched him run off and her heart swelled. This was the first time anyone had ever called her aunt.

The baby in Gina's arms peeked at Caasi, eyeing her curiously.

"Do you think he'll let me hold him?" she asked Gina, putting her hands out to the baby. Immediately, Tommy buried his face in Gina's shoulder.

"Give him a few minutes to become used to you. He's not normally shy, but he just woke up and needs to be held a few minutes."

"Is Donald coming?" Anne asked Gina.

"He'll be here, Mom—you know Donald. He'll probably be late for his own wedding, but I love him anyway."

"Have you set a date?" Caasi questioned as they strolled back to the house.

"In two months."

"The wedding shower's here next month, Caasi. We'd be honored if you came." Anne extended the invitation with an easy grace that came from including everyone, as she probably had all her life, Caasi realized.

"I'd love to. In fact, if you'd like, I could arrange to have the shower at the hotel. I mean, I wouldn't want to take over everything, but that way…" She hesitated; maybe she was offending Anne by making the offer.

"You'd do that?" Gina asked disbelievingly.

"We wouldn't want you to go through all that trouble." Anne looked more concerned than dismayed that Caasi would take on the project.

"It's something I'd enjoy doing, and it would be my way of thanking you for today."

"But we can't let you…"

"Nonsense," Caasi interrupted brightly, enthusiasm lighting up her expression. "This will give Gina and me a better chance to get acquainted."

"Oh, Mom," Gina said and sighed happily. "A wedding shower at the Empress."

"We'll get together one day soon and make the arrangements," Caasi promised.

Tommy was studying her more intently now. "Can you come and see me, Tommy?" Caasi asked encouragingly, holding out her hands to him. The little boy glanced from Caasi to Gina, then back to Caasi, before holding out both arms to her.

"You are such a good boy." Caasi lifted him into her arms. She was sure that at one time or another in her life she'd held a small child, but she couldn't remember when, and she thrilled to the way his tiny hands came around her neck.

"I think you've got yourself a friend for life." Anne laughed and held open the back door for Caasi to come inside. Donald had arrived, and Gina hurried into the living room to greet her fiancé.

Tommy's mother was busy making the salad at the sink, and she smiled shyly when Caasi entered the house carrying Tommy.

"Here." Anne pushed out a tall stool for Caasi to sit on while she put the finishing touches on the meal.

Although Caasi joined in the conversation around her, she was enjoying playing peekaboo and pattycake with Tommy. The little boy's giggles rang through the house.

Her face flushed and happy, Caasi glanced up and saw Blake standing in the doorway of the kitchen. He was watching her, and her breath caught in her throat at the intensity of his gaze. At first she thought he was angry. His eyes had narrowed, but the glint that was shining from them couldn't be anger. A muscle worked in his jaw and his eyes seemed to take in every detail of her sitting in his mother's kitchen, bouncing a baby on her lap.

One of his brothers slapped Blake across the back

and started chatting, but still Blake didn't take his eyes off her.

She broke the contact first as Tommy reached for her hair, not liking the fact that her attention had drifted elsewhere. Suddenly a dampness spread through her linen skirt and onto her thighs. She gave a small cry when she realized what had just happened. Laughing, she handed Tommy to his embarrassed mother, who was apologizing profusely.

Anne led Caasi into the bathroom and gave her a dampened cloth to wipe off her teal blue skirt. Someone called Anne and she left Caasi standing just inside the open bathroom door. Caasi couldn't keep from smiling.

"What are you doing here?" Blake was leaning against the doorjamb. That warm, sensuous look was gone, replaced with something less welcoming.

"Your mom invited me last night," she told him, her eyes avoiding his as she continued to rub at her skirt. "Do you mind? I'll leave if you do. I wouldn't want to interfere with your family. I'm the outsider here."

He was silent for a long moment.

"No," he murmured at last, "I don't mind."

Some of the tension eased out of her. "If you'll excuse me, I'll see if I can help in the kitchen." She laid the cloth on top of the clothes hamper and started out the door. But Blake's arm stopped her.

"How'd you sleep last night?" A strange smile touched the curve of his mouth. Caasi didn't know what he wanted her to say. "Fine. Why?" she asked tightly.

He shrugged, giving the impression of nonchalance.

"No reason." But he didn't look pleased with her response and turned abruptly to leave her.

Anne gave her the job of dishing up the home-canned applesauce, dill pickles, and spicy beets. All the women were in the kitchen helping in one capacity or another. Laughing and joking with everyone, Caasi didn't feel the least like a stranger. She was accepted, she was one of them. It was the most beautiful feeling in the world.

After the meal, everyone pitched in and helped with the dishes. As promised, Caasi played Yahtzee with Todd and a couple of the other children. Blake was playing cards with his father and brothers and future brother-in-law.

While the children watched TV , Caasi joined the women, who were discussing knitting patterns and recipes. Caasi listened with interest, but her studied gaze was on Blake. He looked up once, caught her eye, and winked. Her heart did a wild somersault and she hurriedly glanced away.

"What game are the men playing?" Caasi asked Gina, who was sitting beside her.

"Pinochle. Have you ever played?"

Card-playing was unheard of in the Crane family; even as a child Caasi had never indulged in something her father considered a waste of valuable time.

"No." Caasi shook her head with a sad smile.

"You've never played pinochle?" Gina repeated incredulously. "I thought everyone did. It's a family institution. Come on, let Dad and Blake teach you."

"No...no, I couldn't."

"Sure you could," Gina insisted. "Donald, would you mind letting Caasi sit in? She's never played."

Blond-headed Donald immediately vacated his chair, holding it out for Caasi.

Standing, Caasi looked uncertain. Her eyes met Blake's, but he ignored the silent entreaty. He didn't want her to play, and his eyes said as much. He scooted out of his seat, offering to let another of his brothers take his place.

Caasi felt terrible. The other women hadn't played.

"Come on. I'll coach you," Gina persisted and straddled a chair beside Caasi's at the table.

The other men didn't look half as obliging as Donald, but one look told her he had been losing. Slowly she lowered herself into the vacant seat opposite Blake's father, who was to be her partner.

The cards were dealt after a thorough review of the rules. Gina wrote down the necessary card combinations on a piece of paper as a ready reminder for Caasi. The bid, the meld, and the passing of cards were all gone over in careful detail until Caasi's head was swimming.

They played a practice hand to let Caasi get the feel of the game. Her eyes met Gina's before every move. Once she threw down the wrong card and witnessed her partner's scowl. Caasi's stomach instantly tightened, but George glanced up and offered her an encouraging smile. They made the bid without the point she had carelessly tossed the opponent, and all was well again.

Soon Caasi found herself relaxing enough to enjoy the game. Although playing cards was new to her, the basic principle behind the game was something she'd been working with for years. She studied her opponent's faces when they bid and instinctively recognized what cards were out and which ones she needed to draw. By the time they finished playing, almost everyone else had left—including Blake—and it was almost midnight.

Anne and George walked Caasi to her car, extending an open invitation for her to come again the next week.

"You do this every Sunday?"

"Not everyone makes it every week," Anne was quick to inform her. "This week was more the exception. Everyone was home because of Kathleen's wedding."

Caasi was glad Anne had reminded her. She snapped open her purse and took out an envelope. "Would you give this to Kathleen and her husband for me?" She had written out a check and a letter of congratulations.

"You didn't need to do this," Anne said, fingering the envelope.

"I know," Caasi admitted freely, "but I wanted to."

"I'll see that she gets it."

Caasi could see the elderly couple in her rearview mirror as she drove away. Their arms were around one another as they stood in the light of the golden moon as if they had always been together and always would be. A love that spanned the years.

Caasi was humming as she walked into her office the following morning. Laurie, her secretary, gave her a funny look and handed her the mail.

Caasi sorted through several pieces as she sauntered

into her portion of the office. Pivoting, she came back to Laurie's desk.

"I'd like you to make arrangements for a wedding shower in the Blue Room a week from Thursday. Also, would you send the chef up here? I'd like to talk to him personally about the cake and hors d'oeuvres."

Laurie looked even more perplexed. "I'll see to it right away."

"Thanks, Laurie," Caasi said as she strolled back into her office.

The morning passed quickly, and Caasi ate a sandwich for lunch while at her desk. She hadn't seen Blake all morning, which wasn't unusual, but she discovered that her thoughts drifted to him. She wondered what he'd say when she did see him. Would he be all business, or would he make a comment about her visit with his family?

She stared down at the half-eaten sandwich and nibbled briefly on her bottom lip. His mother and sister had been discussing a quiche recipe that had been in Wednesday's paper. Caasi hadn't thought much about it at the time, but the urge to bake something was suddenly overwhelming. She'd taken a cooking class with Edie once simply because her friend didn't want to attend the session alone, but that seemed a hundred years ago. There was a kitchenette in her suite, although she'd never used the stove for much of anything. The oven had never been used, at least not by her. There hadn't been any reason to. And even if she did make the quiche she'd be eating it all week.

Still…

Impulsively she buzzed her secretary. "Laurie, please get me last Wednesday's paper."

Laurie returned twenty minutes later looking slightly ruffled as she handed Caasi the newspaper.

Caasi spread it across her desk and pored over it until she found what she wanted. Reading over the list of ingredients, she realized that not only would it be necessary to shop for the groceries, but she would need to buy all the equipment, including pots, pans, and dishes. Quickly she made out a list and handed it to Laurie, who stared at it dumbfounded.

"What you can't find and have delivered to my suite, get from Chef," Caasi instructed on her way out the door to a meeting.

Laurie opened and just as quickly closed her mouth, then nodded.

"Thanks," Caasi said.

She was late getting back to her office. Laurie had left for the day, but Caasi wanted to check over the list of phone messages before heading upstairs. She was shuffling through the pink slips when she walked into her office and found Blake pacing the floor.

He took one look at her and frowned.

"Hello, Blake." She smiled nervously, avoiding his piercing glare. "Is something the matter?" The atmosphere in the room was cool. He turned away, his back rigid. "Blake, what's wrong?"

He spun around, obviously angry as his blazing gaze seared over her. "I got a call from my mother this afternoon. She dropped off the card you gave her for Kathleen." His words were harsh. "What is the idea of giving them a check for two thousand dollars?" The challenge in his eyes was as hard as flint.

Caasi swallowed tightly. "What do you mean?"

"They're strangers to you."

"They're not strangers," she contradicted him sharply. "I met them when I was with you Saturday night. Don't you remember?"

"Kathleen and Bob don't need your charity." His eyes were as somber as they were dark.

"It wasn't charity," she returned. Her hands shook, and she clenched them into hard fists at her sides. "I have the money in fact, I have lots of money. What does it matter to you what I do with it?"

"It matters," he shouted in return. "Do you think you can buy yourself a family? Is that it? Are you so naive as to believe that people are going to love and respect you because of your money?"

Caasi blanched, her hand shooting out behind her to grip the edge of her desk. She suddenly needed its support to stand upright. From somewhere she found the courage to speak. "I don't need anyone, least of all you. Now I suggest you get out. I'll send a letter of apology to your cousin. It wasn't my intent to offend her or you or anyone. Now kindly leave."

He hesitated as if he wanted to say something more, but then he pivoted sharply and stalked out of the room.

Caasi lowered herself into her desk chair and covered her face with her hands. She took several deep breaths and managed to keep the tears stinging the back of her eyes at bay. It mortified her that Blake thought she was looking to buy herself a family. His family. The thought was too humiliating to consider. She wouldn't go to the next Sunday family dinner. Maybe keeping her away had been Blake's intent all along.

She stayed a few minutes longer in her office, but any thoughts of returning her phone messages had been sabotaged by Blake's anger. She leaned against the elevator wall on the ride to the penthouse suite, weary and defeated. Blake was right in some ways. That was what hurt so much. No matter how much she tried, she wasn't going to fit into the homey family scene with love and acceptance. She didn't belong. A lump had formed in her throat by the time she let herself into the empty suite. What she needed was a hot bath, an early dinner, and bed.

Dinner... Her mind stumbled over the word. She'd canceled her meal for the evening because she'd planned to bake the quiche. The laugh that followed was brittle. Well, why not? She could cook if she wanted to. Who was to care?

Laurie had done her job well, and the kitchen was filled with the necessary equipment. After a quick survey, Caasi slipped off her high heels and tucked her feet into slippers. Fearing she'd spill something on her suit, she used an old shirt as an apron, tying the sleeves around her waist. Rolling her sleeves up to her elbows, she braced both hands on the counter and read over the recipe list a second time. Lastly, she lined the ingredients up on the short countertop in the order in which she was to use them.

The pie crust was going to be the most difficult; everything else looked fairly simple.

Blending the flour and shortening together with a fork wasn't working, so Caasi decided to mix it with her fingers, kneading the shortening and flour together in the palms of her hands.

The phone rang; she stared at the gooey mixture on her hands and decided to let it ring. Ten minutes later, just as she'd spread a light dusting of flour across the counter and was ready to roll out the dough, there was a loud knock on her door.

"Come on, Caasi, I know you're in there."

Blake.

Panic filled her. He was the last person she wanted to see, especially now.

"Aldo says you haven't left. Your car's in the garage and there's no one in the office, so either let me in or I'll break down the door."

He didn't sound in any better mood than he had when she'd last seen him.

"Go away," she shouted, striving—vainly—for a quiet firmness.

"Caasi." His low voice held a note of warning.

"I'm…" She faltered slightly with the lie. "I'm not decent."

"Well, I suggest you cover yourself, because I'm coming through this door in exactly fifteen seconds."

She caught her lower lip in her teeth and breathed in deeply. Why was it that everything in her life had to end up like this?

"It's unlocked," she muttered in defeat.

Blake let himself in, then stopped abruptly when he saw her framed in the small kitchen. A smile worked its way across his face, starting with crinkling amusement at his eyes and then edging up a corner of his chiseled mouth.

"What are you making?" he asked, hands on his hips.

"What do you think you're doing, coming up to my suite like this? I should have security toss you out."

"Why didn't you?" he challenged.

"Because…because I had dough on my hands and would have gotten it all over the phone."

"That's a flimsy excuse."

Caasi released a low, frustrated groan. "Listen, Blake, go ahead and laugh. I seem to be an excellent source of amusement where you're concerned."

"I'm not laughing *at* you." The humor drained out of his eyes, and he dropped his hands.

"Then say what you came to say and be done with it. I'm not up to another confrontation with you." Her voice trembled and her eyes had a wild look. Blake had the ability to hurt her, and that was frightening.

"To be honest," he murmured gently as he took several deliberate steps toward her, "I can't recall a time I've seen you look more beautiful."

For every step he advanced, she took one in retreat, until she bumped against the oven door. The handle cut into the backs of her thighs.

"There's flour on your nose," Blake told her softly.

Caasi attempted to brush it aside and in the process spread more over her cheek.

His gaze swept over her and he shook his head in dismay. "Here, let me."

"No." She refused adamantly. "Don't touch me, Blake. Don't ever touch me again."

He looked as though she'd struck him. "I've hurt you, haven't I, Cupcake?" he asked gently.

"You can't hurt me," she lied. "Only people who mean something to me have that power."

He frowned, his dark eyes clouding with some unreadable emotion. *Surely not pain,* Caasi mused.

"For what it's worth," he said quietly, "I came to apologize."

She shrugged, hoping to give the impression of indifference.

"I got halfway home and couldn't get that stricken look in your eyes out of my mind."

"You're mistaken, Blake," she said pointedly, struggling to keep her voice steady. "That wasn't shock, or hurt, or anything else. It was..." She stopped abruptly when he placed the tips of his fingers over her lips. Helplessly, she stared at him, hating her own weakness. By all rights she should have him thrown out after the terrible things he'd said.

His hands slid around her waist and she tried to push him away, getting dough on his suit jacket.

"I told you not to touch me," she cried. "I knew something like this would happen. Here, I'll get something to clean that."

"There's only one thing I want," Blake murmured softly, pulling her back into his arms. His mouth settled hungrily over hers.

Caasi's soft body yielded to the firm hardness of his without a struggle. His arms tightened around her waist until every part of her came into contact with him. For pride's sake, Caasi wanted to struggle, but she was lost in a swirling vortex of emotion. She could feel the hunger in him and knew her own was as strong.

His teeth gently nibbled on her bottom lip, working his way from one corner of her mouth to the other. Caasi wanted to cry at the pure sensuous attack. No one had ever kissed her like that. What had she missed? All these years, what had she missed? Her breath came in quick, short gasps as she broke out of his arms. Tears filled her eyes until he became a watery blur.

"Don't," she whispered achingly and jerked around, her back to him as she placed her hands on the counter to steady herself.

His ragged breathing sounded in her ear as he placed a comforting hand on her shoulder. "That's the problem," he said quietly. "Every time I touch you it nearly kills me to let you go. Someday you won't send me away, Cupcake."

"Don't call me that. I told you before not to call me that."

The phone rang and she glanced at it guiltily, not able to answer it with her dough-covered hands.

"Aren't you going to answer it?" Blake demanded.

She waved a floury hand in his direction.

"Wash your hands. I'll get it for you."

Because the water was running in the sink, Caasi didn't hear what Blake said or who was on the line.

"It's someone by the name of June. She sounded shocked that a man would answer your phone."

Caasi threw him an angry glare and picked up the receiver. "Yes, June."

"Who was that?" June demanded in low tones.

"My general manager. No one important." Caasi smiled at Blake sweetly, hoping the dig hit its mark.

"I just got out of the doctor's office and he said that everything is looking great. He also said that I could have someone in the delivery room with me when my time came, and I was wondering if you'd like to be there."

Caasi didn't even have to think twice. "I'd love to, but what about Burt?"

"Oh, he doesn't mind. I can have two people with me, and I wanted you to be one of them."

"I'm honored."

"I'm going to be touring the hospital facilities on Friday. Could you come?"

"Yes, that shouldn't be any problem. I'll phone you in the morning once I've had a chance to check my schedule."

"I'll let you get back to that unimportant, sexy-sounding manager."

Caasi laughed lightly, knowing she hadn't fooled her intuitive friend. "Talk to you tomorrow," Caasi promised and hung up.

When she returned to the kitchen, she discovered that Blake had taken off his jacket, rolled up his sleeves, and was placing the pie crust into the pan with the ease of an expert.

"Just what do you think you're doing?" she demanded righteously.

"I figured you couldn't possibly eat all this yourself and you'd probably want to invite me to dinner."

"You have a high opinion of yourself, Blake Sherrill."

His boyish smile would have disarmed a battalion. "And if you plan to invite me to dinner, the very least I can do is offer a hand in its making."

Five

"Well, don't just stand there," Blake insisted. "Beat the eggs."

Caasi hesitated, her feelings ambivalent. She wanted to tell Blake to leave, to get out of her life. He had hurt her in a way she had never expected. But at the same time he had awakened her to what it meant to be a woman, and she wanted him with her. He made her laugh, and when he touched her she felt more alive than she had in all her twenty-eight years.

Not fully understanding the reasons why, Caasi decided to swallow her pride and let him stay. She took the eggs and cracked them against the side of the bowl one by one. Silently they worked together. Caasi whipped the eggs until they were light and frothy while Blake chopped onion and green pepper and sliced zucchini.

"I'm going to the hospital Friday," Caasi mentioned casually.

Blake paused and turned toward her. "Is something wrong?"

"No," she assured him quickly. "It's one of the most natural things in the world. Babies usually are."

A stunned silence crackled in the tension-filled room. "Did you say 'baby'?"

Caasi was enjoying this. "Yes," she murmured without looking up, pouring the milk into the measuring cup.

"Are you trying to tell me you're pregnant?" Blake demanded.

Caasi had trouble keeping a smile from forming. "I'm not trying to tell you anything. All I did was make a casual comment about going to the hospital Friday."

"Because of a baby?"

Caasi nodded. She could see the exasperation in his expression.

Blake's eyes raked over her, and she noticed the way the paring knife was savagely attacking the green pepper. "Who's the father?"

"Burt."

"Who's Burt?"

"June's husband."

"But that was June on the phone and…" Blake stopped in midsentence, as comprehension leapt into his eyes. "You little tease," he said deeply, "I should make you pay for that."

"Tease? Me?" Caasi feigned shock. "How could you accuse me of something like that? You have to remember, I'm not a real woman, with real blood."

Blake linked his arms around her waist and nuzzled her neck. "I don't know, you're becoming more woman-like by the minute."

"You think so, do you?" A throb of excitement ran through her at his touch. Fleetingly Caasi wondered why she hadn't experienced these sensations with other men.

"Yes, I do." He turned her into his arms, linking his hands at the small of her back. Hungrily, his gaze studied her.

Caasi gave a nervous laugh and broke free. These feelings Blake was creating within her were all too new, too strong. They frightened her.

"I want you to know," Caasi began, taking a shaky breath, "I thought about what you said at the dance—about having ink in my veins."

A silence seemed to fill the small kitchen. "And?" Blake asked her softly.

"And I think you're probably right. Ever since Dad died, I've been so busy with Crane Enterprises that I've allowed that role to dominate my life." She slipped the onion and other vegetables he had chopped into the egg mixture and poured it over the thinly sliced zucchini already in the pie crust. "June and Edie tried to tell me the same thing," she said and gave a weak laugh. "Edie said what I needed was an affair."

"An affair," Blake repeated slowly, his dark eyes unreadable. "So that's what this is all about."

"What?"

"You heard me. What happened then? Did you suddenly look at me and see the most likely candidate?" His words went cold.

"Of course not. I thought Edie was nuts. I'm not the

type of woman who would have an affair. Do you honestly think I'd do something like that?"

"Why not? I won't be around much longer. You can have your fling and be done with me."

Words momentarily failed her as she struggled to control her outrage. "Why do you do this to me? I started out by telling you that you were right in what you'd said about me and suddenly I'm on the defensive again." One hand gripped the oven door, and she knotted the other until the long nails bit into her palm. "June and Edie had noticed that I have no life except the business. All I'm saying is that I'm trying to change that." Irritated with her inability to explain herself in simpler terms, Caasi walked across the suite to stand in front of the large picture window. Her arms hugged her stomach. These changes made her vulnerable to Blake? If these changes only brought pain, then she wanted no part of it.

He came to stand beside her but made no attempt to touch her. "Have you noticed how we can't seem to be together anymore without disagreeing about one thing or another?"

"Oh, yes, I've noticed." Her hands dropped to fists at her side.

"By all rights you should throw me out."

Caasi knew that, but she didn't want him to leave. He might have the power to wound, but just as strong was his ability to comfort and heal.

"I can't do that." A wry smile twisted her mouth. "You made half the dinner." It didn't make sense, Caasi realized, but she wanted him there, liked having him around.

"Truce, Caasi?" His voice was soft and gruff at the same time.

"For how long?" They hadn't gone without fighting for more than a few minutes lately.

"Just tonight. We can get through one night without arguing."

Caasi resisted the temptation to slip her arms around him. "Working together, we can manage it." They'd been a team for years—but soon that, too, would change. The thought was a forceful reminder that Blake had turned in his resignation and would be leaving her soon. She wondered if she'd ever see him again after he left the Empress. The realization that she might not produced a painful sensation in the area of her heart. Blake had always been there. She relied on him. Nothing would be the same after he left. But she couldn't mention that now. Not when they'd agreed on a truce. Every time she said something about him leaving, they argued.

"The quiche has to bake for an hour. Would you like to listen to some music?"

"And have a glass of wine."

Caasi kept a supply of her favorite Chablis available and brought down two crystal glasses. While she poured, Blake reached for his phone.

Music filled the suite as Caasi brought their drinks into the living room.

Blake sat on the couch, holding out his arm to indicate he wanted her at his side. Caasi handed him the wine and sat next to him on the plush leather sofa, leaning her head against his shoulder. A hand cupping her upper arm kept her close. Not that Caasi wanted to be anyplace else.

The music was mellow and soft, the ballad a love song. Oftentimes, after a long day, Caasi would sit with her feet propped up on the coffee table, close her eyes, and let the music work its magic on her tired body. But the only magic she needed that night was Blake.

"June asked me to go into the delivery room with her when her baby is born," Caasi said, elaborating on the earlier conversation. "That's why I'm going to the hospital this Friday. They want to familiarize the three of us with the procedures."

"Three of you?"

"Four, actually," Caasi said, correcting herself. "Burt, June, baby, and me."

"You're sure you want to do this?" Caasi felt his gaze wandering over her as if in assessment. "From what I understand, labor is no picnic, and for someone who's never had a baby it may be more than you can handle."

Caasi stiffened, biting back angry words. "I want to be there and nothing's going to stop me."

Blake glanced at his wristwatch. "Twenty minutes."

"What's twenty minutes?"

"How long we lasted without arguing."

"We didn't fight. I was tempted, but being the mature woman I am, I managed to avoid telling you that I found that remark unnecessarily condescending."

Blake chuckled and took a sip of his wine. "I'm glad. Because then I can admit that sometimes I say things purposely just to see the anger spark in your eyes.

You're beautiful when you let that invisible guard down, and sometimes anger is the only thing that lowers it."

Every part of her was conscious of Blake. Pressed close to his side, she ached for the urgent feel of his arms around her and the hungry taste of his mouth. But their truce wasn't limited to arguments, although they hadn't stated as much. They needed to find a level plane, a happy medium between the fighting and the loving.

"I'm working to change that about myself," Caasi admitted softly. "When Dad was in charge he was firm in his belief about mixing business with pleasure. When he was in the office he was one man and outside the office, another. In some ways I'm a lot like my father. We've worked together five years, Blake, but I never saw you as anything more than my general manager."

"And you do now?"

Her voice was becoming huskier as she strove to keep the emotion out of it. "Yes."

"Because I'm leaving?"

"Say…" She laughed shakily. "Why am I doing all the talking? Shouldn't you make some deep revelation about yourself?"

Blake's answering grin was dry. "I like fine wine—" he raised the glass to his lips and took a sip "—and the challenge of climbing mountains. I love the Pacific and enjoy walks along the beach in the early hours of the morning before the sun rises. Sometimes when the mood comes over me, I paint." He paused. "Does that satisfy your curiosity?"

"In some ways." But he didn't offer to reveal more, and the point was well noted.

The timer on the stove rang and Caasi reluctantly broke from his arms. "I'll check our dinner."

She set the quiche on top of the stove to cool and returned to the living room. Blake was looking out the window at the view.

"Some nights, especially when things are troubling me," Caasi admitted softly as she joined him, "I'll stand here and think."

"So that's why there's a worn spot in the carpet," Blake teased.

"I've been here frequently of late."

"Why?" Blake turned and took a step toward her. Only a few inches separated them.

Caasi lowered her gaze to the floor and shrugged. "Lots of things."

"Anything in particular?"

She ignored the question. "The quiche is ready if you are."

Blake brushed a strand of hair from her face. When his hand grazed her cheek, Caasi was forced to stifle an involuntary gasp of pleasure.

"No," Blake said slowly, his words barely audible. "I'm not ready." His hand worked its way around the back of her neck, his fingers twining into her hair as he brought her mouth up to meet his.

With a small sigh of welcome, Caasi swayed into him, melting against him, her arms reaching instinctively for him. Her response was so automatic she didn't have time to question it.

As his mouth plundered hers, Caasi felt as though

she were on fire, the burning heat spreading down her legs until she was weak and clinging.

This wasn't supposed to happen, they'd promised one another it wouldn't, but they were like two climbers waiting to explore a mountain and would no longer be denied the thrill of the challenge.

Her roaming hands reveled in the feel of the hard muscles and smooth skin of his back. A delicious languor spread through her, and her breath came in sharp gasps.

Blake buried his face in the hollow of her throat and shuddered. "Let's eat," he whispered, and Caasi smiled at the husky timbre of his voice as she realized he was experiencing the same sensations she was.

Neither showed much interest in the meal. Blake commented that she'd done a good job and Caasi was pleased with her efforts, but her mind wasn't on the food.

They hardly spoke, but each intuitively seemed to know what the other was thinking. Caasi wished she had her wine, and without a word Blake stood and brought it to her.

Simultaneously they set their forks across half-full plates, their interest in food entirely gone. Blake stood and held out his hand to her.

Heedless of where he was taking her, Caasi realized she would have followed him to Mars. She placed her hand in his. Blake reached for his phone and once more the music played as he led her back to the sofa.

Caasi slid an arm around him and rested the side of her face close to his heart. Blake rubbed his jaw against the top of her head in a slow, rotating action that was faintly hypnotic. His fingers were in her hair.

Caasi didn't need to look to know that his eyes were closed. This was like a dream, a trance from which she never wanted to wake. The barriers were down.

Caasi didn't know how long he held her. The music had faded long ago, but they made their own. Blake had made that comment to her when he'd given her the dancing lesson, but she hadn't understood him then. Now she didn't even need to close her eyes to hear the violins.

Blake shifted and Caasi was shocked to look at her watch and see that it was almost midnight.

"Walk me to the door," he whispered and kissed the crown of her head, his breath stirring her dark hair.

She nodded, not finding the words to release him readily.

"Our truce lasted," she said softly and added, with a warm smile, "sort of."

"If we're going to fight, let's do it like this. Agreed?" He took her in his arms, gazing down at her upturned face with a warmth that reached all the way to the soles of her feet.

"Yes, I agree." Her hand lovingly stroked his thick, unruly hair. "Are you really going to leave me, Blake?"

He went completely still. "How do you mean?"

Did he think she was asking him to spend the night? If she was honest, she would admit the thought wasn't an alien one. But she had been sincere when she explained that she wasn't one to indulge in casual affairs. She wanted Blake; Caasi couldn't deny it. But she wanted him forever.

"The Empress," she explained. "You're not going to leave, are you?" The minute the words were out she knew she'd said the wrong thing.

Blake looked as if she'd physically struck him. He pulled her arms away, severing the contact. "So that was what this was all about." Impatience shadowed his face.

"Blake, no!" But he wasn't listening as he sharply turned, opened the door, and left.

"There's a Gina Sherrill to see you," Laurie announced over the intercom the following Monday.

"Send her in," Caasi replied. "And, Laurie, could you see to it that we're not disturbed?"

"Of course."

Gina stepped into the office a moment later.

"Hi, Caasi." She looked uncertain, her eyes taking in the expensive decor of the room. "Wow, you've got a great view from up here, haven't you? How do you ever get anything done?"

"It's hard, especially on a sunny day like today when it seems that the whole world is outside this window and ready to be explored."

"We missed you Sunday."

Caasi rolled a pencil between her palms. "I had a previous engagement." The lie was only a small one.

"Everyone likes you, and we were hoping you'd come again."

"I will," Caasi assured her but secretly doubted that she could. Not with Blake in his present state of mind. Another confrontation with him was to be avoided at all costs. They treated one another like polite strangers. Blake had hired his replacement and was training the middle-aged man now. Caasi liked Brian Harris and had recognized almost instantly that she wouldn't have any trouble working with him.

Blake's last day was scheduled for the end of the month, less than ten days away.

"Let's go down to the Blue Room and you can tell me what kind of decorations you want. Are the other women coming?" Caasi asked. Gina had asked to include her maid of honor and bridesmaids in the shower planning.

"They're in the lobby. We didn't feel like we should all descend on you."

"Why not?" Caasi asked, setting the pencil aside. "I'm looking forward to meeting them."

"Blake's leaving, isn't he?" Gina's question came as a surprise.

Caasi nodded with forced calm. "Yes, he handed in his resignation not long ago."

"I'm surprised." Gina wrinkled her nose. "I didn't think Blake would ever leave you."

That was the crux of the problem—Caasi hadn't thought so either.

"Shall we go now?" Caasi wanted to divert the conversation from Blake.

"Sure," Gina answered eagerly.

Riding the elevator down to the lobby Gina announced, "All the invitations have been mailed. Everyone is impressed that the shower's at the Empress. I'm still having problems believing it myself."

"I'm glad to do it." Caasi meant that.

"You'll be there, won't you? I know it's in the middle of the day and everything, but you wouldn't have to stay long and I'd really like everyone to meet you."

Caasi hesitated. There was an important meeting scheduled with some architects the afternoon of the shower, and if past experience was anything to go by, she could be held up for hours.

"I won't make any promises, but I'll see what I can do."

"Great," Gina enthused.

They met the others in the lobby, and the small party took the broad, winding stairs built against a mirrored wall to the second floor where the Blue Room was situated.

"Oh." Gina sighed with excitement. "It's perfect, just perfect."

Caasi stayed only a few minutes longer. She wanted to have some time to herself before she had to leave for a luncheon engagement that was scheduled with the Portland Chamber of Commerce; they would be discussing plans for a basketball players' convention that winter.

Briefly Caasi explained to Gina that she'd ordered the flowers delivered Thursday morning and had asked the chef to provide a sketch of the cake.

"The cake," Gina said happily, "is larger than the one for the wedding."

Glancing at her wristwatch, Caasi sighed. "I've got to run, but I'll see you Thursday afternoon."

"Oh, thanks, Caasi. I can't tell you how excited I am about this."

"To be honest, I'm having as much fun as you, doing it."

Caasi took the elevator back to her office. As the huge doors glided open, Caasi stepped into the wide hallway—and nearly bumped into Blake.

His hands shot out to help her maintain her balance and their eyes clashed. "Are you all right?"

Caasi couldn't take her eyes from his face. For the first time in days there was a faint flicker of something more than polite disregard. Every angle of his jaw was lovingly familiar, and she longed to ease the lines of strain from his eyes and mouth.

"Caasi," he said sharply.

Her eyes studied the floor, and she struggled to maintain the thin thread of her composure. "I'm fine."

He released her slowly. "Will you have time this afternoon to go over the Wilson figures?"

"Yes, that shouldn't be any problem. I'll be back around two."

"Fine," he said in clipped tones. "I'll send Harris into your office then."

"Harris." She repeated the name. She knew the man was replacing Blake, but she had yet to deal with him directly. "Yes." Her voice faltered a bit. "That'll be fine."

Caasi stepped into her office and retrieved her purse. "I'm leaving now."

Laurie looked up at her blankly. The luncheon wasn't scheduled for another hour. "But Mr. Gains is due to see you in twenty minutes."

"Send him in to Blake," Caasi said curtly. "You know where to reach him."

Caasi took the Mercedes, heading east down Sandy Boulevard until she located Broadway. She drove around for several fruitless minutes. It had to be around here somewhere. Finally she recalled seeing that small mom-and-pop grocery and knew she was headed in the right direction. For all her years in Portland, she'd been to Rocky Butte only once. With Blake, the night of his cousin's wedding.

She parked her car in the same area Blake had. The scene was all the more magnificent during the day. The snow-capped mountain peaks of the Cascade range, the flowing Columbia and Willamette rivers, could all be seen from there. Washington State was just on the other side of the Columbia River Gorge, and once powerful Mount Saint Helens was in full view. No wonder Blake loved it up there so much.

The park itself was a different matter. Someone had broken beer bottles against the steps, and Caasi avoided the sharp pieces of glass as she climbed the flights of rock-hewn stairs for the second time. Walking to the parapet, she studied the view again. Faint stirrings of love and appreciation for what lay before her brought an involuntary smile. Caasi, born and raised in Portland, Oregon, was unaware of her city's charm and beauty. A shame, she mused dejectedly.

Caasi sauntered into the office a little after two, having decided to send Harris to the luncheon. Laurie glanced up at her nervously.

"Mr. Sherrill's in your office."

"Thanks, Laurie." Her assistant's tone told her Blake wasn't in a mood to exchange pleasantries.

"Problems, Blake?" she quizzed as she entered.

He swiveled and jammed his hands into his pockets. His gaze hardened. "Gains had the appointment with you. Where were you?"

"Out," she snapped.

"You don't give important people like Gains the brush-off like that. The banker was furious, and with good reason."

Perfectly calm, Caasi sat at her desk and glared at him. "Do you presume to tell me how to run Crane Enterprises now? Criticizing my personal life isn't enough?"

Blake clamped his mouth closed. "You're in no mood to discuss this rationally."

Caasi's laugh was sarcastic and brittle. "This is getting better every minute," she said, refusing to let him talk down to her. "Send Harry in with the Wilson figures, please."

"The man's name is Harris."

The contempt in Blake's eyes was enough to make her cry. Maybe tears would dissolve the lump of loneliness within her. Maybe tears would take away the pain of what Blake was doing. But somehow Caasi doubted it.

Thursday afternoon, fifteen minutes before her scheduled meeting with the architects, Caasi took the elevator to the Blue Room, where Gina's wedding shower was in progress.

She stood in the entry watching the young girl open her gifts. The turnout was a good one, and Caasi recognized several people from Kathleen's wedding.

The bouquets of blue and white flowers harmonized beautifully with the room's decor. The chef had outdone himself with the huge sheet cake.

Gina saw Caasi just inside the doorway and gave a squeal of delight. The young bride-to-be hurried to proudly introduce Caasi to her friends.

Caasi's appearance was only a token one, and she made her farewells, sorry to learn that she'd missed Anne. She would have enjoyed seeing Blake's mother again.

Laurie smiled when Caasi returned to the office. "There was a Mrs. Sherrill here to see you. I told her you'd gone down to the Blue Room."

Caasi smiled sadly. She'd just missed Anne again. But that was the way her life was headed. Always close but never close enough.

She'd barely sat down at her desk when Blake slammed into her office, nearly taking her door off the hinges when he closed it.

"What was my mother doing here?" he demanded.

"Your mother was here because of Gina's shower," Caasi replied calmly.

"Gina's wedding shower?" He was pacing the floor like a caged lion eager for the opportunity to escape and hunt the closest victim.

"Yes. It's in the Blue Room."

"My family can't afford the Blue Room."

"But I can. I'm doing this for Gina."

Blake froze, and his anger burned from every pore. "You did what?"

"I would have said something earlier if we'd been on better terms. Everything I do lately angers you. There are only a few days left until you're free of me. Must you fight me at every turn?"

Blake marched to the far side of the office and raked his hand through his hair. "I want you to add up every cent that this fiasco has cost and take it out of my next paycheck."

"What?" Caasi exploded, bolting out of her chair.

"You heard me. Every cent."

Tears sprang into her eyes, blinding her. She lowered her gaze so Blake wouldn't notice.

"Why?" she asked, amazed that her voice could remain so steady when she felt as though the world was crumbling apart beneath her.

"I told you before that you couldn't buy yourself a family. Least of all mine."

"Yes, of course." She swallowed at the painful hoarseness in her throat. "Now, if you'll excuse me."

She nearly walked into Laurie. "Conference Room A is ready for..." Laurie stopped sharply. "Miss Crane, are you all right? Do you need a doctor?" The woman looked flabbergasted to see Caasi in tears. Hurriedly she supplied Caasi with a tissue.

"Cancel the meeting, Laurie." Her voice trembling, Caasi fought down a sob. "Please extend my sincere apologies." With as much self-possession as she could muster, Caasi walked out of the office.

Blake came up behind her. "Caasi." Her name was issued grimly.

She ignored him and stepped into the elevator. When she turned around their eyes met. The tall, lean figure swam in and out of her vision.

"You have so much, Blake. Is it that difficult to share just this little bit with me?" The huge metal doors swished shut and Caasi broke into sobs that heaved her shoulders and shook her whole body.

Six

Caasi leaned against the penthouse door, her face buried in her hands as her shoulders shook. If this horrible ache was part of being a woman, she wanted none of it. Ink in her veins was preferable to the pain in her heart. But it was too late and Caasi recognized that.

Arms hugging her stomach, she tilted her face to the ceiling to keep the tears from spilling. She was tired. The weariness came from deep within.

Blake was leaving; why shouldn't she? She hadn't been on a real vacation in years, not since she took over Crane Enterprises.

Wiping the moisture from her cheeks, she took a quivering breath and stood at her favorite place by the window. She'd be fine. All she needed was a few days away to gain perspective.

Her leather luggage was stored in the bedroom closet. Caasi wasn't exactly sure where she'd go. It would be fun just to drive down the coast. Oregon had some of the most beautiful coastline in the world.

The soft knock on the door surprised her. Probably Laurie. The secretary had been shocked to see Caasi cry…and little wonder. Caasi wasn't the weeping female type.

"Yes," Caasi called softly, striving to sound composed and confident. "Come in."

When Blake strolled into the living room, Caasi felt ice form in the pit of her stomach. "These are my private quarters," she told him in a voice that was dipped in acid. "I don't know who or what has given you the impression that you may come up here, but that has got to change. Now, get out before I call Security." She marched out of the room and into her bedroom, carelessly tossing her clothes into the suitcase.

"Caasi, listen." There was an unfamiliar pleading quality to his voice as he followed her. "Let me apologize."

"Okay," she said without looking up. "You're sorry. Now leave."

"What are you doing?" His eyes followed her as she moved from the closet to the suitcase, then back to the closet.

"That's none of your business."

"If you're going someplace, I need to know."

"I'll leave the details of my trip with Laurie." She didn't look at him; she was having enough trouble just keeping her composure intact.

"Isn't this trip a bit sudden?"

"Since when do you have the authority to question me?" She whirled around, placing her hands challengingly on her hips.

"Since you started acting like an irrational female," he returned sarcastically.

"Me?" Caasi exploded. "Of all the nerve!" She stormed across the room and picked up the phone. "Security, please."

"I'm not leaving," Blake threatened. "Call out the National Guard, but I'm not leaving until we understand one another."

"Understand?" Caasi cried. "What's there to understand? I'm the boss, you're the employee. Now get out."

"No."

"Yes." Caasi spoke into the receiver. "This is Miss Crane. I'm having a problem here. Could you send up security?" She hung up the phone and tossed Blake a hard look. "Oh, before I forget," she said and gave him a saccharin smile, "be sure and have accounting give you an employee discount on the Blue Room." She slammed the lid of her suitcase closed and dragged it off the top of the bed.

Taking a smaller case, she entered the master bathroom and impatiently stuffed brush, comb, shampoo, hair dryer, and an entire cupboard of cosmetics into it. When she whirled around, Blake was blocking the doorway.

"Will you kindly step out of the way?"

"Not until we talk."

Expelling a long sigh to give the impression of boredom, Caasi crossed her arms and glared at him. "All right, you win. Say what you want to say and be done with it."

Blake looked surprised but determined. He paused and ran his hand over his jaw.

"What's the matter, has the cat got your tongue?" she taunted unfairly.

Confusion flickered across his brow. "There's something about you, Caasi, that makes me say and do things I know are going to hurt you. Yet I do them."

"This is supposed to be an apology?" She faked a yawn.

Blake's thick brows drew together in a pained, confused expression. Caasi doubted that her feigned indifference could create a fissure in the hard wall of his defenses.

The phone rang, diverting her attention to the other room.

"If you'll excuse me."

"No, not now." His arm across the door prevented her from leaving.

"Blake." She groaned in frustration. "This is ridiculous. Look at you. Now, for heaven's sake, will you let me out of the bathroom so I can answer the phone?"

He didn't budge.

"Please," she added.

Blake dropped his hand and turned his back to her. As she hurried past him, Caasi noted fleetingly that he looked as weary and defeated as she felt.

"Hello," she answered on the fourth ring, her voice slightly breathless.

"Caasi?" The male voice on the other end was only faintly recognizable.

"Burt?" Caasi felt all the blood drain from her face.

"It's June. She's in labor. She said I should phone you now."

"Now?" Caasi repeated with a sense of unreality. "Isn't this early?"

"Only ten days. The doctor assured us it wasn't anything to worry about. I'm at the hospital; the nurse is checking June and said she'd prefer I stepped out for a few minutes." Burt sounded worried and unsure.

"I'll be there in five minutes." Caasi's heart was singing with excitement as she replaced the telephone receiver.

"Who was it?"

Caasi had forgotten Blake was there. "Burt. June's in labor." She grabbed her purse from the end of the bed and hurried out of the suite. A security man met her just outside the door.

"You wanted me, Miss Crane?"

"Yes," she shouted and shot past him to the elevator. "I mean, no, everything's been taken care of. I'm sorry to have troubled you."

"No trouble, miss." He touched the brim of his hat with his index finger.

"Caasi," Blake called as he followed her out of the suite. "I'll meet with the architects and we can talk about it in the morning."

"Fine." She'd have agreed to anything as long as it didn't delay her.

The car engine roared to life when she turned the key. Caasi wondered if June was experiencing this same kind of exhilarated excitement. Burt and June wanted this baby so much and had planned carefully for it. For *her,* Caasi corrected her thoughts. June's deepest desire was for a little girl.

The visitors' parking lot was full, and Caasi spent several frustrating minutes until she found a space on the street. On her visit the previous Friday, she had learned that once Burt phoned she was to go directly to the labor room on the third floor. Stepping off the elevator, her shoes clapped against the polished, squeaky-clean floor.

"I'm Caasi Crane," she announced at the nurses' station. "Can you tell me which labor room Mrs. Kauffman is in?"

The uniformed nurse with white hair and a wide smile glanced at the chart. "Number 304. I believe her husband is with her."

"Thanks," Caasi said with a smile.

The room was the second one on the left side of the hall. The door was closed, so Caasi knocked lightly.

Burt opened it for her, looking pale and worried.

"Is anything wrong?" Caasi asked anxiously.

"No, everything's fine or so I've been assured." He ran his hand through his hair. "June's doing great."

Caasi smiled. "How come you look like *you're* the one in labor?"

"I don't know, Caasi, I can hardly stand to see June in pain like this."

"Caasi?" June looked flushed against the white sheets. "Is that you?"

"I'm here."

"I suppose I got you out of some important meeting."

"Nothing I wasn't glad to escape from," Caasi assured her and pulled up a chair so she could sit beside the bed. "I've read that babies aren't particularly known for their sense of timing."

June laughed weakly. "At least not this one. The pains woke me up this morning, but I wasn't really sure this was the real thing. I didn't want to trouble you if it wasn't."

Burt came around to the other side of the bed and took his wife's hand in both of his. "How do you feel?" His eyes were filled with such tenderness that it hurt Caasi to look at him. Would any man ever look at her like that? The only thing she'd seen in Blake's eyes lately was disdain.

"I'm fine, so quit worrying about me. Women have been having babies since the beginning of time."

Burt looked up at Caasi. "I'll say one thing; having a baby is a lot different than I thought."

Caasi smiled reassuringly. "I don't imagine it's much what June thought either." She glanced down to note that June's face was twisted with pain. Instinctively, Caasi gave June her hand. Her friend gripped it the way a drowning man would a life preserver. The young face relaxed.

"The pains last about thirty seconds, but it's the longest thirty seconds of my life," June whispered.

"The last time the nurse checked, she'd dilated to five centimeters. She has to get to ten centimeters in the first stage of labor."

Caasi had been reading the book the doctor had given her in preparation for the big event. Once June was fully dilated, the second stage of labor, when the baby entered the birth canal, would begin.

"The nurse said that won't be for hours yet," June told her.

"Not to worry, I've got all day. What about you?"

"Well, if the truth be known, I'm missing a big sale at Lloyd Center," June admitted with a weak smile.

The hours passed quickly. Caasi was shocked to look up from timing a contraction to note that it was after seven, and she hadn't eaten lunch. But she was too busy to care about food.

When the hard contractions came, Burt coached his wife, while Caasi, her hand on June's abdomen, counted out the seconds. Time and again Caasi was astonished at her friend's fortitude. June and Burt had decided in the beginning that they wanted natural childbirth, and although the pains were excruciating, June's resolve didn't waver. Burt didn't look as confident.

When the time came to move into the delivery room, Caasi and Burt were asked to don surgical gowns.

"I didn't realize I would have to dress for the occasion," Caasi joked as June reached for her hand.

A small cry slipped from June as the pain crescendoed. As it ebbed, June lay back on the pillow, panting.

Burt carried June's fingers to his lips. Then, tenderly, he wiped the moisture from her brow.

"I love you," June whispered, the soft light of love shining in her eyes.

Strangely, Caasi didn't feel like an intruder on the touching scene; she felt she was a part of it—a wonderful, important part.

"I've never loved you more than I do right this minute," Burt whispered in return.

Another pain came and June bit into her lip with the grinding agony, panting and breathless when it waned.

"One more pain and you should be able to see the head," the doctor told them. A round mirror was positioned near the ceiling, and all eyes focused on the reflection as another pain came and passed. June gave Caasi a happy but weak smile.

The baby started crying once the head was free of the birth canal, the doctor supporting the tiny skull.

"Good pair of lungs," Burt said excitedly. "It must be a girl."

One final contraction and the baby slipped into the doctor's waiting hands.

"It's a girl," he announced.

June gave an exhilarated cry. "Oh, I wanted a girl so badly. Burt…a girl." Laughing and crying at the same time, she threw her arms around her husband's neck, hugging him fiercely.

"Seven pounds, twelve ounces," the nurse said as she lifted the squalling baby from the scale.

Unabashed tears of happiness flowed down Caasi's cheeks. She had never felt such wondrous joy in her life. To have had even a small part in the baby's birth produced warm emotions that touched the softest core of her heart.

"Caasi." June gripped her hand. "You're crying. I don't think I've ever seen you cry."

"It's all so beautiful. And your daughter's beautiful."

"Should I tell her?" Burt looked down with love

at his wife. At June's confirming nod, he glanced up. "June and I decided if we had a daughter we would name her Cassi—two *s*'s, one *a*."

"After a lifelong friend we both love and respect," June added.

Caasi couldn't push the words of love and appreciation past the lump of happiness in her throat.

"And, of course, we want you to be her godmother," Burt continued.

"Of course," Caasi confirmed, tears winding a crooked path down her face.

An hour later, Caasi walked to her car parked on the deserted street. A look at her watch confirmed that it was almost ten. She felt like skipping and singing. Tiny, sweet baby Cassi was adorable, and Caasi couldn't love her any more if she were her own.

Caasi pulled onto the avenue and merged with the flow of traffic. She felt wonderful and rolled down the window, singing as she cheerfully missed the turn that would lead her back to the downtown area and the Empress.

Before she could reconsider, she took the turnoff for Gresham and Blake's house. He'd said something about wanting to talk to her after the meeting that afternoon, but that wasn't the reason she had to see him. If she didn't tell someone about the baby, she'd burst.

There wasn't a streetlight to guide her as she drove down the winding road. She had to pull over to the side of the road a couple of times, having difficulty finding her way in the night. Finally she pulled into the driveway, the old weeping willow the only reminder she required.

The kitchen lights were on, and Caasi paused before climbing out of the car and slowly closing the door. Maybe coming to Blake's wasn't such a good idea after all. They'd been fighting when she left.

The back door opened and Blake came down the steps. "Caasi." He sounded shocked. "Is anything wrong?"

She shook her head. "June had a baby girl."

"That's wonderful. Come inside and I'll make you a cup of coffee."

"I'd like that."

A hand at her elbow guided her up the stairs. The coffeepot was on the kitchen counter. Caasi glanced into the living room and saw an open book lying across the arm of an overstuffed chair. Blake had been spending a quiet evening at home reading.

He handed her a mug and Caasi took it, leaning against the kitchen counter as she hugged the coffee cup with both hands.

"June and Burt are naming her Cassi—two *s*'s, one *a*. She's so beautiful, all pink and with the tiniest hands. She's perfect, just perfect. Before they moved her out of the delivery room, the nurse let me hold her for a few minutes. It was the most incredibly marvelous feeling I've ever experienced, holding this new life. I still can't believe it," she finished breathlessly.

A warm smile appeared on his face and was reflected in his eyes as he watched her. "Come and sit down in the living room. You can tell me all about it."

"I don't even know where to start." She sat in the chair opposite his and lifted the lid from a candy jar nearby, popping a couple of pieces of hard candy into her mouth. "I'm starved. I hope you don't mind if I help myself."

"Didn't you eat dinner?"

Caasi shook her head. "Not lunch either. No time," she explained while sucking the lemon drops. The sugary sweetness filled her mouth, making her hunger more pronounced.

"Let me fix you something."

"No, I'll be fine, really," she asserted.

Blake ignored her, returning to the kitchen and opening the refrigerator as Caasi trailed after him. "There are leftover pork chops, eggs, bacon. What's your pleasure?"

Caasi bit into the side of her mouth to keep from saying: *You.* The thought nearly squeezed the oxygen from her lungs. Never had she wanted a home and husband more than she did at that moment. They even looked like an old married couple, standing in the kitchen, roaming through the fridge and looking for leftovers.

"Caasi?" Blake glanced up, his look questioning.

She shook her head. "Anything's fine. Don't worry about a meal, a sandwich would do as well."

"Bacon and eggs," he decided for her, taking both from the refrigerator and setting them on top of the counter.

Caasi pulled out a chair and sat at the table while Blake peeled off thick slices of bacon and laid them across a skillet.

"June was marvelous," Caasi continued. "She was a real trouper. Burt and June had decided they wanted natural childbirth and she did it. She refused to give up. The doctor tried to encourage her to use the anesthesiologist a couple of times—it would have made his job easier. But June refused." She paused and smiled. "It's a good thing the doctor didn't ask Burt. He could barely stand to see June suffer. Instead of watching, he closed his eyes along with her. Don't get me wrong— he was wonderful too. I don't know how any woman can have a baby without her husband's help. I know I couldn't." Caasi swallowed tightly. But then, she probably wouldn't have a child. Some of the enthusiasm left her and she stared into the coffee mug.

A disturbing silence filled the kitchen.

"The meeting with Schultz and Son went fine. But they'd like you to make a trip to Seaside next Tuesday, if you can."

"I don't see why not." Eagerly Caasi picked up the conversation. "I don't remember that anything's scheduled. I'll check with Laurie in the morning." Her index finger made a lazy circle on the tabletop. "Will you be coming?" Blake sometimes traveled with her, depending on the circumstances.

"It looks as if I'll have to. We'll leave Harris in the office, which will be good experience for him."

"Sure," she agreed, feeling somewhat guilty. Not once in the past week had she made an effort to meet or talk to Brian Harris. The man only served to remind her that Blake was leaving, and she hadn't accepted that. *Couldn't* accept it. Not yet.

The bacon grease was sizzling in the frying pan when Blake cracked two eggs against the side and let them slide into the hot fat. With the dexterity of an accomplished chef he flipped down the toaster switch.

"Hey, I didn't realize you were that skilled in the kitchen," Caasi murmured, uneasy with the fact that he could cook and she couldn't.

"Practice makes perfect, and I've cooked plenty of solitary meals in my time," he said as he slid the fried eggs onto a plate. He set the meal in front of her and straddled a chair, drinking his coffee while she ate.

Everything was delicious and she said as much. "I don't remember a time I've enjoyed a meal more." At his skeptical look, Caasi laughed and crossed her heart with her finger. "Honest."

"Then I suggest you have a talk with that expensive chef you imported."

Blake had never approved of her hiring the Frenchman who ran the Empress kitchen.

"I'd be willing to do away with the whole kitchen staff if you'd agree to stay."

Forcefully Blake expelled his breath, and Caasi realized that she'd done it again.

Lowering her gaze to the empty plate, she tore a piece of crust from her toast. "That was a dumb joke. I didn't mean it." For once, just tonight, when she was so happy, she didn't want to say or do anything that would start a disagreement.

"Didn't you?" he asked in a low, troubled voice.

Caasi peered at him through thick lashes. "Well, it's

true I don't want you to go, but my reasons are entirely selfish."

"You don't need me anymore."

Oh dear heaven, if only he knew. "I guess not," she agreed reluctantly, "but you've always been there, and it won't be the same when you're gone."

"Sure it will."

How could he sound so casual about leaving the place that had been his second home for eight years? Apparently she didn't mean much to him. Instead of seeking answers to the nagging doubts, Caasi scooted out of her chair and stood.

"I'll do the dishes. Anyone who does the cooking shouldn't have to do the dishes."

"Caasi Crane doing dishes," Blake said mockingly. "This I've got to see."

"Well, just who do you think did them the night we baked the quiche?" she declared righteously. "I am a capable person, Blake, whether you care to admit it or not."

She washed while he dried and put away. Wordlessly they worked together, but it wasn't a strained silence.

When they finished, Caasi noted that it was very late…they both had to be at work in the morning. There wasn't any reason to stay, but she didn't want to go.

"I suppose I should think about heading back," she murmured as she dried her hands on a kitchen towel.

Blake agreed with a curt nod, but he didn't look as though he wanted her to leave either.

Caasi glanced at the oil painting over the fireplace.

"Have you done any artwork lately?" Maybe some small talk would delay her departure.

"Not much to speak of." He shrugged his shoulders. "I'm thinking about concentrating more on my painting after the first of the month."

After the first—when he would no longer be at the Empress and wouldn't be troubled with her anymore.

"Let me know; I'd like to buy something from you."

Blake laughed outright. "I only dabble in art. The Empress displays paintings from some of the best in the country. Those artists would be insulted to have my work hanging beside theirs."

Caasi hadn't been thinking of hanging it in the hotel, but in her suite. It would give her something tangible to remember him by. But rather than admit it, she said nothing.

"We did it," Caasi murmured as they strolled toward her car.

"Did what?"

"Went the whole night, or at least a portion of it, without fighting. That's a record, I think."

"You mentioned my resignation only once."

"I won't admit how many times I've had to bite my tongue," Caasi teased.

"Is my leaving that difficult for you to accept?" Blake leaned against the front of her car and folded his arms across his chest.

Caasi shrugged both delicate shoulders. "Yes," she admitted starkly. "But I'm beginning to understand how selfish I'm being toward you. There's something about having you with me.... I trust you, Blake—sometimes more than I do myself. Looking back, I can see the mistakes I've made in my enthusiasm to live up to Dad's expectations. I allowed Crane Enterprises to become everything to me."

For a long second he looked at her. "But not anymore?"

"I don't know," she admitted honestly. "But I'd do anything if you'd change your mind."

Indecision flickered in his narrowed gaze. "You're handing me a powerful weapon; you know that, don't you, Caasi?"

"You're worth it."

"To Crane Enterprises?"

She nodded. "And me," she told him softly.

He was silent for so long that Caasi wasn't sure if he'd heard her.

"Let me think about it," Blake said. Looking away, he took a deep breath, as if struggling within himself.

"How soon before you can give me an answer?" Her heart was beating double time. If Blake stayed she would have the opportunity to explore the relationship that was developing between them. The thought of losing him now—just when she was discovering Blake, the man—was intolerable.

"I'll let you know by the first of the week."

"Great," Caasi agreed. At least there was a chance.

Seven

Monday morning Caasi strolled into the outer office and greeted her secretary with a cheerful, "Good morning."

Laurie glanced up. A frown drove deep grooves into her wide brow. "Good morning, Miss Crane."

Caasi was sure Laurie didn't know what to think of her anymore. Her secretary probably attributed the wide swings in her moods to Blake's resignation. Not immune to office gossip, Caasi was aware that there was heavy speculation as to his reasons.

Today she would know his decision. How could he refuse her after all that they'd shared recently? How could he walk away from her on a day as gorgeous and sunny as this one? He wouldn't, Caasi was sure of it.

In her office, she buzzed the intercom. "Laurie, would you ask Mr. Sherrill to come to my office when he arrives?"

"I think he's in now."

"Good."

Caasi released the switch and sauntered to the far side of the room. So much had changed between her and Blake in such a short time. Mostly there was Blake to thank for that. And he'd see that she was changing and that would be all the incentive he'd need to stay.

Friday she'd watched him, studied his body language as well as his speech. He didn't want to leave, she was sure of it. Her father had warned her of the hazards of being overconfident, but she didn't feel the necessity to heed his counsel this morning. Not this glorious morning.

Caasi had spent Sunday with June, Burt, and baby Cassi. June had come home from the hospital, and while Burt had fussed over his wife, Caasi had sat and held the baby. Cradling the tiny being in her arms had filled her heart with love. This was what it meant to be a woman, whole and complete. The overwhelming tenderness she'd experienced holding the baby lingered even now, a day later.

Sunday night Caasi had lain awake staring at the ceiling, unable to sleep. So much depended on Blake's decision. Her father had taught her to hope for the best but plan for the worst. She'd asked herself over and over again what would change if Blake decided to leave. Ultimately nothing. Brian Harris seemed capable enough of assuming Blake's duties.

But losing Blake the man would be more than Caasi could bear. Not now, not when she was just coming into her own. Surely he'd see the changes in her and withdraw his resignation.

"Good morning," Blake said as he entered the room. "You wanted to see me?"

"Yes." Caasi nodded, standing at her desk. One look at Blake and a nauseous feeling attacked her stomach. He looked terrible. "Blake, are you ill?"

"No," he denied with an abrupt shake of his head. "I suspect you want to hear my decision."

"Of course I do," she said somewhat sharply. What she wanted to do was scream at him to say what she needed to hear: the promise that he'd never leave her, that he'd stay with her all her life.

Blake rubbed a hand over his eyes. "This decision hasn't been easy," he said softly.

"I know," she whispered in return. *Dear God,* her mind screamed, *don't let him leave me.*

"I can't stay, Cupcake."

Caasi slumped into her chair, fighting to disguise the effect of his decision by squaring her shoulders and clamping her hands together in her lap. "Why?"

Blake lowered himself into the chair on the other side of her desk. "Not for the same reasons I originally resigned," he explained.

"I see," Caasi replied stiffly. "In other words—"

"In other words," Blake interrupted, "things have changed between us."

"For the better," she inserted, not easily dissuaded. "I've tried so hard."

"Too hard, Cupcake."

Caasi couldn't respond as the continued waves of disappointment rippled over her.

"In light of my decision, maybe it would be best if Brian Harris accompanied you tomorrow."

Somehow, with a determined effort, Caasi managed to nod.

"My last day is Wednesday, but if you think you'd like me to stay a few more days…"

"No." She whispered. "No," she repeated softly a bit more in control of her voice now. "If you've made your decision, then don't prolong the inevitable."

"You're beginning to sound like your father again."

"Again?" Caasi asked with a dry smile. "I've always sounded like Dad. Why shouldn't I? After all, I am his daughter."

"Caasi…" Blake sounded unsure.

"If you'll excuse me, I've got a meeting to attend." She spoke crisply and centered her gaze just past him on the seascape hanging on the wall.

The door clicked and Caasi realized that Blake had left. Taking deep breaths helped to calm her pounding heart. She was stunned, completely and totally shocked.

"Laurie." Her hand was surprisingly steady as she held down the intercom switch. "Do I have anything pressing this morning?"

Her secretary ran down a list of appointments.

"Would you reschedule them at a more convenient time, please? I'm going out for a while."

"Going out?" Laurie repeated disbelievingly. "But there's the meeting with Jefferson at nine."

"I'll be here for that, but cancel everything else."

"The whole day?"

"No." Caasi pressed a hand to her forehead. She was

overreacting. She had to come to grips with herself. "Just this morning."

An hour later Caasi couldn't have repeated one word of the meeting with Jefferson. The accountant seemed to be aware of her lack of attention and called their time short. Caasi didn't return to her office but went directly to the parking garage and took out her Mercedes.

The drive to the Lloyd Center was accomplished in only a matter of minutes. Leaving her car in the underground parking garage, she took the escalator to the second-floor shopping level. Standing at the rail, she looked down at the ice-skating rink situated in the middle of the huge complex.

A sad smile touched her eyes as she watched the figures circle the silvery ice. Most of the skaters were senior citizens, loving couples with their arms around one another as they skillfully glided around the rink. Thirty years from now she could picture June and Burt skating like that. Thirty years from now and she would remain an observer, standing on the outside of life— exactly as she was now.

In the mood to spend money, Caasi went from store to store, buying whatever took her fancy. She bought baby Cassi enough clothes to see her into grade school. She also bought toys, blankets, shoes—whatever attracted her attention. Caasi held up one frilly outfit after another and understood why June had wanted a baby girl.

Returning to the hotel garage, she left instructions for the packages to be taken to her quarters. The last thing she needed was for Blake to see what she'd bought and accuse her of buying herself another family.

Laurie glanced up and smiled when Caasi stepped into the outer office.

"Happy Monday," Caasi said and handed her secretary a small box.

"What's this for?" Laurie pulled the gold elastic ribbon off the box.

"Just a thank you for rearranging the day."

Her announcement was followed by a short gasp of pleasure from Laurie. "Chocolates from How Sweet It Is. But they're fifty dollars a pound."

"You deserve only the best."

For the first time in years, Laurie looked completely flustered. "Thank you, Miss Crane."

"Thank *you,* Laurie," Caasi stated sincerely.

The stack of phone messages was thick. Caasi shuffled through them and paused at the one from Dirk Evans from The International Hotel chain. He'd phoned several times in the past few years, eager to talk to her about acquiring the Empress. International was interested not only in the Portland Empress but also in several others in California and along the Oregon coast.

She stared at the pink slip for several moments while pacing the floor. Pausing at the window, she examined her options. Her father would turn over in his grave if she were to sell. But why did she need the hotels? Why did she need any of this? Even without the hotels she was a wealthy woman. No, the thought of unburdening herself was tempting at the moment, but the Empress was her family, the only family she'd ever known, the only family she would ever know. She couldn't throw that away, not on a whim.

Laurie buzzed and broke into her thoughts. "Call from Edie Albright on line one."

"Thanks, Laurie." Caasi released one button and pushed down another. "Edie, how are you?"

"Fine."

"You don't sound fine. What's wrong?"

"Freddy's in New York and I'm bored. I don't suppose you'd be interested in dinner with me tonight? Nothing fancy. I could come to the Empress if you'd like."

"I'd like it very much. I'm feeling a little down myself." That was a gross understatement, but if she admitted as much they'd both be crying in their salads.

"Great." Edie cheered up immediately. "What time?"

"Any time you like."

Edie paused. "My goodness, you're accommodating today. I expected an argument at the very least. You don't go out that often."

Caasi smiled drily. "And how would you know that?"

"Honestly, Caasi, June and I are your best friends. We know you."

"Apparently not well enough," Caasi couldn't resist adding. "I'll meet you at seven in the main dining room."

"Wonderful. You don't know how much I appreciate this," Edie said with a sigh. "I've got lots to tell you. This pregnancy stuff isn't all it's cracked up to be."

Caasi replaced the receiver a few minutes later and stared into space a while longer. Seeing Edie that night was just what she needed. Her friend, scheming and crazy, had a refreshing way of helping her see the bright side of things. And she'd need a lot of talking to see the pot of gold at the end of the rainbow as far as Blake's leaving was concerned.

The afternoon passed in a whirl of appointments and phone calls. By six Laurie had left, and although there were several items on Caasi's desk that needed her immediate attention, she decided to deal with them Wednesday. The next day she'd be flying to Seaside with Brian Harris to meet with the architects. The time spent with Harris would help her become acquainted with the man. They'd be working closely in the future, and there was no reason to delay knowing one another. *No reason,* her mind repeated, and a curious pain attacked her heart.

Wednesday would be Blake's last day. As she pushed the elevator button, Caasi wondered how or where she would get the courage to relinquish him as unemotionally as possible.

Her living room was filled with packages from that morning's shopping spree. Caasi decided to ignore them until after her bath. She didn't want to keep Edie waiting.

The bathwater was running when there was an abrupt knock on her door.

Caasi wasn't sure it was someone at her door until the sound was repeated. "Just a minute," she called and hurried to turn off the water. She was grateful that she hadn't completely undressed. Grabbing a housecoat, she tied the sash as she walked across the living room carpet.

"I thought I said seven in the dining room," Caasi murmured good-naturedly as she opened the door. Her jaw must have sagged.

"Can I come in?" Blake looked at her, his eyes sparkling with amusement as he surveyed her appearance.

"I… I'm not dressed for visitors," Caasi stammered, her heart pounding wildly.

"Get dressed then, if it'll make you feel more comfortable."

Numbly, she stepped aside, swinging open the door.

"I'll only take a minute of your time," Blake promised with a half smile.

"I think I'd prefer to be dressed even if it is only for a minute," she said. Naturally she was curious as to why he'd come. She wasn't ready to deal with him. Not that night, not after he'd announced his decision. "If you'll excuse me." She turned around and nearly choked. The packages from her shopping spree covered the sofa and chair. She closed her eyes and groaned inwardly. The only thing she could do was ignore them now. If she called Blake's attention to the parcels and boxes that covered the sofa it would only invite comment.

Her fingers shook as she hurriedly donned her blouse, fumbling with the tiny buttons. Stuffing the silk tails into her skirt, she returned to the living room.

"Yes," she said crisply. "What is it?"

Blake turned around with a slightly guilty look. "I'd say this is a little small, wouldn't you?" He held up one of the dresses she'd purchased for June's baby.

"It's not for me," she said stiffly, refusing to meet his laughing eyes.

"I'd guessed as much," he returned seriously. "Is all this for little Cassi?"

Caasi jerked the dress out of his hands and stuffed it back into its paper sack. "That's none of your business," she told him. "And don't you dare..." She paused to inhale a quivering breath. "Don't you *dare* say I'm buying myself a family."

"You *are* their family, Cupcake," Blake said gently.

Caasi jerked her face up and their eyes met. His were warm and oddly indulgent. She wanted to yell at him not to look at her like that. How could he do this when only hours before, he'd told her he wanted nothing more to do with her or the Empress. He was the one who wanted out, not her. Heaven knew she didn't want him to go.

Abruptly, Caasi turned away. "Was there something you wanted to tell me?" she asked in a clipped, businesslike tone.

"Yes." Blake walked to the other side of the room and ran his hand through his hair. "Harris won't be able to go with you tomorrow. His son's involved in a high-school championship baseball game. So it looks like you're stuck with me for one last trip."

Terrific, her mind threw out sarcastically.

Some of her thoughts must have shown in her expression. "Don't look so pleased," Blake chided. "We'll be back by afternoon. I assume after all these years that we can manage to get along for a few hours."

"Sure." The word nearly stuck in her throat, then came out sounding scratchy and weak. "Why not?"

"You tell me," Blake said in a low voice.

Caasi pivoted sharply and walked to her favorite place by the window. "No reason," she said and shrugged her shoulders.

"I'll see you in the morning, then."

Without turning around, she answered, "It looks that way." She stood poised, waiting for the click of the door. When it didn't come, she turned to find Blake watching her.

"Caasi?"

"Was there something else?" she asked politely.

His searching eyes narrowed on her, and Caasi had the impression he wanted to say something more. "No." He shook his head. "I'll see you tomorrow."

"Fine."

Edie was already seated in the dining room when Caasi arrived. Caasi returned her small wave as she entered the room.

"You look positively…" Edie paused and sighed longingly. *"Skinny."*

Caasi laughed. "You always did have a smooth tongue."

"The only reason I'm so candid is that for every ounce you've lost, I've gained three." Elbows on the table, Edie leaned forward. "I'm telling you, Caasi, I'm going crazy."

"What's wrong?" Edie had always been the dramatic one, so Caasi wasn't overly concerned.

"Well, for one thing, I can't stop eating peanut butter. I woke up at two this morning and ate it straight out of the jar. Freddy couldn't believe it and for that matter neither could I."

"At least peanut butter is a high source of protein."

Edie groaned and closed her eyes. "That's what Freddy keeps telling me."

"Why the worry?"

"My dear Caasi, have you any idea how fattening peanut butter is?"

"I haven't checked out any calorie counters lately," Caasi responded and fought to hide the smile that teased the corners of her mouth.

"Well, it's fattening, believe me. The shocking thing is I've hated the stuff since I was a kid."

"There are worse things." Caasi attempted to soothe a few of Edie's doubts.

"Okay," Edie agreed and took a sip from her cocktail. "Listen to *this*. I was watching the Blazers play basketball the other night. The center missed two free throws at the foul line and all of a sudden tears welled in my eyes and I started crying. Not just a few silent tears, but gigantic sobs. Freddy didn't know what to think. He was finishing up a report in his den and came rushing in. I'm sure he thought the telecast had been interrupted and someone had just announced that my mother had died or something."

The small laugh could no longer be contained. "Listen, Edie, I'm no expert on the subject, but isn't this all part of being pregnant?"

"Dear sweet heaven, I hope so," Edie said fervently.

"Have you talked to June? She'd probably be more help than me."

"June," Edie repeated and shook her head dramatically. "You know June; she's the salt of the earth. The entire time she was pregnant she acted as if she was in heaven. June's the kind of woman who would deliver her baby and go back to work in the fields an hour later. *I'm* going to need six months' rest on the Riviera to recover."

The maître d' handed them the menu and gave Caasi a polite nod of recognition.

Edie opened the menu, took one look, moaned, and folded it closed.

"What's the matter?" Caasi asked.

"I was afraid this would happen. Everything looks divine. I want the first four entrées and chocolate mousse for dessert."

"Edie!" Caasi couldn't prevent her small gasp of shock. Of the three, Edie had always been the most weight-conscious.

"I can't help it," Edie hissed.

"If you eat that much, *I'll* get sick."

"All right, all right," Edie said, "you choose for me. I don't trust myself."

The waiter took their order and filled their water glasses.

"Enough about me." Edie took a sip from the steaming cup. "I want to hear what's been going on in your life. I don't suppose you've picked up any tall, dark, handsome men lately, have you?"

Caasi shrugged and looked away uncomfortably. "Not recently. You know I went into the delivery room with June and Burt, don't you?"

"Don't tell me a thing about it. I don't want to hear." Edie shook her head and squinted her eyes closed.

"It was one of the most beautiful experiences of my life," Caasi reminisced softly.

"Sure—it wasn't *you* going through all that pain."

Caasi didn't bother to try to explain. Edie wouldn't understand. At least, not until her own baby was delivered.

"Have you had any thoughts about what I was saying the last time we were together?" At Caasi's blank look, Edie continued, "You know, about having an affair and maybe getting pregnant yourself?"

Caasi nearly choked on her coffee. "Edie, I wish you wouldn't talk like that."

"Maybe not, but it's what you need. I bet you've lost five pounds since the last time I saw you. Believe me when I tell you a man can do wonders."

"Maybe," Caasi conceded, feeling the color seep up her neck.

"I take it that it didn't work out with the hunk you met here the last time?"

Caasi's hands surrounded her glass of water. She stared at the melting ice and felt the cold move up her arm and stop directly at her heart. "No. It didn't work out."

"It was only your first try, so don't let it discourage you. Would you like me to pick out someone else?"

"No," Caasi returned forcefully. "I'm perfectly capable of finding a man myself. If I want one."

"*If?*"

Their dinner arrived, and thankfully Caasi was able

to steer the conversation from Edie's questions to the light banter they normally enjoyed.

After their dinner they decided to visit the lounge although Edie wouldn't drink. The same piano player was at the keyboard and a fresh crowd was gathered around the bar.

The cocktail waitress brought Caasi a drink and Edie cranberry juice. They sat listening to the mellow sounds of a love song.

"Hey," Edie whispered excitedly. "Don't turn around now, but guess who just came in!"

"Who? The Easter Bunny?"

"No," Edie remarked seriously. Her eyes didn't waver. "Mr. Incredible."

"Who?" Caasi whispered.

"The same guy who was here the other night. You remember—you've got to," Edie admonished, her voice dipping incredulously.

Caasi moved her chair so that she could look at the newcomer. She didn't need a second guess to know it was Blake.

Edie's eyes widened appreciatively. "He really is something, isn't he?"

"If you go for that type," Caasi replied with a flippancy she wasn't feeling.

"He's everyone's type," Edie said without taking her eyes off Blake. "Did you notice how every woman here perked up the minute he walked in?"

Caasi certainly had. Her stomach felt as if a hole was being seared through it. The burning sensation didn't lessen when a tall, attractive blonde slid onto the empty stool beside Blake. Caasi's eyes narrowed as the woman leaned close and whispered something to Blake.

"Watch," Edie advised. "This blonde knows what she's doing. You might be able to pick up a few pointers."

Caasi smiled weakly, her fingers linked into a hard fist in her lap. For one crazy moment she felt like screaming in outrage. Blake was hers! But he wasn't, not really—he had made that clear that morning. Rather than watch the exchange between the two, she lowered her gaze to her fruity drink.

"Well, I'll be," Edie murmured unbelievingly.

"What?" Caasi demanded.

"Weren't you watching?"

"No," Caasi whispered, her voice shaking.

"As slick as a whistle, Mr. Incredible gave the blonde the brush-off. I wouldn't have believed it. This fellow is one tough character. Little wonder you didn't have any luck."

"Little wonder," Caasi repeated.

Edie continued to study Blake. "You know, just watching Mr. Incredible I'm getting the distinct impression he's hurting."

"Hurting?" Caasi asked and swallowed tightly.

"Yes. Look at the way he's leaning against the counter. See the way his elbows are positioned? He doesn't want to be disturbed and his body is saying as much, discouraging anyone from joining him."

"Why doesn't he just sit at a table?" Caasi whispered, revealing her curiosity.

"Because that would be an open invitation for company. No, this man wants to be left alone."

"Just because he wants his own company doesn't mean he's eating his heart out."

Thoughtfully, Edie shook her head. "That's true. But he's troubled. Look at the way he's hunched over his drink. He looks as if he's lost his best friend."

Caasi felt Edie's slow appraisal turn to her. "So do you, for that matter."

"So do I—what?" Caasi feigned ignorance on a falsely cheerful note.

"Never mind," Edie murmured thoughtfully.

"I was looking through some travel brochures the other day…." Caasi quickly changed the subject before Edie managed to stumble onto something she could only escape by blatantly lying. "Do you realize I haven't had a vacation, a *real* vacation," she amended, "in over five years? I was thinking of a cruise."

"I'll believe it when I see it." Edie tilted her chin mockingly. "You wouldn't know what to do with yourself with empty time on your hands."

"Sure I would," Caasi argued. "I'd take a few classes. I've always wanted to learn how to do calligraphy. And get back to reading. I bet there are a hundred books I haven't had time to read in the last five years. They're stacked to the ceiling in my bedroom just waiting for me. I'd bake, and learn how to sew, and volunteer some time at the local—" She stopped abruptly at the peculiar look Edie was giving her.

"I can't believe this is Caasi Crane speaking!" Edie looked shocked.

Caasi laughed, hoping to make light of her own enthusiasm and squelch Edie's growing curiosity. "It's been on my mind a lot, that's all."

"What's been on your mind?" Edie asked. "Those weren't things you'd do on vacation. They're things an everyday housewife does."

"A housewife?" She gave Edie a surprised look. "And what's wrong with a housewife and mother?"

"Nothing." Edie was quick to amend her attitude. "Heavens, June's one, and I'll be one shortly. Think about it, Caasi. You, a housewife? A baby on each hip, diapers that need to be changed with dinner boiling on top of the stove. Can you picture yourself in that scene?"

Caasi pressed her mouth tightly closed. She longed to cry out that she'd never wanted anything more. If she could run ten hotels effectively, she could manage a single home. The only condition her mind demanded was that Blake share that loving picture with her.

Her eyes drifted across the room to the dejected figure sitting at the bar. It took everything within her not to go to him. But she couldn't see that it would do any good. She'd bared her heart and he'd rejected her. Just remembering the shock she'd felt at hearing his decision caused her to bite into her bottom lip.

"Caasi?" Edie's soft voice broke into her musings.

Gently Caasi shook her head. "Sorry." She turned her attention back to Edie. "What were you saying?"

Edie's attention was focused in the direction of the bar. "Look who's coming our way," she whispered in shocked disbelief.

Blake strolled to their table and nodded politely at

Edie. "We didn't set a time for tomorrow morning. Is eight too early?"

"Fine." Caasi managed to answer with some difficulty.

"I'll see you then."

Edie looked stunned as Blake turned and walked away. "All right, Caasi Crane," she whispered in a shocked voice, "you've got some explaining to do."

Eight

The whirling blades of the helicopter stirred the early morning air. With her purse clutched under her arm and her head bowed, Caasi rushed across the landing pad. Blake supported her elbow as she climbed aboard.

The volume of swirling sound made conversation impossible, which was just as well. There was little Caasi had to say to Blake. Not anymore. A week before, even less, she would have been excited about this trip with him. It would have been a chance to talk, another opportunity to learn more about this man who had been invaluable to her for the past several years. Now it would be torture to sit beside him and know that the next day he would be walking out of her life.

"Caasi."

Blake's hand against her forearm recalled her from her musings.

"It's not too late. We can make the drive in less than—"

"No," she interrupted him and, closing her eyes,

leaned her head back against the seat cushion. When they'd met at eight that morning, the first thing Blake had done was propose that they drive instead of taking the helicopter. Caasi couldn't understand why he would make such a suggestion. He wasn't any more eager to spend time alone with her than she was to endure the stilted silence that would have existed in the comparative quiet of a car.

When they didn't take off immediately, Caasi opened her eyes and noted that Blake was talking to the pilot. A frown creased his brow before he nodded abruptly and climbed back aboard.

"Is everything all right?" she asked.

"Nothing to worry about," Blake assured her.

A wobbly sensation attacked her stomach as the helicopter rose. To hide her anxiety, Caasi clenched her hands, closed her eyes, and turned her head as if she were gazing out the window.

Blake placed his hand over hers; Caasi sat up and shook her hand free. She didn't want his comfort or assurance or anything else. The day was torture. If he was going to get out of her life, then he should go. Why prolong the agony?

They didn't say a word as Portland disappeared. A small smile flickered across Caasi's face at the memory of Edie's reaction when Blake had stopped at their table the night before. Her friend had been stunned speechless. Caasi couldn't remember a time in all the years they'd known each other that Edie didn't have an immediate comeback.

"You sly fox," Edie had gasped a full minute after Blake had sauntered away from the table.

"Don't get excited," Caasi returned with a nervous smile. "Blake works for me. He's been around for eight years."

Edie shook her head in disbelief. "You have worked with that hunk all these years?"

"His last day is Wednesday." Something in Caasi's voice must have revealed the pain she felt at the thought.

Edie's look was thoughtful. "I noticed something was different almost from the moment you came into the dining room tonight. At first I was sure I was imagining things. Somehow, you're…softer. It's in your eyes, even in the way you walk, if that's possible. You have, my dear, dear Caasi, the look of a woman in love."

Caasi tried to laugh off Edie's announcement. "Who, me?"

"Yes, you!" Edie declared adamantly. "Now tell me, why is Blake leaving?"

Sadly Caasi shook her head. "I don't know. I've tried everything I know to convince him to stay."

"Everything?"

Hot color suffused Caasi's face and she lowered her gaze, unable to meet Edie's probing eyes. "It wouldn't do any good. Blake's mind is set."

"Is there any chance of you two getting together?"

Caasi shook her head, unable to answer with words. A terrible sadness settled over her heart. The pain was as potent as it had been at her father's death. In some ways, the hurt was the same. Blake would be lost to her. Just as she would never have her father again, she would never have Blake.

"What about your baby hunger?" Edie asked.

"My what?" Caasi jerked her head up.

"The last time we were together we talked about you and a baby, don't you remember?"

"Yes, but a baby usually requires a father."

Edie gave a sophisticated shrug. "Not always. You're a successful career woman. You're strong, independent, and financially capable. Any child would be lucky to have you as a mother."

"I can't believe what I'm hearing." Caasi gripped her hands in her lap so that Edie wouldn't see how her fingers were trembling. "You're not really suggesting I get pregnant with Blake's child?"

"Of course I am. He's leaving, isn't he? You want a baby, not a husband. As far as I can see, the setup is perfect."

Even now, with Blake sitting beside her, Caasi couldn't help shaking her head in disbelief at her friend's suggestion. Sometimes it was astonishing that two women so completely different could be such good friends.

An hour later, with a cup of coffee in front of her, Caasi reviewed the architects' plans. The piece of beach was prime property, and Caasi realized how fortunate she was to have obtained it. No, she had Blake to thank for that. He was the one who had handled the negotiations.

Seaside was a tourist town. The economy depended

on the business of travelers. With only a few weeks left until summer and a flux of vacationers, the community was preparing for the seasonal traffic.

The morning passed quickly. Leaving the architects' office, Caasi donned a hard hat and visited the building site. Everything was ahead of schedule; where she had pitched a shovelful of dirt only a few weeks before now stood the empty shell of the latest Empress Hotel.

Caasi walked around, examining each area. Once she would have experienced an intense satisfaction at the venture; now she was surprised to feel nothing. The lack of emotion shocked her. What did she care if there were ten or a hundred Empress Hotels? Would breaking ground for another hotel bring her happiness? Perhaps at one time it would have. But no longer. Blake was responsible for that. He was responsible for a lot of things.

Her smile felt frozen as she entered the restaurant where the chamber of commerce was holding its luncheon.

After they ate, Caasi stood before the group and spoke a few introductory words before turning the presentation over to Blake. As he was talking, Caasi observed the way the men in the room responded to him. In some ways their reactions were like those of the women in the cocktail lounge the night before. Blake was a man's man. The magnetism about him defied barriers.

Caasi's fingers were tender from all the handshaking she'd done by the time they returned to the copter. The pilot, a middle-aged man with a receding hairline, removed his hat as they approached. He shook his head, seeking Blake's eyes.

"Is something wrong?" Caasi asked Blake.

"I don't know, but I'll find out."

Blake and the pilot talked for several minutes and when Blake returned, his jaw was tight, his look disturbed.

"Well?"

"There's something wrong with the chopper. Dick noticed that one of the gauges was malfunctioning when he revved it up this morning. That was why I suggested we drive."

Caasi closed her mouth tightly to bite back bitter words. Blake hadn't been eager for her company that morning. Had she been fooling herself with the belief that he would have enjoyed an intimate drive from Portland?

"How long will it take to check it out?"

"An hour, two at the most."

Unwilling to spend an extra minute in Blake's company, Caasi announced, "I'll wait for you on the beach, then."

Blake didn't acknowledge her as she turned and walked the block or so to the ocean.

Wind whipped her hair about her face as she stood looking out over the pounding surf.

A flight of concrete stairs led to the beach. Caasi walked down to the sand, removed her heels, and strolled toward the water until her nylons felt the moisture.

Once, when she was a little girl, her father had taken

her to the ocean. A business trip, Caasi was sure. Very little in Isaac Crane's life had been done for pleasure. Caasi could recall vividly how the thundering surf had frightened her and how she'd clung to her father's leg.

Funny, Caasi mused, she hadn't thought about that in years. She couldn't have been more than two, maybe three, at the time. The incident was her earliest memory.

Swinging her high heels in her hands, Caasi walked for what seemed like miles, enjoying the solitude, the fresh, salt-scented air, and the peace that came over her. Blake would go and she'd hurt for a time, suffer through the regrets for the love they could have shared. But the time would come when that, too, would pass. And she'd be better for having loved him.

When she turned around to return to the street, she noticed Blake standing at the top of the concrete steps watching her. He was a solitary figure silhouetted against the bright sun, hands in his pockets and at ease with the world. That disturbed her somehow. He was leaving her without a second thought, without regrets, without looking back.

As she neared the steps, Blake came down to meet her. "I just talked to Dick."

"And?" she prompted.

"The problem is more extensive than he thought. It looks as if we'll have to spend the night."

"Spend the night?" she cried in frustration. "I won't do that."

"There isn't much choice," Blake returned with limited patience.

"Rent a car. And if you can't do that, then buy one! I'm not spending the night here."

"Caasi." Blake drew in a slow, angry breath.

"You're still my employee," she said bitterly and glanced at her watch. "For another twenty-three and a half hours I expect you to do what I ask. After that, I don't care what you do."

Caasi regretted the words the minute they slipped out. She watched Blake's struggle to hide his anger. His fists knotted at his sides until his knuckles were white.

"I didn't mean that," she said in a low voice and released her breath slowly. "Make what arrangements you can. I'll phone Laurie and answer any necessary calls from here."

Fifteen minutes later Caasi walked across her hotel room, carrying her cell with her as she spoke. A knock on her door interrupted the conversation.

"Could you hold a minute, Laurie?" she asked before unlocking the door and letting Blake into the rented quarters.

"It's Blake," she said into the receiver. "I'll give you a call in the morning before we leave." She hung up and turned to him. "Yes?"

"I thought you might need a few things." He handed her a small sack that contained a toothbrush and toothpaste.

"Thanks." She smiled her appreciation. "But what I could really use is a good martini."

"Dry, of course."

"Very dry," Caasi agreed.

The cocktail lounge was deserted; it was too early

for the predinner crowd and too late for the business-luncheon group.

It amazed Caasi that they could sit companionably at a minuscule table and not say a word. It was almost as if they were an old married couple who no longer needed words to communicate. Caasi focused her attention on the ocean scene outside the window. The view was lovely, but she had seen so much breathtaking scenery in her life. That day it failed to stir the familiar chord of appreciation.

Without asking, Blake ordered another round of martinis for them. Slowly, Caasi sipped her drink. The bitter liquid seared its way down her throat. The lounge was quickly filling now; after two martinis Caasi could feel the coiled tension ease out of her.

"Are you ready for dinner?" Blake asked.

"Sure," she agreed readily, "why not?"

His hand cupped her elbow as he escorted her into the dining room. The food was good, though not excellent.

"I should have Chef share some of his recipes," Caasi remarked as she set her fork aside.

"You and that chef. I don't know when I was more upset with you than when you imported him."

Caasi's smile didn't quite reach her eyes. "Oh, I can tell you. Several times you've looked as if you wanted to wring my neck, all within the last couple of weeks too."

Blake's expression was weary and he conceded her observation with a short shake of his head.

The soulful sounds of a singer drifted into the dining room from the lounge.

"Shall we?" Blake asked softly.

Caasi couldn't find an excuse to refuse. All there was to do in her room was watch television. "All right," she agreed, somewhat reluctantly. When they reentered the lounge, she saw that a few couples occupied the tiny dance floor, which was little bigger than a tabletop.

They sat for a long time, so close their thighs touched, listening to the music and not speaking. For the first time Caasi admitted to herself how glad she was that the helicopter needed work. The repairs afforded her this last chance to be with Blake. She didn't speak for a long time, fearing words would destroy the moment.

"Caasi."

Their eyes met and she drew a shaky breath at the intensity of his look.

"Dance with me, Blake," she whispered urgently. "Hold me one last time."

He answered her by standing and giving her his hand. They didn't take their eyes from one another as Caasi slid her arms around his neck, her body's movement joining his in a rhythm that was uniquely theirs.

His fingers were pressed against the small of her back as he molded her body to him. His mouth was mere inches from hers as his warm breath fanned her cheek.

The music stopped—but they didn't. If Blake released her now, she'd die, Caasi mused.

She released an uneven breath when the singer

began again. A love song. Caasi bit into the corner of her bottom lip and sighed. Tomorrow Blake would go—but for tonight he was hers.

Caasi lost track of how long Blake held her, how many songs they danced to, barely moving, oblivious to the world surrounding them.

When the music stopped, Caasi led the way off the dance floor, but instead of stopping at their table she continued out of the lounge and down the wide hall to their rooms, which were opposite one another.

Her hands shook as she inserted the key and opened the door to her room. It was dark and silent.

Blake's dark eyes bore into hers as she stepped inside the room and extended her hand to him. A look of indecision passed across his face. Caasi's eyes pleaded with him, and gradually the expression on his face softened as his look became potent enough for her to drown in.

He took one step inside and Caasi released a deep sigh of relief. He couldn't turn away from her. Not now. Not tonight.

She slid her arms around his neck and stood on the tips of her toes as she melted against him.

He groaned her name, reaching out to close the door as she fit her body to his.

She wouldn't let him talk, her open mouth seeking his. He hadn't kissed her in so long, so very long.

"Caasi." He groaned, repeatedly rubbing his mouth over hers. "You don't know what you're doing." His voice was husky and hungry.

"I do," she insisted in a low murmur. "Oh, Blake, I do."

Again and again his mouth cherished hers, eager, hungry, seeking, demanding, giving, taking. The soft, gentle sounds of their lovemaking filled the silence. They whispered phrases of awe as passion took control of their bodies.

Caasi paused long enough to tug the shirt free at Blake's waist. Her eager fingers fumbled with the buttons until she could slip her palms over his chest. The sensations were so exquisite she wanted to cry.

"Caasi, no," Blake whispered gruffly. "Not now, not like this." The shirt fell to the floor.

"Yes, like this," she pleaded. "Only tonight, it's all I want." She felt the tears well in her eyes. Her body trembled wildly against his, and Blake released an anguished groan as he swung her off her feet and carried her across the room.

Caasi wanted him so desperately, she could no longer think. Pressing her face to his neck, she gave him tiny, biting kisses and felt his shudder as he laid her on the bed.

Her arms around his neck, Caasi refused to release him, half lifting herself as she kissed him long and hard, her mouth slanting under his.

His eyes looked tortured in the golden glow of the moon as he pulled her arms from his neck. "Caasi," he whispered in a voice she hardly recognized. "Are you drunk? Is this the liquor?"

"Yes, I'm drunk," she whispered, "but not from the martinis. You do this to me, Blake. Only you."

"This isn't the way I wanted it, but heaven knows I haven't got the strength to let you go," he murmured, his lips above hers. His hands ran down her smooth body, exploring, touching, until Caasi was sure she would die if he didn't take her. She arched against him and sighed with a longing so intense that it sounded like a mournful cry.

Impatiently he worked at her clothing, freeing her from the constricting material. The feel of his hands against her bare skin was an exquisite torture.

"Tonight," she whispered in a quivering breath. "For tonight, I'm yours."

"Yes," he agreed, his mouth seeking hers again.

"I'm freeing you from any...consequences." She stammered slightly.

He froze. For a moment he didn't even breathe. "You're what?" He sat up, holding her away from him, a rough hand against each bare shoulder.

"I'm freeing you from any responsibility," she murmured, confused. What had she said that upset him so much? Wasn't that something a man wanted to hear?

Sitting on the edge of the bed, Blake leaned forward and buried his face in his hands as if he needed time to compose himself.

"Blake," she pleaded in a soft whisper, "what did I say?"

He didn't answer as he reached for his shirt and rammed his arms into the sleeves. Not bothering to fasten the buttons, he started across the room.

"Blake," she begged, "don't do this to me. Please don't do this to me."

He turned to her in the moonlight. She had never seen a man look more upset. His face was contorted with anger, his mouth twisted, his eyes as hard as flint.

Caasi sagged against the bed, closing her eyes against the pain that went through her heart, a pain so deep that it was beyond tears.

For hours Caasi lay exactly as she was, staring dry-eyed at the ceiling. She had offered Blake everything she had to give and he had rejected it all.

Even her makeup couldn't camouflage the dark circles under her eyes the next morning. The mirror revealed pale, colorless cheeks, as if she were recovering from a long illness. Caasi doubted that she would ever recover. Not really. She'd go on with her life, would probably even laugh again, but something deep inside her had died last night. In some respects she would never be the same.

It gave her little satisfaction to note that Blake looked as if he hadn't slept either.

Dick was at the helicopter when they arrived, assuring them that everything was fixed and ready to go.

Blake didn't offer her his hand when she climbed inside, which was just as well, since she would have refused it. They sat as far apart from each other as possible.

The atmosphere was so thick that even Dick was affected, glancing anxiously from one to the other, then concentrating on the flight.

As Caasi ran the bathwater in her quarters back at the Empress, she realized there was nothing about the short flight home that she could remember. The pain of being so close to Blake was almost more than she could bear. Her mind had blotted it from her memory.

Blake had stepped out of the helicopter and announced stiffly that he was going home to change and would be back later to clear out his desk and pack up what remained of his personal items. It was Wednesday. His last day with Crane Enterprises.

Caasi hadn't bothered to answer him but had turned and gone directly to her suite.

Some of the staff had planned a small farewell party for Blake, but she hadn't contributed anything. Not when seeing him go was so painful. There would be an obligatory statement of good wishes she would make. Somehow she'd manage that. Somehow.

A hot bath relieved some of the tiredness in her bones, but it had little effect on her heart.

Dressed in a prim business suit, Caasi walked briskly into the office and offered Laurie a short nod before entering her own.

Her desk was stacked with mail, telephone messages, and a variety of items that needed her immediate attention.

"Laurie," she called to her secretary, "send in Brian Harris."

"Right away."

If the man was there to take Blake's place, she had best start working with him now.

By noon Caasi's head was pounding. She wasn't one to suffer from headaches, but the pain was quickly becoming unbearable.

"Are you all right?" Laurie asked as she came into Caasi's office for dictation.

"I'm fine," Caasi said with a weak smile. She stood at the window, her fingertips massaging her temples as she shot off one letter after another, scarcely pausing between items of correspondence.

Laurie sat on the edge of her chair, her glasses delicately balanced on the bridge of her nose as her pencil flew across the steno pad.

"That'll be all." Caasi paused. "No, get me Dirk Evans of International on the phone."

Laurie returned to her office and buzzed Caasi a minute later. "Mr. Evans is on line two."

"Thanks, Laurie," Caasi said with a sigh. "Would it be possible for you to find me some aspirin?"

"Of course."

"Thanks." Five years since she took over for her father, and this was the first time she'd ever needed anything to help her through the day.

The aspirin had little effect on the pounding sensation that persisted at her temples well into the afternoon.

Laurie came into her office around four to tell her that the farewell party for Blake was in progress.

"I'll be there in a minute," Caasi said without looking up, her fingers tightening around her pen.

Hands braced against the side of her desk, Caasi inhaled deeply, closing her eyes and forcing herself to absorb the silence for a couple of moments before rising and going to join the party.

Someone had opened a bottle of champagne. Caasi

stood on the outskirts of the small crowd and watched as everyone toasted Blake and wished him success. One of the women had made a farewell cake and was serving thin slices. Caasi recognized her as Blake's personal assistant but couldn't recall her being so attractive.

Caasi felt far removed from the joking banter that existed between Blake and his staff. There wasn't one who didn't regret his leaving. Yet he had chosen to do exactly that.

Someone slapped him across the back and he laughed but stopped short as his eyes met hers.

Quickly Caasi looked away. A hush fell over the room as she walked to the center, Blake at her side.

"I think we can all agree that you'll be missed," she said in a voice that was surprisingly steady. "If my father were here I'm sure he would say how much he appreciated the excellent job you have done for Crane Enterprises for the past eight years. I'm sure he'd extend to you his personal best wishes."

"But not yours?" Blake whispered for her ears alone.

Stiffening, Caasi continued somewhat defiantly, "My own are extended to you in whatever you pursue. If there's ever a time you feel you'd like to return, you know that there will always be a place for you here. Goodbye, Blake."

"What? No gold watch?" he mumbled under his breath as he stepped forward and shook her hand. "Thank you, Miss Crane." Those dark, unreadable eyes stared into hers, and Caasi could barely breathe.

Grateful for the opportunity to escape, she nodded

and stepped aside as Blake's assistant approached with a small wrapped package. Hoping to give the impression she was needed elsewhere, Caasi glanced at her watch. "If you'll excuse me, please."

"Of course." Blake answered for the group.

Without another word, she turned and walked away, not stopping until she reached her desk.

Caasi forced herself to eat dinner. For two days she hadn't been able to force down more than a few bites of any meal.

The headache was now forty-eight hours old. Nothing seemed to relieve the throbbing pain. She hadn't slept well either. After several hours of tossing fitfully she would fall into an uneasy slumber, only to wake an hour or two later more tired than when she'd gone to bed.

The phone rang Saturday when she returned from a spot check at the Sacramento Empress.

"Hello," she said, with little enthusiasm.

"Is this Caasi?"

Faintly Caasi recognized the voice over the phone. Her home phone had a private listing and she seldom gave out the number.

"Yes, it is."

"Caasi." The young voice sounded relieved. "This is Gina. Gina Sherrill."

"Hello, Gina. What can I do for you?" Caasi's hand tightened around the receiver. The girl had phoned three times in the last few days, and Caasi hadn't returned the calls. She had completely severed herself from Blake and wanted every painful reminder of him removed from her life.

"I'm sorry to bother you like this, but I haven't been able to get hold of you at your office."

"I've been busy lately." She hoped the tone of her voice would effectively convey the message. She didn't want to be purposely rude to the girl.

"I knew that, and I hope you'll forgive me for being so forward, but I did want to tell you that everyone would like it if you could come to dinner on Sunday."

Everyone but Blake, Caasi added silently. "I'm sure I'd like that very much, but I'm sorry, it's impossible this week. Perhaps another time."

Caasi heard a sigh of disappointment come over the line. "I understand."

Maybe she did, Caasi mused.

"I'd like to talk to you someday when you've got the time."

"I'd enjoy that, Gina, but I really am busy. Thank you for calling. Give my love to your family."

"I will. Goodbye, Caasi."

Caasi heard the drone of the disconnected line sound in her ear. Replacing the receiver, she walked to the window and studied the view of miniature people and miniature cars far below.

Someone knocked on her door, and she wanted to cry out in irritation. Why couldn't people just leave her alone? Everything would be fine if she could have some peace and quiet in her life.

"Just a minute," she answered shortly as she strode across the floor. She opened the door to discover...

Blake. Her heart leapt into her throat, and she was too stunned to move.

"I hope you haven't eaten yet. By the way, where were you all afternoon?" he asked as he walked past her into the living room.

Nine

"Where was I?" Caasi repeated, nonplussed. What was Blake doing here? Hadn't he left her, decided to sever his relationship with her and Crane Enterprises?

"Yes—I've been trying to get you all day."

Her hand on the doorknob, Caasi watched his relaxed movements as he sauntered to the sofa, sat back, and positioned his ankle on his knee.

"I do have a business to run." She hated the telltale way her voice shook, revealing her shock.

"Yes, but it wasn't business that kept you out. I know, because I checked."

"You checked?" Caasi demanded. "Then I suggest you question your sources, because it most certainly *was* business."

"Instead of standing all the way over there and arguing, why don't you come and sit with me?" He held out his hand invitingly. "I certainly hope you're hungry, because I'm starved."

Caasi closed the door but didn't sit with him as he

requested. Instead she walked to the window, her arms cradling her waist.

"What you're wearing is fine," he assured her. "Don't bother to change."

Her gaze shot to him. The friendly, almost gentle light in his eyes was enough to steal her breath. His ready smile was warm and encouraging.

"I thought you wanted out of Crane Enterprises."

"I did."

"Then why are you here? Why come back? Don't you know how hard it was for me to let you walk away? Are you really that insensitive, Blake? I don't want you flitting in and out of my life when the mood strikes you. I haven't seen you in…"

"Three days," he supplied. "I know. I wanted you to have time to think things through, but I can see you haven't figured anything out yet."

Caasi's hands became knotted fists and fell to her sides. "I hate it when people play these kinds of games with me. If you have something to say, then for the love of heaven just say it."

Blake released a frustrated sigh. "Are you really so dense you can't see?"

"I don't need to stand in my own home and be insulted by you, Blake Sherrill." She stalked across the room and opened the door. "Perhaps it would be best if you left."

"Caasi." A hint of anger reverberated in his husky voice. "I didn't come here to argue."

"Well, you seem to be doing a bang-up job of it."

He stood and rammed his hands into his pockets.

He strode to the window, his back to her as he gazed at the panorama.

Caasi could see and feel the frustration in the rigid set of his shoulders. She didn't want to fight. The desire to walk to him and slip her arms around his waist and press her face to his back was almost overwhelming. The headache that had persisted since Blake left was her body's method of telling her how miserable she had been without him.

A hundred times since Wednesday she'd had to stop herself from consulting him, remembering that Blake was no longer available to ask. Softly she exhaled and closed the door.

At the sound of the click, Blake turned around. "Can we start again, Cupcake? Pretend I'm an old friend who's come to town for the weekend."

Caasi lowered her gaze. "Don't call me Cupcake," she murmured stiffly. "I'm not a little girl. That's the last way I want you to think of me."

The sound of his robust laugh filled the room. "There's no worry of that."

Indecision gripped Caasi. All her life she'd been in control of every situation. She had always known what to expect and how to react. But not with Blake and this new ground he seemed to want to travel with her. Of one thing Caasi was sure: she couldn't tolerate much more of the pain he inflicted when he walked away.

"Dinner, Caasi?" His arched brow contained a challenging lift.

Her compliant nod was as weak as her resolve. She

would accept what little Blake was willing to offer and be grateful.

His smile crinkled the lines at his eyes. "Come on. I've got fat steaks ready for the barbecue."

Caasi took a light jacket out of the closet. "Where are we going?"

"To my place."

"Your place?"

"Then after dinner I thought we'd try our luck at the horse races."

"Horse races?" she repeated.

Blake looked around, stared at the ceiling, and shook his head. "This room seems to have developed an echo all of a sudden."

Caasi smiled. It was the first time she could remember smiling since Monday, when Blake had announced he would be leaving her and Crane Enterprises.

They rode in his T-Bird convertible with the top down. The wind ruffled her sleekly styled curls, and Caasi closed her eyes to savor the delicious sensations that flowed through her. She was with Blake, and it felt right.

The barbecue could be seen in the backyard, a bag of briquets leaning against its base, when Blake pulled into the driveway. He came around and opened her car door for her. Leaning over the rolled-down window, he lightly brushed his mouth across hers. He straightened and his eyes looked deeply into hers. With a groan his arms surrounded her, half lifting her from the car as she arched against the muscular wall of his chest. Caasi slipped her arms around his neck and surrendered fully to his kiss. Gradually his grip relaxed and he tenderly brushed the tangled hair from her temple. "I've missed you."

Still caught in the rush of emotion he could evoke, Caasi didn't speak. A happy smile lifted the corners of her mouth in a trembling smile. "I've missed you too."

"I'll cook the steaks if you fix the salad. Agreed?"

Eagerly, Caasi nodded. He helped her out of the car, his arm cupping her shoulders as he led her up the back stairs and into the kitchen.

"I'll get the barbecue going and leave you to your task," he instructed.

Almost immediately he was out the back door. Taking off her jacket, Caasi draped it over a chair and looked around. She really loved this house. A gentle feeling warmed her. Any woman would be proud to be a part of this.

The ingredients for the salad were in the refrigerator, and she laid them on the counter. Next she searched through the cupboards for a large bowl. A salad shouldn't be difficult, she mused happily. Her culinary skills were limited, but a salad would be easy enough.

She was at the cutting board chopping lettuce when Blake came back for the steaks and a variety of spices.

He paused, watching her as she slid the knife across the fresh lettuce.

"Is something the matter?" She tensed and looped a strand of hair behind her ear. What could she possibly be doing wrong in making a salad? It was the simplest job he could have given her.

"No. It's just that it's better to tear apart the lettuce leaves instead of cutting them."

"Okay." Feeling incredibly naive in the kitchen, Caasi set the knife aside.

"Did you wash it?" Blake asked her next.

Caasi swallowed at the painful lump that filled her throat. With tight-lipped grimness she answered him with a negative shake of her head. Dumping the cut lettuce into the bowl, she carried it to the sink and filled the bowl with water. Pure pique caused her to pour dishwashing liquid over the green leaves. "Like this?" She batted her long lashes at him innocently.

Not waiting for his reaction, she moved into the living room and stared sightlessly out the front window. A hand over her mouth, she took in several deep breaths. What was she doing here with Blake? This wonderful homey scene wasn't meant for someone like her. She was about as undomesticated as they came.

The sound of footsteps told her Blake had moved behind her. His hand on her shoulder sent a silky warmth sliding down her arm.

"I apologize," she whispered. "That was a stupid thing to do."

"No—I should be the one to apologize." The pressure of his hands turned her around. Gently he pulled her into his arms, his chin resting against the top of her head.

"It's just that I'm so incredibly dumb." Her voice was thick with self-derision.

"You, stupid?" Soft laughter tumbled from his throat, stirring the hair at the crown of her head. "Maybe you won't be competing in the same class as Chef, but not because you lack intelligence. You've just never learned, that's all."

"But will I ever?"

"That's up to you, Cupcake."

Caasi winced. "You're using that name again when I've asked you repeatedly not to."

He didn't comment for several tense moments. "I don't think I'll ever forget the first time I saw you. I'd been working with your father for several months. Isaac didn't talk much about his private life. I think I was at the Empress six months before I even knew he had a daughter. We were in his office one day and you came floating in as fresh as spring and so breathtakingly beautiful I nearly fell out of my chair." He stopped and gently eased her away so that he could look at her as he spoke. "I watched this hard-nosed businessman light up like a sparkler on the Fourth of July. His eyes softened as he held out his arms to you and called you Cupcake. I've never thought of you as anything else since."

"I was only twenty."

A finger under her chin lifted her face to his. "The amazing part is that you're even more beautiful now." Ever so gently, he placed his mouth over hers.

No kiss had ever been so incredibly sweet. Caasi swayed toward him when he released her and sighed with all the love in her heart. "I hope you've got another head of lettuce. I'm afraid I've ruined the first one."

"I'll start cooking the steaks now." He kissed her on the tip of her nose and released her. "How do you want your steak cooked? Rare?"

"No, medium."

Blake looked dissatisfied. "You honestly should try it cooked a little less sometime."

"Blake." She placed her hands on her hips and shook her head. "We seem doomed for one confrontation after another. I happen to prefer my meat medium. If you'd rather, I can cook my own."

"I'd like to see that."

"Steak," she asserted, "I can do. There's nothing to it but flopping it over the grill a couple of times."

"It's an art."

"You overrate yourself," Caasi insisted. "How about I cook the steaks and you make the salad?"

Blake chuckled, shaking his head. "I hate to see good meat wasted, but it'll be worth it just to prove my point."

Caasi was in the backyard readjusting the grill so that it was closer to the fire when Blake walked out.

"I thought you were making the salad."

"I did," he said teasingly, his eyes twinkling. "I slapped a hunk of lettuce on a plate, added a slice of tomato, and poured dressing over the top. What's happening to my steak is of much more interest to me."

"On second thought..." Caasi moistened her dry lips. "I'd hate to ruin your meal. Why don't we each cook our own?"

"That sounds fair," Blake agreed with a smile.

The thick steaks sizzled when placed across the grill, flames curling around the edges of fat.

"Who lowered this? It's too close to the fire," he said irritably.

Guiltily, Caasi handed him the pot holders she was holding. "Sorry," she muttered.

Blake didn't look pleased. He obviously took his barbecuing seriously. He'd flipped his steak over before Caasi had a chance to add salt and pepper to hers.

When he lifted the barely warmed meat from the grill, Caasi dropped her jaw in disbelief. "That couldn't possibly be done."

"This is a rare steak."

"That's not rare," she declared with tight-lipped insistence. "It's raw. A good vet would have it back on its feet in fifteen minutes."

What had been a light, teasing air was suddenly cold and sober.

"You cook your meat the way you like it and I'll have mine my way. As far as I can see, you're not in any position to tell me what's right or wrong in the kitchen."

Caasi felt the color drain out of her face. Quickly she averted her eyes.

"Caasi," Blake said, forcefully expelling his breath. "I didn't mean that."

"Why not?" She gave a weak smile. "It's true. You go and eat. I'll join you in a few minutes."

Caasi ate little of her dinner and noted that Blake didn't either. Her steak was burned crisp around the edges and was far more well-done than she normally enjoyed. The whole time they were eating she waited for Blake to make some sarcastic comment about her cooking. She was grateful that he didn't.

Blake didn't say anything when she left the table and took her plate to the sink. The bowlful of sudsy lettuce leaves was there to remind her of her childish prank. This new relationship Blake apparently wanted to build wasn't going to work; she couldn't be with him more than ten minutes without fighting. She didn't know how to respond to him on unfamiliar ground. Crane Enterprises had been a common denominator, but now that was gone.

Gathering the wilted greens in her hands, she dumped them into the garbage.

"You could use the disposal instead of…"

"I think I've had enough of your 'instead ofs' to last me a lifetime." She made a show of glancing at her watch. "On second thought, maybe we should forgo the races for another time."

"I couldn't agree with you more," he snapped. He stood abruptly, almost knocking over his chair in the process. Pointedly he took the car keys from his pocket.

They didn't say a word during the entire drive back to the Empress. Caasi sat upright, her arms crossed determinedly in front of her. The entire evening had been a fiasco.

Blake pulled up to the curb in front of the hotel. His hands clenched the steering wheel as he stared straight ahead. "We need to talk, but now isn't the time. Neither one of us is in the mood for a serious discussion."

Caasi released a pain-filled sigh. "What do you want from me, Blake? When you worked for the hotel I knew exactly where we stood, but now all I feel is an uncertainty I can't explain." She watched as Blake's hand tightened on the wheel until his knuckles were white.

"You haven't figured it out yet? After all these years

you still don't know, do you?" He was so angry that Caasi knew any kind of response would only fuel his irritation. "Maybe it is too late, maybe you're so impossibly wrapped up in Crane Enterprises that you'll never know." A resolute hardness closed over his features.

She'd barely closed the car door before he drove away. As the car sped down the street, she stood alone on the deserted sidewalk. Blake was always leaving her.

Later that night, as she lay in bed staring at the dark ceiling, Caasi thought about his parting comment. Obviously she had been horribly wrong not to recognize his motives.

Rather than suffer through another day of self-recrimination over her relationship with Blake, Caasi drove to June and Burt's on Sunday afternoon.

"Welcome," June said and gave Caasi a hug after letting her in the screen door. "I'm glad you came. The first pictures of Cassi have arrived. You wouldn't believe how much she's changed already."

"Sure I would." Caasi walked into the house and handed June a small gift she'd picked up for the baby while in Sacramento.

"Caasi," June protested, "you've got to stop buying Cassi all these gifts. Otherwise, she'll grow up and not appreciate anything."

"Let me spoil her," Caasi pleaded and lifted the sleeping baby from the bassinet. "She's probably the closest thing I'll ever have to a daughter. And I love her so much, it's hard not to."

"I know." June sighed and shook her head in defeat.

"But try to hold it down. There isn't any more room in her bedroom to hold all your gifts."

"I hope that's not true."

"Almost," June said. "She's due to wake up any minute and will probably want to eat. I'll get you a cup of coffee now. Burt's working in the back, building one of those aluminum storage sheds."

Cradling the sleeping baby in her arms, Caasi sat in the rocking chair. Her eyes misted as she watched the angelic face. It never failed to materialize, the powerful, overwhelming surge of love she experienced every time she held this child. If this was what she felt with June's baby, how much more would she feel for her own? The question had been on her mind ever since her dinner with Edie. What had Edie called it? Baby hunger. But it was more than that, far more than a passing fancy because her two best friends were having children. When June and Edie had married she hadn't had the urge to go out and find herself a husband. These feelings were different.

A home and family would be worth more than all the accumulated riches of Crane Enterprises. Her father had worked himself into an early grave, and for what reason? All those years he had slaved to build a fortune for her. But she didn't want wealth. The greatest desires of her heart were for a simple life. A home and family, maybe a dog or two. Certainly, money alone couldn't provide all that.

The baby stirred and, opening her tiny mouth, arched her back and yawned.

"Diaper-changing time," Caasi announced as she

carried little Cassi into the bedroom and laid her across the changing table. Within a matter of minutes Caasi handed the baby to her mother.

June sat in a rocking chair and unbuttoned her blouse to nurse. "Every time I see you with the baby I'm amazed at how natural you are with her," June said as she smoothed the soft hairs away from her daughter's face. "To be honest, I was afraid you wouldn't do well around children, but I was wrong. You're a natural. I wish you'd marry and have children of your own."

The coffee cup sat on the end table, and Caasi's hand tightened around it. "I've been giving some serious thought to exactly that."

"Caasi, that's wonderful!" June exclaimed. "You don't know how glad I'll be to see you get away from that hotel. It's dominated your life. I swear, it's been like a monster that's eaten away at you more and more until you were hardly yourself. Who's the lucky man?"

Caasi shifted uncomfortably, crossed and uncrossed her legs, then set her cup aside. "I wasn't thinking of getting married."

June's eyes widened incredulously. "You mean…" She stopped and looked flustered. "You're just going to have a baby?"

"Something like that," Caasi explained cheerfully. "A husband is a nice extra but not necessary."

"I don't get it. Why not marry? You're an attractive woman, and you have so much to offer."

"Maybe," Caasi returned flippantly, "but in this case a husband would be an encumbrance I can live without."

"What about the baby? Doesn't he—or she—have a right to a father?"

"That's something I'm thinking about now."

"This whole idea doesn't even sound like you. Where did you come up with…" June stopped, a knowing look lighting her eyes. "Edie. This sounds exactly like one of her crazy schemes."

"Maybe." A smile tugged at Caasi's mouth. "And when you think about it, the idea isn't all that crazy. Single women are raising children all the time."

"Yes, but…" Slowly June shook her head, her eyes narrowing with concern. "Have you chosen the father? I mean, have you said anything to him?"

"Not yet."

"Then you *have* chosen someone?"

"Oh, yes. You've never met him, but he…" Caasi paused and swallowed. "He used to work for me. Actually, I think my method is a better idea than Edie's. She suggested I pick up someone in a bar. I swear, that woman is looney sometimes."

"I'm going to have a talk with her," June muttered between tight lips.

"Don't. To be honest, I think she was only kidding. She didn't expect me to take it all so seriously, but I have and I am."

"You know, Caasi, I've never advised you about anything. You've never needed my advice. There's confidence in everything about you—the way you talk, the way you stand, the way you look. Think about this, think very seriously before you do something you might regret all your life."

"I will," Caasi assured her with a warm smile. "I've never done anything haphazardly in my well-ordered existence, and I'm not about to start now."

Monday's mail included an invitation to Gina and Donald's wedding. She felt badly at having snubbed Blake's sister the past Saturday. Gina was a warm and loving young woman. Caasi took her checkbook and wrote out a generous amount. Staring at the amount, she pictured her confrontation with Blake after she'd sent his cousin a wedding gift. She could imagine what he'd accuse her of if he saw this. Defeated, Caasi tore the check in two and wrote another for half the amount of the first.

"What the heck," she muttered with frustration. What gave Blake Sherrill the right to dictate the amount or kind of gift she gave anyone? Angrily she tore out another check and wrote it out for the amount of the original one. After scribbling an apologetic letter declining the invitation, she added her congratulations and hoped the couple could put the money to good use.

The letter and money went out in the afternoon mail.

Tuesday Caasi met with her lawyer. If he thought her request was a little unusual he said nothing, at least not to her. He did admit, however, that he hadn't handled anything like that in the past and would have to get back to her. Caasi told him there wasn't any rush. She hadn't heard from Blake since their Saturday-night clash.

Wednesday morning Caasi was in her office giving dictation to Laurie when Blake burst in.

"There'd better be a good explanation for this." He slapped a newspaper on top of her desk.

Completely calm, Caasi turned to Laurie. "Maybe it would be best if you excused us for a few moments, Laurie. It seems Mr. Sherrill has something he'd like to say."

The secretary stood up, left the office, and closed the door behind her. Blake waited until they were alone.

"Well," he demanded and stalked to the far side of the room.

"I knew this would happen." Her hand gestured impatiently. "I knew the minute I put the money in the mail that you'd come storming in here as if I'd done some terrible deed. Quite frankly, Blake Sherrill, I'm growing weary of your attempts to dictate my life."

"Dictate your life!" he repeated and rammed both hands into his pants pockets, then just as quickly pulled them out again and smoothed back his hair. Even when angry, Blake was a fine male figure. His body was rock hard as he continued to pace the carpet. "I couldn't believe it. I still am having trouble." He stared at her as if he'd never seen her before. "Caasi, what would your father say?" He was deadly serious as his narrowed gaze captured hers.

"My father?" She shook her head in bewilderment. "My father has been dead for five years. I don't think he'd care one way or another if I sent your sister a generous wedding present."

"My sister?" he said, confused. "What has Gina got to do with this?" He spread the newspaper across her desk and pointed to the headlines in the business section: International Rumored to Buy Empress Hotels.

"Oh, *that*." Caasi sighed with relief. "I thought you were talking about…"

"I know what you thought," he shouted. "I want to ask you about this article. Is it true?"

She gestured toward the chair on the other side of her desk. "Will you sit down?" she requested calmly, her even words belying her pounding heart. "We need to talk, and there's no better time than the present."

Blake lowered himself into the soft leather chair, but he sat on the edge of the seat as if ready to spring up at the slightest provocation.

"Well?" he demanded again. "Is it true?"

"Yes," she said, confirming his suspicions. "But I'm only selling eight hotels. I'm keeping the Portland Empress and the Seaside Empress."

"Caasi." He groaned in frustration. "Do you know what you're doing?"

"Yes." She nodded. "I've never been more sure of anything in my life. I don't have the time to manage the hotels and everything else."

"Everything else? What?" he demanded. "What could possibly be more important to you than Crane Enterprises?"

Sitting opposite him, Caasi watched his face intently as she spoke. "A baby," she murmured softly.

"A baby," he exploded and shot to his feet.

Caasi closed her eyes and emitted a bittersweet groan. "Blake, I wanted to have a nice logical discussion with you. But if you insist on overreacting like this, then I'm simply going to have to ask you to leave."

"You don't say things like that and expect me to react as if you've asked for the sugar bowl."

"Okay, okay," she agreed with limited patience. "When you've cooled down I'd like to have a calm, rational discussion."

He said nothing for several moments as though trying to calm himself. After a while he asked, "Are you pregnant?"

"Not yet."

"Not yet?" Impatience showed in the set of his mouth.

Caasi lowered her gaze and struggled to keep a firm grip on her composure. "I've met with a real estate agent and have started looking at houses. I don't want my baby growing up in a hotel the way I did."

Blake straightened in the chair, his back ramrod stiff.

"I've also talked with an attorney, and he's drawing up the necessary papers. I think…the father…should have some rights, but I'd be foolish not to protect myself and the baby legally."

Blake's face was hard, his eyes blazing. Yet he was pale, as if his grip on his temper was fragile. "And the father?" he asked curtly.

"Yes, well…" Caasi felt the muscles of her throat tighten as the words slipped out. "I'd like you to be my baby's father."

Ten

Blake's razor-sharp gaze ripped into her. "What did you say?"

Caasi had trouble meeting his eyes. "You heard me right."

Blake propelled himself out of the chair and stalked to the far side of the room. "Have you seen a doctor?" He ground out the question, his back to her.

"No, not yet. I didn't feel that would be necessary until I was fairly certain I was pregnant," she explained tightly.

Blake swiveled around, his brow knit with questioning concern. "I'm not talking about that kind of doctor."

"Honestly, Blake. Do you think I need a psychiatrist?" Her smile was tense and nervous.

"Yes," he insisted, "quite frankly, that's exactly what I think. You've been working too hard."

Caasi's spirits sank and she lowered her head. Her fingers toyed with a stack of papers on her desk. "I'm not working any harder now than I have for the past five years."

"Exactly." His hand sliced through the air.

"Blake, the Empress has nothing to do with this. I woke up, that's all. I've decided I want something more out of life than money and an empty suite." She didn't elaborate that he was the one responsible for awakening her. "I'm a woman with a woman's desires. Is it so wrong to want to be a mother? I can assure you I'll be a good one." She inhaled deeply. "June says I'm a natural with the baby and I'd make—"

"Why pick me?" he interrupted, a grim set to his jaw.

"Why not?" she said and shrugged. The heat seeped into her face, reddening her cheeks. "You're tall, good-looking, and possess certain characteristics I admire." Nervously she stood up and walked around to the front of the desk. Leaning her thighs against the flat top, she crossed her arms.

"Just how do you propose to get pregnant? By osmosis?" Blake taunted.

"No...of course not," she stammered. "Listen, Blake, I'm not doing a very good job of explaining this. I really wish I hadn't said anything. At least, not until I'd heard from the lawyer. But aside from anything else, I'd like you to know I'm willing to make this venture worth your while."

His mouth twisted into a cynical smile. "You don't have enough money to pay me for what you're asking. I'd like to tell you what to do with your proposition,

Cupcake, but your face would burn for a week." Slowly he turned and walked to the door.

"Don't go, Blake. Please."

His hand on the doorknob, he turned; his gaze was concentrated on her, disturbing her even more. "There's nothing you can say. Goodbye, Cupcake."

Just the way he said it made her blood run cold. His voice expressed so many things in those few words. Frustration. Disappointment. Contempt. Disbelief.

Caasi sagged against the desk as the door closed. Blake couldn't be feeling any more confused than she was. He had been angry. Blazingly angry. She'd seen him express a myriad of emotions over the years. And plenty of anger. But never like this. This kind of anger went beyond raised voices and lost tempers. This time it came from Blake's heart.

The thought of working was almost impossible. Caasi tried for the remainder of the morning, but her concentration drifted, and every page seemed to mirror Blake's look as he walked out the door. At lunchtime she announced to Laurie that she didn't know when she'd be back. Laurie rounded her eyes with frustration but said nothing.

Caasi let herself into the penthouse suite and slowly sauntered around the empty quarters. She shouldn't have approached Blake that day. Even the most naive business graduate would have recognized that this wasn't the time to propose anything to him. He'd been upset even before she'd opened her mouth. Her sense of timing couldn't have been more off-kilter. That wasn't like her. She knew better.

Staring out the window, Caasi blinked uncertainly. She needed to get away. Think. Reconsider.

After changing out of her smart linen business suit into capris and a pink sweater, she took her car out of the garage and drove around for a while. It was true that she wanted a baby. But what she hadn't realized until that morning was that she wanted Blake's child. If he wouldn't agree, then she would have to abandon the idea completely.

She had to talk to Blake and make him understand. All the way to Gresham, she practiced what she wanted to say, the assurances she would give him. Nothing in her life had ever been so important.

His driveway was empty when she turned into it. She had counted on his being there. Just as she climbed out of her car, it started to rain. Staring at the skies in defeat, Caasi raised the collar of her jacket and hurried up the back steps, pounding on the door on the off chance he was inside. Nothing.

Rushing back to her car, she climbed inside and listened to the pelting rain dance on the roof. An arc of lightning flashed across the dark sky. *Wonderful,* she reflected disconsolately. Even nature responded to Blake's moods.

Ten minutes passed and it seemed like ten years. But Caasi was determined to stay until she'd had the chance to explain things to Blake.

Half an hour later, when the storm was beginning to abate, she got out of the car a second time. Maybe Blake had left his back door unlocked and she could go inside.

The door was tightly locked, but Caasi found a key under a ceramic flowerpot. It looked old and slightly rusted. Briefly Caasi wondered if Blake even knew it was there. After several minutes spent trying to work the key into the lock, she managed to open the door.

Wiping her feet on the mat, she let herself into the kitchen. Blake's dirty breakfast dishes were on the table and she carried them to the sink. It looked as if he'd been reading the morning paper, found the article about the rumored sale of the Empress, and rushed out the door, newspaper in hand.

To fill the time, she leafed through several magazines. But nothing held her interest, so she straightened up the living room and ran warm, sudsy water into the kitchen sink to wash the breakfast dishes. She had just finished scrubbing the frying pan when she heard a car in the driveway.

Her heart thumped as though she'd just run a marathon when Blake walked in the door. Turning, her hands braced on the edge of the sink behind her, Caasi smiled weakly.

"Who let you in?"

Involuntarily, Caasi flinched at the cutting edge in his voice.

"There was a key under the flowerpot." Her voice nearly failed her. Turning back to the sink, she jerked the kitchen towel from the drawer and started drying the few dishes she'd washed. At least she could hide how badly her hands were shaking.

"Okay, we'll abort that how and go directly to why.

Why are you here?" The dry sarcasm in his voice knotted her stomach.

"Would you like a cup of coffee?" she asked brightly. "I know I would."

"No!" he nearly shouted. "I don't want any coffee. What I'd like is a simple explanation." His narrowed gaze swung to her as she took a mug from the cupboard and helped herself to the fresh pot of coffee she'd made.

"Caasi." The tone of his voice as he spoke her name revealed the depth of his frustration.

Pulling out a chair, she sat down, her eyes issuing a silent invitation for him to do the same.

He ignored her and leaned against the kitchen counter.

She didn't look at him as she spoke. "You once accused me of having ink in my veins. At the time you were right. But the ink is gone and there's blood flowing there now." Briefly her gray eyes slid to him. His stance didn't encourage her to continue.

"So?" His arms were crossed as if to block her out. He drew his head back, pride dictating the indifference he so vividly portrayed.

"So?" she repeated with bitter mockery. "*You* did this to me. You're the one responsible...."

Blake straightened slightly. "Does that make it my duty to fall in with these looney plans of yours? Do you have any idea of how crazy you sound? You want to pay me to father your child, so you can be a mother. What in heaven's name do you have against marriage?"

"Nothing. I... I think marriage is wonderful."

"Then if you're so hot for a family, why don't we get married?"

She stiffened with angry pride as she met his glare. "Is this a proposal?"

"Yes," he snapped.

Caasi felt as if someone had punched her in the stomach, effectively knocking the oxygen from her lungs. Tears brimmed in her eyes.

"Well?" His voice softened perceptibly.

One tear slid down her drawn face and she wiped it aside with the tips of her fingers. "Every girl dreams about having a man ask her to marry him. I never thought my proposal would be shouted at me from across a kitchen."

"I'm not exactly in a romantic mood. Do you want to get married or don't you?" he barked. "And while we're on the subject, let's get something else straight. We'll live right here in this house and on my income. Whatever money is yours will be put into a trust fund for the children."

A soft curtain of hair fell forward to cover her face as she stared into the steaming coffee. "My mother died before I knew her," she began weakly. "Maybe if she'd lived I would know a better way to say these things. To me, marriage means more than producing children. There's love and commitment and a hundred different things I don't even know how to explain. The quiet communication I witnessed between your mother and father. That look in Burt's eyes as June was delivering their child. Do you see what I'm trying to say?"

Blake was quiet for so long, she wondered if he'd

heard her. "Maybe as time goes by you could learn to love me," Blake said with slow deliberation. "I think we should give it a try."

"Learn to love you?" Caasi repeated incredulously. "I love you already." She raised her eyes to his, her gaze level and clear. "I don't want any baby unless it's yours. I don't want any other man but you...ever."

In the next instant, she was hauled out of the chair and into his arms. "You love me?" Roughly he pushed the hair from her eyes, as if he had to see it himself, couldn't believe what she was saying and had to read it in her face.

Her hands were braced against his chest. "Of course I do. Could I have made it any more obvious in Seaside?" Her lashes fluttered closed as she struggled to disguise the pain that his rejection still had the power to inflict. "But you...you..."

"I know what I did," he interrupted, a grim set to his mouth. "I walked out. It was the hardest thing I'd ever done in my life, but I turned away and left you." He released her and twined his fingers through his hair. "I was half a breath from telling you how much I loved you. Then I heard you say that you were absolving me from any responsibility. Here I was ready to give you my heart and you were talking to me like a one-night stand."

"Oh, Blake." She moaned, lifting the hair from her forehead with one hand. "I wanted you to understand that I didn't expect anything of you. You didn't have to love me, not when I loved you so much."

Tenderly, his eyes caressed her. "How can any two people misunderstand each other the way we have?"

Sadly, Caasi shook her head. "Why did you resign? Why did you leave when I wanted you so desperately to stay?"

He took her back into his arms, and his lips softly brushed her cheek. "Because loving you and working with you were becoming impossible. I've loved you almost from the moment you floated into your father's office that day. I kept waiting for you to wake up to that fact. Then one day I realized you never would."

"Why didn't you say something? Why didn't you let me know?"

"Caasi, I couldn't have been any more obvious. All the times I made excuses to touch you, be with you. Anything. But you were so caught up in Crane Enterprises you didn't notice. And, to be truthful, your money intimidated me. One day I decided: why torture myself anymore? You were already married to the company, and I was never going to be rich enough for you to believe I wasn't attracted to you for your money."

"But, Blake, I didn't think that. Not once."

"But then, you didn't guess I loved you either."

Smiling, Caasi slid her arms over his shoulders and looked at him with all the love in her heart shining from the blue-gray depths of her eyes. "But now that I know, Blake Sherrill, I'm not letting you go. Not for a minute."

Tenderly he kissed her as if she were a fragile flower and held her close as if he'd never release her.

"I love you so much." She curled tighter into his

embrace. "And, Blake, we're going to have the most beautiful children."

"Yes," he murmured, his lips seeking hers. "But not for a year. I want you to myself for that long. Understood?"

"Oh, yes," she agreed eagerly, her eyes glowing with the soft light of happiness. "Anything you say."

Five months later Caasi stood on the back porch as Blake drove into the driveway. Even after three months of marriage, just seeing her husband climb out of the car at the end of the day produced a wealth of emotions.

"Hi—how was your afternoon?" she greeted him, wrapping her arms around his neck and kissing him ardently. She worked mornings at the Empress but gradually was turning her responsibilities over to Blake so that the time would come when she could pursue some of the things she wanted.

Lifting her off the floor, Blake swung her around, his mouth locating the sensitive area at the hollow of her throat, knowing the tingling reaction he'd evoke.

"You're being mighty brave for five-thirty in the afternoon," she teased.

"It doesn't seem to matter what time of the day it is, I don't think I'll ever stop wanting you," he whispered in her ear. "Fifty years from now, I'll probably be chasing you around the bedroom." His voice was deep and emotion-filled.

"I don't think you'll have to chase too hard."

"Good thing," he said as he set his briefcase aside so

he could hold her tightly against him. "Your cooking is improving, because whatever it is smells delicious."

"Yes—that reminds me." Caasi groaned and broke from his embrace. "I have good news and bad news. Which do you want first?"

Blake's eyes narrowed fractionally. "Knowing you, I think I'd better hear the bad news first."

"Promise you won't get angry?"

"I'm not making any promises." He pulled her back into his arms and nuzzled her throat playfully.

Giggling and happy, Caasi blurted out, "The bad news is I burnt the roast. The good news is I went out and got Kentucky Fried Chicken."

"Caasi, that's twice this month." Blake groaned, but there was no anger in the way his eyes caressed her.

"That's not all," she added, lowering her eyes. "Honey, I tried, but I can't make Ekalb into a decent name for a boy or a girl."

Blake laughed. "What are you talking about now?"

"Your name spelled backwards, silly. I wanted to name the baby after you, and Ekalb just isn't going to do it."

A stunned silence fell over the room. "Baby?" Blake repeated. "What baby?"

"The one right here." She took his hand and pressed it against her flat stomach. "I know you said a year, but eight months from now it will be almost that long."

"Caasi," Blake murmured as if he couldn't believe what he was hearing. "Why didn't you say something sooner?"

"I couldn't. Not until I was sure. Are you upset?"

"Upset?" He chuckled. "No, never that. Just surprised, that's all." His smile was filled with an intense satisfaction as he pulled her into his arms.

Closing her eyes, Caasi slid her arms around her husband's neck and released a contented sigh as she drew his mouth to hers.

* * * * *

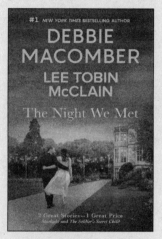